Praise for Beverly Rae's
Dance on the Wilde Side

"Beverly Rae does it again with her outstanding second addition to her CANNON PACK series. Be prepared to be taken on a wild adventure with DANCES ON THE WILDE SIDE. Its explosive storyline, mouth watering alphas, and sweltering encounters grabbed my attention from the get go. Ms. Rae does a great job fleshing out her main characters while adding to her plot even more with her cleverly done supporting characters. This is one steamy little shifter series you'll want to get your paws on."

~ *Romance Junkies Reviews*

"Beverly Rae has written a wonderful story that is both sexy and adventurous. You'll lose yourself in this fascinating world where shifters abound, and stooge like hunters track them. It's a very enjoyable read with an interesting premise, an excellent cast, a surprise twist, and tons of heat. I couldn't put it down and finished it in one sitting. Werewolf lovers have to give this one a taste. I loved Dance On The Wilde Side."

~ *Long and Short of It*

Look for these titles by *Beverly Rae*

Now Available:

Touch Me
Wailing for Love
To Fat and Back

Wild Things Series
Cougar

Para-Mates Series
I Married a Demon
I Married a Dragon

Cannon Pack Series
Howling for My Baby
Dance on the Wilde Side

Print Anthology
Magical Mayhem

Dance on the Wilde Side

Beverly Rae

A Samhain Publishing, Ltd. publication.

Samhain Publishing, Ltd.
577 Mulberry Street, Suite 1520
Macon, GA 31201
www.samhainpublishing.com

Dance on the Wilde Side
Copyright © 2010 by Beverly Rae
Print ISBN: 978-1-60504-783-6
Digital ISBN: 978-1-60504-719-5

Cover by Angela Waters

This book is a work of fiction. The names, characters, places, and incidents are products of the writer's imagination or have been used fictitiously and are not to be construed as real. Any resemblance to persons, living or dead, actual events, locale or organizations is entirely coincidental.

All Rights Are Reserved. No part of this book may be used or reproduced in any manner whatsoever without written permission, except in the case of brief quotations embodied in critical articles and reviews.

This book has been previously published under the title Dancin' in the Moonlight and has been revised from its original release.
First Samhain Publishing, Ltd. electronic publication: October 2009
First Samhain Publishing, Ltd. print publication: August 2010

Dedication

For my husband, who supports me in every way.

Thank you to the many readers who made the first book in my Cannon Pack series, Howling for My Baby, a wonderful success.

Chapter One

"Five."

"No way. He's not even a four."

"Okay. So how about that guy?"

"Which one?"

Carly rolled her eyes at Tala. "The lean, mean-looking one by the bar. The one staring at you."

Tala darted her eyes toward the bar then whipped her gaze back to her Cosmopolitan. "Figures."

"Just because he looks mean, doesn't mean he is mean, Tala. Besides..." Carly licked sugar off the rim of her glass. "I like 'em a bit rough around the edges."

Tala took another sip—and another peek at the man in question. "Rough is one thing, but ragged is another."

Carly, Tala's friend since childhood, leaned against the back of her stool and regarded her with cool eyes almost the same blue as her own. "Just how long can you last, girl? Four months and counting without any sex? How the hell do you keep from going insane?"

"I spend a lot of money on batteries." Tala chuckled at Carly's expression. "Hey, don't knock it. I can have a different fantasy every night. One night I can savage Brad and the next night I'm licking up and down Orlando's body." She laughed again even though her joke hadn't had the desired effect on her friend. "Besides, four months isn't very long. I mean, for most of us. Lighten up."

"I'd rather die than go four long, lonely months without male companionship. Much less without the Big O. Still—"

"Still, no man is better than an asshole, right?" Tala flicked a loose strand of hair away from her eye. "It's a sad fact, but the guys I've met lately aren't worth the time of day."

"Honey, I've been there. There is definitely a lack of quality fish swimming in our dating pond."

Tala nodded vigorously. "Exactly. Besides, I'm good to go, at least until my vibrator dies." Her friend snorted. "But hey, don't mind me. If you want to search for your perfect man—" she added finger quotes to the description, "—then, by all means, don't let my self-imposed celibacy stop you."

"Uh-oh, Tala. Don't look now, but Mr. Lean-and-Mean is headed your way." Carly's warning barely made it out of her mouth before the man appeared at Tala's side.

The stench of alcohol and smoke smothered the atmosphere and Tala had to shift her head to the side to gasp in semi-clean air. His hand slid behind her, stopping to rest on the top of her stool. "Hey, beautiful. You're Tala Wilde, right? Name's Fred. How about you join me for a nice, private drink?"

Oh, shit. A fan. He must have recognized her from the zoo's public service and promotional spots, *Tala Wilde's Animal Facts*. Although she loved being a vet and owning her own veterinary clinic, consulting at the zoo gave her the chance to work on more than dogs, cats and the occasional ferret. But how she'd let the zoo's administrators talk her into going on television, she would never know.

She tilted her head up and batted her eyes at him. "Wow, Fred, I haven't had such an enticing invitation in a really long time. How can I possibly refuse?"

His stained, toothy leer didn't do anything for his bloodshot eyes. "You can't." He snaked his hand around her arm and tugged her closer. "Come on, babe, let's go back to my place and you can show me what you've learned from all those wild animals. In fact, I bet you're the wild animal. You know. In bed. With Fred?"

Tala slipped her thumb under his fingers and ran her fingers over the top of his hand. "Let me give you a little tip, Fred. Unless you want a broken hand, back off. Now."

Carly shot him a look of warning. "She's been taking karate."

Fred scoffed and feigned an air of indifference. "Aw, but she wouldn't hurt me." Yet he carefully withdrew his hand before adding, "Would you, babe?"

Damn, how she hated anyone calling her "babe". But before she could open her mouth, Carly twisted on her stool, tipping over her drink. The cool liquid splashed onto Fred's bright orange shirt and green pants, a dark stain spreading over his crotch.

"Oh, I'm so, so sorry!" Carly feigned a contrite expression and winked at Tala.

Although they tried to hide their amusement, Fred's curse only added to their enjoyment. With a groan of disgust, he flicked drops off his hands. "You bitches are crazy." Adding a few more choice expletives, he slinked back to his hole at the bar.

"Thanks, girlfriend." Tala high-fived Carly. "Fred doesn't realize he got off easy."

Carly grabbed a rag from the waitress who arrived to clean up the spill. "I'll take care of this." She gestured toward Tala. "You can get the drink my friend here is buying me."

Tala sipped her Cosmopolitan. "You bet. You deserve it for saving the man's life. Or at least his hand." She shook her head, refusing the waitress's offer to get her another drink. "I think I'm going to call it a night."

"Already?" Carly pointed an accusing finger at her. "Come on, Tala. You need to let yourself go. Free your inner goddess. Run naked through the woods. Live a little."

Tala sputtered into her drink. "Oh, sure, I can see it now.

Me, bare-assed, frolicking with the wildlife." Although she had to admit, if she could find the wild man of her dreams, she'd shed her inhibitions and her clothes in a sec. Until then, however, she'd keep her clothes on.

Carly sat up straighter, thrusting out her generous chest. "You can't go until at least one of us finds our perfect man." She copied Tala's earlier use of finger quotes. "After all, this is the hottest club in Denver. If we can't score here, we may as well become nuns."

Tala's sarcastic laugh turned heads in her direction again. Lowering her voice, she explained. "For Pete's sake, there's no such thing as the perfect man. It's an oxymoron, not to mention an impossibility."

But Carly picked up where they'd left off. "Stop with all the negativity and start hunting. The night's getting old."

"Okay. But only for a little while longer. And first, I'm getting some fresh air. I'm still choking from Fragrant Fred." She slid off the stool and snatched up her bag.

"You'd better not take off and leave me here alone." Carly pulled Tala's drink closer. "I'm holding your Cosmo hostage until you return."

Leave it to Carly to turn a simple night out into a hostage situation. "Fine. But don't you dare do any unapproved sipping." She pointed at her friend and strode toward the side door of the club.

Thank goodness for fresh air. Outside, Tala took another deep breath and leaned against the wall of the club. Although she was fairly certain she could get back in, she kept her foot wedged between the door and frame. The alley was dark, too dark, but she'd needed the break from the smoke and other aromas inside. A break from all that, as well as a moment to herself. A moment to reflect again, as she'd done so many times, about the dream.

She hadn't been able to shake it. At first, the dream had come sporadically and she'd written it off as her imagination added to something bad she'd eaten, or a distorted memory of a television show. But during the past two weeks the same dream had started coming every night, growing clearer, more familiar, more urgent in its intensity. What had been an oddity had turned into a daily event.

Her mind drifted off again, letting the image form in her mind's eye. Within seconds, the form appeared, drawing her deeper into her trance.

His long, toned body, sleek and glistening in the moonlight, slowly rose from a crouched position. Muscles rippled across his chest, highlighting the broad expanse while large brown nipples accented his hardened pecs. A sprinkling of silky black hair running from his six-pack abs led to the full curly patch below, and Tala wetted her mouth at the sight of his richly endowed shaft. Yet even more magnificent than his body, his face drew her attention away from his torso. Straight black hair teased the tips of his shoulders and flowed around his angular face, while his strong square jaw beckoned for a woman's touch.

And then she saw his eyes.

Amber eyes. Golden, compelling, magnetic eyes drawing her to him. Commanding her to be his, promising to be hers. Eyes she recognized from pleasurable nights of lustful dreams.

Her breaths shortened with the ache, the need clutching at her heart. Did he exist? Even as she wondered, he bent, inching back into a crouch. His image morphed, blurring the lines of his physique while outlining another. She blinked, trying to see him better but, instead, lost the vision for a moment. She whimpered a small, tortured sound.

Blinking again, Tala saw the new image. The eyes were the same. Amber eyes. Golden, compelling, magnetic eyes. She blinked again and stared into the eyes of a black wolf.

"Tala? Hel-*lo*? Tala? Are you okay?"

She jerked to awareness to find Carly gawking at her. Then she noticed why. She was down on the pavement, on all fours, gravel digging into her knees and palms. She must've fallen over after having too much to drink. *Funny. I don't remember drinking a lot.* "What's going on?"

Carly reached over and helped her to her feet. "Well, for one thing, you're sweating like a pig. Gross!" Releasing Tala's hand, she wiped her palm on her jeans. "Having hot flashes already?"

Tala shook her head to both answer the question and to clear the remnants of the dream lingering inside. She noticed the clamminess of her hands and copied Carly's gesture. "I, uh, guess I'm a little hot. Probably just the alcohol."

"Yeah. Sure." Carly's tone left no doubt of her disbelief.

Tala glanced around her, clarity forming again, and tried to make a joke. "What's the big deal? I zoned out for a minute and fell over. Too much drink, I guess. No biggie."

Carly patted Tala's arm, bringing her into a hug in the process. "You haven't been ill lately, have you?" She shot her a nervous grin. "Or are you just drunk off your butt? Literally."

Tala broke free and stepped away. "I'm fine."

"Uh-huh." Carly flipped open her cell phone.

"What is the matter with you?" Her nerves strung tighter, Tala gritted her teeth. "You're acting like I've gone over the edge."

Several tense moments passed until Carly broke the silence. "I'm not the one acting strangely, Tala. You are."

"Damn it all to hell and back, all I did was fall down."

Carly held her cell phone out. "Just look at the picture."

"Ugh." Tala pushed the phone away. "Just tell me." For some unexplainable reason, she didn't want to look.

Taking a deep breath, Carly answered. "You howled."

Tala's mouth dropped. "I did what? You're kidding."

From the expression on her friend's face, joking was the last thing on her mind. "I swear to God, Tala. You lifted your head, stared at the full moon, and howled."

"I did not." No way could she believe such an outlandish

accusation. She'd had a daydream, sure. But howled?

Carly lifted an eyebrow at her. "Take a look at the picture, honey. Head laid back, baying at the moon in full color. Pictures don't lie."

Tala shook her head, still holding out hope for a better explanation. "No, but—"

Carly dipped her chin and raised both eyebrows. "Girl, I'm dying if I'm lying. And I am not lying to you. You stood there and let loose with an actual throw-your-head-back, no-holds-barred, canine-loving howl. Hell, I thought we'd have a wolf pack on us before the sound died out."

"I did?" Had she really howled? If she had, she needed to come up with a good explanation and quick. "Hey, I was just kidding around." She forced out a laugh. "And you fell for it."

Carly glanced at the image on her phone before arching a skeptical eyebrow at her. "Looked real enough to me. Too real."

☾

"Oooh, Devlin. Fuck me. Fuck me harder."

Devlin rammed into the female as hard as he could, nearly knocking her off her hands and knees. He grasped her ample bottom tighter and closed his eyes. Focusing on the feel of her wet warmth wrapped around his cock, he tried to block out her voice.

She's not the one. She's not the one. Almost as an accompaniment to his thrusts, his chant continued to harangue his thoughts. He growled, wanting to rid his mind of the image fighting for control.

She howled for me. Damn it, she howled for me.

For several nights he'd tried unsuccessfully to rid himself of *her*. He'd taken female after female to his bed, yet none of those women had managed to rid him of the sound of *her* voice calling to him. Sure, he'd seen her enough times in his dreams, but he'd never heard her. Until he'd heard her call, he'd been able to convince himself that they were just dreams—hot wet dreams of an imaginary woman.

Damn. He wanted to stay free and unburdened—especially of her. With everything going so well in his life—his business thriving and his role in the pack secure—he didn't want this. Not when he had enough women to take to bed. Not when he had his freedom to do as he wished. Not when he had everything he'd ever wanted. Not *now*.

But the female he'd heard wouldn't let him go. And he knew why. Whether he liked it or not. Whether she fit into his plans or not. Now was the time.

As though she'd heard his thoughts, a picture of her—almost as clear as a photograph—popped to the forefront, scattering all his attempts to keep it at bay. Her face was almost angelic in its innocence. Penetrating blue eyes seared into him and he sensed the urgency sparkling in their depths. Silky golden hair cascaded around her, creating a halo for the purity of her face. But her body was the ilk of lust-filled fantasies. Firm breasts taunted him, daring him to take hold while the smooth skin of her stomach invited him to feather-kiss his way over it.

He groaned, half out of frustration, half out of his need for her. Leaning backward, he opened his eyes, gritted his teeth and slammed into the woman again. The power behind his thrust forced her to her forearms and she twisted around to look at him.

"Hey, harder is good. But not too rough, okay?"

"Sorry." He gently ran his hands over her hips. "You're just so sexy I got carried away."

She smiled and bent her torso lower, raising her ass higher for him. "Oh, Devlin, you make me so hot. I love feeling you in my ass."

His attempt to return her smile failed. Instead, he studied her face. Maybe if he could memorize this face, he'd forget his dream woman's. But could he ever forget the sound of her howl?

The sound ripped through him, jolting him as it had done the first night he'd heard it. Her tone, hesitant yet demanding, reverberated through him, making him suck in a breath and hold it. Her melodic vibrato flowed into his heart, awakening a need he'd never thought he'd experience.

Had it been real this time? Or only a whirlwind of imagination encased in his mind? He bent his head to check the expression of the woman in front of him. Nope, she hadn't heard anything.

Shit.

The howl had been for him. And only him. Just like the woman who'd called to him. The woman he was destined to take. The woman who would have his children.

My mate.

He couldn't believe this day had finally come. Yet hadn't he known all along that it would? Hadn't he seen others find their mates the same way? All pack members knew that one day their one true mate would call for them. All of them knew and accepted it.

My mate.

Taking his shaft out of the female, he rolled off the condom and stroked himself, urging the end to come. The woman—*what the hell is her name?*—whipped around, wrapped her hand around him and took over his job. He dug into her red hair, holding on to her, forcing her to keep her mouth on him. Fondling one of her large breasts, he ran his gaze over her sexy body, desperately trying not to compare hers to *hers*.

What's-her-name kept glancing up at him, obviously wanting more of a reaction. However, the more she peered at him, the less he liked it. *Just do it, Who-ever-you-are, and get it over with.* He cringed. When had he grown so cold?

Pushing the callous thoughts from his mind, he forced himself to concentrate on the warm mouth around his shaft. At last, sweet relief came and he moaned. Now if he could only get relief from the image of the woman in his head. He wiped his cock clean with the sheet. Wanting to make up for his earlier harsh thoughts, he positioned the woman on her back and slipped between her legs to return the favor. Sucking and nipping her clit in rapid succession, he made her writhe and moan. Soon she screamed with her climax.

With a kiss on What's-her-name's cheek, he stepped away from the bed. The memory of *her* howl ripped through him again, making him unsteady on his feet and he knew. He had to accept what he knew to be true. He couldn't ignore her call any longer. It was time to find his mate.

☾

Devlin scanned the valley below him, enjoying the twinkling of the city's lights. But the smell from the city offended him so he rubbed his nose in the dirt to get rid of the stench. Soon he'd change back into human form, but he traveled faster on four paws than on two feet.

She was his destiny and she'd called to him. He knew the truth in his heart, in his very soul. Her call had drawn him to the city and, like his father before him, he would find his mate among the humans.

Some of the pack never ventured into town, preferring the wild—and their wolf forms—to the city. He, too, preferred to conduct as much of his business as he could through associates, leaving the interaction with humans to others. Running his business from a distance had proven surprisingly easy, allowing him to stay in the mountains and have as little contact with the city and its noises as possible. Fortunately, his childhood friend Conrad handled the day-to-day operations, allowing Devlin to oversee the company from their mountain home.

But now he'd return to claim his mate, the one destined for him. The one he'd trust with his life. The one he'd trust with his heart. Unlike before, he let the vision of her play in his head. Her sparkling eyes now held a welcoming glow and she waved at him, beckoning him to come to her. She swayed, her hair floating over her shoulders, making him long to reach out and touch the silky strands. Lifting her head, she howled.

The sound no longer jarred him and he grinned with anticipation. She was beautiful and strong. And soon she would be his.

He loped toward the train yard spreading out below the hills. The satchel he carried on his back held what few supplies he needed. Stretching out his long legs, he lengthened his gait, anxious to reach the city.

Devlin reached the first track at the same moment the moon reached its zenith in the starlit sky. Ducking behind an empty boxcar, he checked to make sure he'd arrived unnoticed, then let the transformation start. Within seconds his human form materialized and he stood naked, the night breeze spreading goose bumps over his skin.

After pulling on jeans, a denim shirt, and well-worn boots, Devlin discarded the empty pack and ran a hand through his hair, checking his reflection in the metal of the car. Would his mate consider him handsome? Did it matter? They were soul mates. Their lives were already connected.

Rotating, he tried to determine which direction to go. He sniffed the air and caught her scent, slight and almost nonexistent, but there. Somewhere in this city of brick and steel, she waited for him.

Her aroma drew his attention to the left and he sniffed once more. Although he didn't know her name, her age or her exact location, he knew her smell. No other female could have called to him. Determined to answer her, he sped up, his feet pounding on the concrete surface below.

Office buildings grew fewer and farther between, while neighborhoods and subdivisions sprang up around him. The barking of a dog protecting his turf slammed him to a dead stop until he realized the dog couldn't escape from behind his six-foot fence. Uttering a low growl, he met the canine's gaze and snarled a dare. The dog whined, tucked his tail between his legs, and scampered into his doghouse.

"Don't start what you can't finish, pooch." Devlin cocked his head and again moved toward his mate's scent.

Her heady fragrance, filling his nostrils more with every step he took, drew him forward, bringing him to her as no compass or lighthouse beacon could. The nearer he got to her, the longer his strides became, until he broke into a comfortable run, his panted breaths matching the rhythm of his footfalls.

He was almost there. Along with her scent came a tug at his heart, an excitement, a thrill of the future with her. Rounding a corner, he jogged up the sidewalk, past the open gates and into an apartment complex.

Sounds of humans playing, arguing, living in the small dwellings stacked one on top of the other drifted to his ears. Devlin lifted his nose to the air and sniffed. Her spicy fragrance led him along the narrow pathway to the rear of the apartment building.

The last row of apartments backed up to a wooded lot, keeping the area more secluded than the rest of the complex. One lamppost lit the area behind the apartments, casting a yellow glow over the ground. Another light shone from a second-story window, highlighting a shadow on the blinds. He inhaled, caught wind of her, and smiled.

The dark form playing across the curtains glided back and forth, arms outstretched, almost as if in flight. Her shape, enticing in silhouette, dipped and weaved, dancing in time with the sensual music coming from inside the apartment. She twirled, sending her hair flowing away from her body, a flag waving an invitation to his heart. Her movements entreated him, sending a primal urge to dance with her flaring within his soul.

My mate.

Where once those words had irritated, even angered him, now he welcomed them. How he had changed once he'd accepted his destiny, their destiny to be together!

After scanning the area for any onlookers, he crouched and jumped, hurling his body onto the side of the balcony rails, and pulled himself up for a good look. Secured with both hands, he paused when she stopped moving, holding his breath as he waited. Had she seen him?

"What 'cha doing?"

Devlin dropped in surprise, hanging on with his fingertips, and gaped at the curly-headed girl peeking out of the first-floor apartment's sliding doors. He grinned, scrunched up his face, and let one hand release its grip. Scratching under his armpit, he uttered noises he hoped sounded like a monkey and prayed the little girl found him funny.

The child giggled, hopping up and down in delight. "Mommy! Mommy!"

Devlin stopped the monkey antics and put a finger to his lips. "No, little girl. Don't tell Mommy or the monkey will go away."

"Tracy? What are you doing up at this time of night?"

Devlin prepared to run, certain the mother would show at any second.

"There's a monkey outside, Mommy."

Oh, crap. Again, he put his finger to his lips. *Please, little girl, hush.*

"Don't be silly, honey. You go to sleep this instant and stop waking up Mommy."

Devlin held his finger to his lips again, hoping the third time would be the charm. This time, Tracy copied his gesture and brought her finger to her lips. Softly, she whispered, "Shush, Mr. Monkey. Don't wake up Mommy." She waved at him, turned and disappeared.

Devlin let out a relieved sigh and let his body hang loose for a moment. Just as he started to pull himself up again to watch, he heard the swish of curtains sliding open and then a glass door—*her* door—squeak wide. He grabbed the slatted boards of the balcony floor and slipped underneath the floorboards. The woman's shadow crossed over him, her feet narrowly missing his fingers as she moved to the railing.

Taking shallow breaths, he waited, knowing he could keep his hold for hours. He peeked through the slats to see the silky robe she'd wrapped around her body. Suddenly, he wished he could wrap his arms around her, taking the place of her robe.

She leaned against the rail and sighed.

Was she thinking of him? Of the mate she longed for? Was she aware that he'd heard her call?

He listened to her breathing, soft and easy, and dragged in her sweet aroma. *Ahhh.* Her body's own fragrance was sweeter than any perfume or flower he'd ever smelled. She needed nothing more to entice him.

Taking another deep breath of the intoxicating bouquet, he considered moving to the edge of the balcony to pull his body over the railing and meet her. Then decided against it. He had to be careful about their first meeting.

She pushed away from the railing and moved inside. He heard the *click* of the sliding door and frowned. Waiting, seconds turning into minutes, but he didn't hear the slide of the curtains.

Damn it, man. Be careful. He chastised himself, yet his grin grew wider. Although he wanted their first meeting to be special, what harm could a little pre-meeting snooping do? After all, destiny, instinct and scent told him she was the right one for him, so she'd better get used to his playful side, right? Not that he normally showed that side of himself, but with her he would be different; more open, more fun.

Devlin swung like a kid on a jungle gym up to the edge of the balcony. Changing his grip to lock his hands around the vertical boards, he did a pull-up and held his head inches above the flooring. With his chin braced on the edge and his arms tense under the strain, he peered into the apartment. He sucked in a breath when he saw that she hadn't closed the curtains.

She's magnificent.

Swaying to the sultry music, the woman—his woman— turned slowly in a circle, letting go of the robe to stretch her arms outward. The robe fell open, exposing the firm body underneath it. The sight of her clad only in skimpy underwear and bra sent a hum of desire through him. Momentarily forgetting to stay hidden, he started to climb onto the balcony. In the last second, however, he remembered and growled his frustration. *Be patient. I'll meet her when the time is right.*

She flowed in front of him, twirling in a waltz for one. Dipping and swaying, she put on a coquettish show, slipping her robe off one shoulder only to pull it back up, then doing the same with the other, teasing an unseen audience. Was she teasing him? He hoped so. Watching her moves, he drank in each inch of flesh she exposed then covered. What would she do next?

Take the robe off. Devlin silently pleaded with her, commanding her to obey his wish. As though hearing his request, she tossed her lustrous hair and shrugged the silky material down her back. Her hair, waving against her skin, hid the robe until it dropped to her waist where she caught it. With her arms still in the sleeves, she shimmied the silk against the appealing curve between her spine and the rise of her ass, keeping her bottom covered. He concentrated on the way the material slid over her rounded curves to give him a peek at her tan line, loving the temptress in her while quietly praying to see more. At last, yet in some inexplicable way too soon, she shrugged off the robe and threw it on a nearby chair.

Had she instinctively heard him? Yet Devlin didn't care about the why of it as long as she'd dropped the barrier to the treasure lying beneath. She continued to dance, moving her hips in a provocative rhythm. Like a seductress, she skimmed her hands over her body, pausing to press her palms against the curves of her breasts before sliding them down her hips and over her bottom. Grasping her cheeks, she stuck out her buttocks toward him, perfect melons below the slope of her hips. His mouth flooded with saliva while his shaft jerked in response. Long blonde hair rippled like a golden waterfall down her back to kiss the tip of her ass.

And then she whirled around.

At the sight of her firm, ripe breasts almost spilling out of her bra, he loosened his hold and dropped, scraping his chin against the edge of the balcony. He dangled, suspended by one hand, and clung on with the other while his head—both heads—rejoiced at what he'd seen. Grunting, he stretched upwards to regain his position and view.

Bending slightly forward and tilting her head, she spilled her glorious mane down to hang in front of her. Devlin's palms itched to touch her hair, to run its softness through his fingers. Still swaying to the music, she shook her head, whipping the golden strands across her body, feathering the softness across the tips of her breasts.

He let his claws grow and dug into the wood, intent upon restraining himself from leaping over the railing, breaking through the glass door and making her his.

Tossing her hair back, she straightened, her eyes still closed. Devlin licked his lips and watched as lust filled her face. At that moment, he would've given anything for her to look at him with the same desire.

She rotated her hips in a sexy imitation of a hula dance, giving him a good idea of how she would undulate under his body. Sultry and hot, she traced her fingers along one arm, from her elbow upward to her shoulder. She slowly slid her palm along her shoulder to push the bra strap down. Crossing her arms, she slipped the other strap off until the bra inched down to the swell of her breasts to stop, barely covering her nipples. She reached behind her, unhooked her bra and twirled it away. Taking her breasts, she fondled them, running her fingers over the taut buds.

Devlin swallowed and silently urged her to do what he wanted her to do. When she licked her lips, he nearly lost his grip.

She lifted one breast and dipped her head to her nipple. Devlin held his breath. *Please suck it.* Instead, she wickedly teased him, trailing her tongue along her smooth tanned skin and over her nipple. *Holy shit! Suck it. Please.*

At last she seemed to hear Devlin and tugged the bud into her mouth. Juices flowed in his mouth as he imagined what she was feeling, tasting at that second. He watched, mesmerized. *I bet she tastes like sweet honey. No. She'll be saucy, spicy, and tangy all rolled into one.* When she treated the other tit to the same attention, he groaned and had to use one hand to readjust his dick away from the zipper digging into the expanding flesh.

She let go of her breasts, nearly breaking his heart until she slipped her hands lower. Lower still until she traced a path along the edge of her panties with her fingertips. Devlin ran his tongue over his lips and tried not to anticipate too much. But he couldn't help it. He let his imagination wander down that tantalizing path. *Is she going to do what I hope she's going to do?* He blew out pent-up air and waited, afraid to hope. Wiggling to the tempo, she granted his fondest wish.

She pushed her fingers beneath the lacy fabric and, in an excruciatingly slow trek, eased her hand between her legs.

Yes! Devlin bit his bottom lip to keep from shouting his joy. *Come on, baby. Pleasure yourself and please me at the same time.* He squinted, unsure if she'd started touching herself or not. *Go on. Do it. Show me.*

She lifted her head toward the glass, eyes still closed, and the rapt expression on her face almost knocked him to the ground. *This is my mate.* The thought of having her as his mate brought a silly grin to his face.

No longer dancing, she moved her legs apart, making room for her to glide her hand into place. Her actions pushed her panties lower and he quickly prayed that she'd push them all the way down. His prayer was answered, but the real prize remained hidden. His mate found her pleasure spot. Working her hand up and down, she rubbed herself.

Damn it, let me see. If I don't get to see, I don't know what I'll do. His breaths came in ragged puffs. He'd wanted women before, lusted after many, but he'd never wanted anyone as much as he wanted *her*.

She turned, placing her side to Devlin, but kept her hand in place. Running her other hand over her breast, she pinched her nipple. Gracefully, she lowered herself to the floor. Her hair tumbled around her, slinking over the tops of her breasts and he ached to touch the glossy strands almost as much as he ached to touch the silkiness between her legs. If only he could lie between her legs and give her real satisfaction.

The need to have her splintered his resolve to stay hidden. Now was not the time to meet, but oh how he needed her under him, squirming with her desire, feeding his every need, bringing to life his every dream, all while he gave everything he had to her. Yet instead of following his instincts, he used all the strength he had, dug his claws into the wood and imagined it was his hand rubbing her instead of her own.

Tala knew she should close the blinds, yet something primal stirred within her, wanting to turn the animal inside her loose. How often had she dreamed of being totally free, uninhibited like the wolves at the zoo? How often had she imagined breaking the rules of society, running wild in the woods, doing only as her instincts told her.

Closing her eyes, she let the music fill her, taking her away from her apartment into another world. A world she thought of often. A world where *he* lived.

She sighed, letting the image of her animal-man ease into

her thoughts.

His hard body lengthened in the moonlight and he stretched, cat-like yet more compact, more powerful. If she could touch him, she knew granite would feel softer. She knew if she could curve her fingers over his wide shoulders that she would feel nothing less than if she'd clung to the inflexible edges of a mountain. His lean form, all sharp angles and cut diamonds, left her sucking in a breath, surprisingly unprepared for the lust rocketing through her. Surprising only because she'd experienced the yearning so many times before.

Dark hair curling at the corners of his jaw cushioned his face, yet somehow didn't soften the strength there. His nostrils flared and she saw him sniff the air around her, dragging her scent into his nose. He parted wide full lips and she waited, transfixed by the hope that he would lean toward her and kiss her. When she couldn't wait any longer, she took a breath and raised her eyes to his.

His eyes, perhaps his most sensual attribute, raked over her, sending her pulse racing. Darkness melted away into amber richness, dragging her into their depths. She swallowed, unable to break free from their hold on her.

He's the one.

She knew, as well as she knew her own name, that he was the one she needed. He was the one she'd waited for, passing over other men, knowing that one day he would come.

At last she managed to tug her gaze away from his and was drawn downward, over the enticing lips, past the square chin, down the hardness of his chest. The curly black hair running from his touch-me abs led her mental gaze to the darker patch below and her gaze lingered *there*.

He was perfect. The hair covering his mound made her ache to run her fingers through it. But not for long. Not when the real prize lay beneath. Her gaze fell on his manhood and she inhaled. The length alone was impressive, but the width made her knees weak. As though hearing her thoughts, it jerked, teasing her. She swallowed and moved her hips seductively, temptingly. Had he grown longer? Bigger? She finally exhaled and wet her lips. God, she needed him. Wanted him. Had to have him.

When another jerk came, she decided she'd heed the call of his shaft and the large balls supporting it to reach out and grasp them. And in her mind's eye, she did just that.

He moved back from her with an arch of one eyebrow tempting her, toying with her. Would he deny her what was hers to take?

Tala tempted him, slipping one side of her robe off a shoulder, then the other. In her fantasy, his eyes deepened with lust. She danced like a mysterious temptress, swaying her body, promising him the riches between her legs. With a come-and-get-me move, she shed her robe and twirled it once, twice, then tossed it away. Her bra followed slowly, letting it dip until it hung on the edge of her breasts. The bra, too, however, was soon discarded.

She mewed, a soft sound yet one she knew her dream-man would hear. Lifting her breast, she swept her tongue over her skin and played with the hardened bud. Kneading her firm breasts, she teased herself, until at last, the urge to suck her nipple overcame her. She drew her nipple into her mouth and whipped her tongue over it, around it.

Wetness dampened her crotch and she slipped her hand into her panties. Finding her pleasure spot, she rubbed, imagining his hand instead of hers. His tongue instead of his hand. She spread her legs, keeping the massage going and slid her other hand up her side to capture her aching nipple between two fingers. She mewed softly, pulling on her tit and fondling her breast.

Raging heat flashed through her and she quickened her fingers' work. Lifting her nipple to her lowered mouth, she sucked on her tit. She pulled on it, sucked on it, hoping to entice the man in her thoughts to come closer.

Dance on the Wilde Side

Her legs grew unsteady and, lowering herself to the floor, she stretched out. In one smooth motion, she rid her body of her panties. Bending her knees, she let her legs fall to the side, opening her pussy to her explorations.

Her breathing grew faster, shorter, echoing the speed of her finger against the hot wetness. Folding her arm over both breasts, she toyed with one nipple and rubbed her forearm against the other. She tensed, fought to stay relaxed, but knew she fought an impossible battle.

Moaning, she imagined him coming to her at last. Crouching next to her, he gazed at her, letting his eyes tell her of the storm brewing inside him. Knowing what she wanted, he moved to her feet, took her legs and spread her wider.

She sighed and caught the gleam in his eyes. He would resist her no longer.

Going to his knees, he flattened his hands on either side of her and lowered his body to the floor. She lifted up on her elbows to watch. With a sly smile, he slid up to her vee and softly blew on her snatch.

A hurricane couldn't have left her panting any more than his seductive breath. The shock of it spiraled through her, rushing over her skin to send countless smaller shockwaves through her. She gasped and threw her head back.

Had she thought his puff of air incredible? She had, but it was nothing compared to the swipe of his tongue across her pussy. She shuddered and fell with her back on the floor. But he was only beginning. Parting her lips with his fingers, he latched onto her already throbbing nub and sucked. Licked. And sucked more. Until she could stand it no longer.

She gripped the carpet beneath her and let out a cry.

When she lay down on the floor to pleasure herself more, Devlin couldn't take it any longer. He groaned, aching more than he had ever ached for any woman. He had to have her, take her, make her his.

Was this spectacular show for his benefit? After all, she'd called him to her, so maybe she'd planned to entice him with a performance using her female charms? Why else would she have left the curtains open at such a perfect time? Devlin considered the chances of her having seen him and his shaft grew thicker. The idea of her treating him to such an alluring exhibition hardened him further and he moaned at the tightness of his jeans over his crotch. If she'd meant to simultaneously torment and enthrall him, she'd achieved her goal. He only hoped the delicious anguish would go on forever.

When the music ended, Devlin's heart stopped along with it. *No, don't stop! Keep going. I know I shouldn't, but I can't wait any longer. I have to get inside.* He regained his grip on the railing, forcing down the urge to leap onto the balcony and race inside to beg her to continue. Could he dare hope she'd come out and greet him, relieving him of the burden to stay away? *Come to me.*

She cried out in ecstasy, wrenching him apart in his agony to be with her. Yet, once her cries had subsided and her breathing evened out, she rose without a glance his way, placing her back to him. She scooped up the robe to wrap around herself and slid into a chair.

Why isn't she coming to me? Surely she knows I'm here. Right?

"Hey! What're you doing? Yo, Caroline! We got us a pervert peeking inside the apartments."

Devlin's head jerked to his left. A wiry, unkempt man wearing hunter's camouflage stood a few yards away, with arms crossed to steady the shotgun he cradled. Devlin's fight-or-flight instinct clicked into high gear. Flight wasn't the best option so he readied himself for the fight. Bracing himself, he swung forward and backward, gaining the thrust he needed.

"Hoo-ee! You, my man, are b-u-s-t-i-d, bus-ted!"

Swinging around with the skill of an Olympic gymnast, Devlin released his hold on the railing and flung himself at the man. Devlin struck the hunter head-on, sending them both tumbling to the ground and the gun flying. They stayed together, rolling over each other until they banged into the trunk of a tree. With a grunt, they stopped, still clinging to each other, each fighting to be the first to gather his wits and breath.

On top, Devlin fought to control the power surging within him but couldn't keep the flow of energy from leaking through. The man's eyes went wide and a desperate cry escaped his lips when Devlin snarled, exposing long, sharp fangs.

"Shit! What the hell are you?"

Devlin growled and rolled to the side. Crouching, he bared his teeth again at the terrified man and tried to stay in human form.

He failed.

Clothes ripped from his body as the transformation took over and he shifted from man to wolf in seconds. The hunter, shuddering, opened his mouth and yelled a strangled, incomprehensible cry. But it was another's cry that caught Devlin's attention.

"Bobby Lee!"

Devlin, in full wolf glory, wrenched his head around to see a woman in an adjacent first-floor apartment bursting onto her patio. Together, they glanced at the shotgun lying at the edge of the grass. Without further hesitation, she scooped up the gun and pointed the barrel at him.

"Get away from him, you beast!"

"No! Stop!"

Devlin swiveled toward the second voice, a voice melodic even while raised in a mix of fear and anger, and saw her—his woman—standing next to the other woman. Her eyes, sparkling blue against the paleness of her startled face, caught him, making him forget about the man, the woman with the shotgun—*Caroline?*—and even about the danger. He'd seen those eyes before. In his dreams. In impossible, desire-driven dreams.

His woman grappled with Caroline, trying to yank the gun out of her hands.

"Tala, he's after Bobby Lee! Let go of the gun."

However, his woman—*Tala*—continued to wrestle for possession.

A loud *pop* fractured the air, sending pellets flying toward them, and Devlin hunched his shoulders in reaction. He ducked, crunched his body together, and prayed for luck.

But luck wasn't on his side. Or Bobby Lee's.

The buckshot found its targets and pain seared through him, wrenching a howl from him and a howl from Bobby Lee. *Shit! She shot me!*

Bobby Lee yowled again. "Shit! Y'all shot *me*! Shoot the wolf, you crazy women!"

"Damn it, Tala. Why'd ya go and shoot Bobby Lee?" Caroline gaped at her.

"It was an accident. I didn't mean to shoot anyone. Or anything. And I don't want you to, either."

Devlin threw an enraged look at Tala, but knew by her horrified expression that she was telling the truth. She was still hanging onto the gun, keeping the other woman from shooting him. His anger left him, replaced by the knowledge that she, like any good mate, was trying to help him.

But he wasn't out of danger yet. He cringed at the burn coursing through him at the same instant he noticed blood running down Bobby Lee's shirt. Growling, Devlin stumbled toward the woods, falling once as the pain raked up his flank.

He skidded to a stop, whipped toward Tala again and met her stare. For a moment he could sense a connection, their unspoken bond. She stood frozen in place, obviously still stunned, yet no longer frightened. He smiled a wolfish grin, hoping she would understand his gesture.

Smile at me, Tala. Let me know you understand. Let me know you danced for me.

Instead, she broke the bond between them and jumped her stare from him to the hunter.

"Hang on, Bobby Lee. I'll call for help." She fled into her apartment.

Snarling his disappointment, Devlin bolted into the woods.

Chapter Two

"Shit, Dev. Pull yourself together so we can do this. I'm not about to let some female you haven't even met fuck up your mind." Conrad giggled, an odd sound coming from such an enormous body. "Fuck your body? Hell yes. Fuck your mind? Hell no."

Devlin squinted at his friend, trying to make the blurry images in front of him focus into only one face. Aside from his rough exterior, rather like a pirate with his long reddish-blond beard and hair, Conrad was the perfect right-hand man. "Hey, just watch whazzu say about my fe-uh, woman."

"Sure, sure. Don't cough up a fur ball."

The sign on the front door read Wilde's Veterinary Hospital. *Tala's clinic? What the hell am I doing here?* Devlin swayed unsteadily on his feet and forced his beer-sloshed brain to remember. After getting shot in the ass—which had had Conrad bellowing with laughter—Devlin had needed a change of clothing and someone to listen to him vent. Who else would he call but Conrad? Not only did Devlin trust his childhood friend with his business, but with his life as well.

After a few hours guzzling drinks, he'd nearly fallen off his barstool when "Tala Wilde's Animal Facts" appeared on the bar's television. Her commercial obviously showed that she cared about animals, which had intrigued and pleased him. *Although she did put the animals in cages. Still...* Nudging his buddy, he had pointed at the screen and told everyone within hearing distance that she was his mate.

Conrad, however, hadn't been impressed. In fact, he'd been downright pissed. How dare Devlin's future mate shoot him? Even by mistake, it was an insult. So after several more beers, Conrad had come up with a plan to show Tala "who the alpha male in this relationship is". Together, they would break into her clinic and free the canines. Hell, they might even free the damn cats, too.

"On second thought—*belch*—I'm not sure this is, uh, you know, a good idea. I mean, it was an accident." Devlin glanced down, found that he was holding a beer can and took a swig. *How many does this make? Never mind.* However many, it wasn't enough to ease the pain in his ass—or his heart.

"Accident, smackadent. Damn it, man. First you let her tease you with her sexy dance and then you let her shoot you with a butt-load of buckshot," Conrad snarled and wiggled the doorknob. "I'm not letting you get kicked around like this. Fuck no."

"She didn't kick me." Devlin winced at the throbbing in his backside. "She s-shot me." He poked a finger at his friend and tried again. "By accident."

"Yeah, right. So you say." With a growl, the big man stepped back, took one last look at the door, kicked out his booted foot and banged into the doorframe.

Devlin snorted. "Ha! Ya missed."

With a low growl, Conrad bent over to study the door, stepped back and tried again. A loud *crack* later and the door hung by its hinges.

Devlin stared at the splintered wood a few moments. *I wonder if Tala's gonna be mad that we broke her door?* "Wait a sec, C-man. Lesss think about—"

"Not a chance." Before Devlin could regroup, Conrad dragged him through the lobby and into the back room.

Cages filled with dogs of various sizes—*Ow! Shut the hell up*—barked at them. A few—*yuck*—cats hissed at them from a row of cages a few feet to his right. Devlin dropped his beer and clamped his hands over his ears. "Damn, man, c'mon. Lesss get the hell outta here. All this fuckin' racket is killin' me."

Although Conrad covered his ears, too, he shook his head emphatically. "Hell no. We're finishing this."

Devlin bent over to pick up his beer can—*maybe I can lick off another few drops*—then lost his balance and half-fell, half-stumbled toward the felines. Trying to recover, he gripped the bars of the nearest cage. "Shit!" Pain ripped through his hand. Yanking it away from the squalling hell-cat spitting at him from inside the cage, he gaped at the three lines of red marking his hand. "Damn thing schliced me."

Conrad, however, wouldn't be sidetracked from the plan. "Will you quit playing with the pussy? We've got a rescue mission to do."

An image of a naked Tala playing with her pussy—the only kind of pussy he'd ever want to play with—flashed through his mind. If only he'd jumped onto her balcony and joined her. He would've given her what she craved.

Conrad pointed at the large dog in the nearest pen. "Looks like he could be a half-breed. You know, sort of a stepbrother." With a come-on wave, he lurched toward the back door. "You let 'em out and I'll open the door."

"Okay, okay. Stop hollering. My head's getting bigger and everything's getting fuzzier." Devlin saluted and tried to focus on the animal that looked like a cross between a German Shepherd and a wolf. The idea of leaving him in the cage was unbearable. Devlin pushed away from the cat and staggered toward the half-breed's pen. Taking a step closer to the animal, he stumbled, landed against the cage, slid to the floor and fumbled with the latch. He finally got the latch unhooked and, pulling himself to a standing position, threw open the door and waved his arms in a sweeping gesture. "Run, my friend. Run free. Run wild." *Wilde. Tala Wilde.* My *Wilde.*

The dog raced past him and through the door Conrad held

open. Devlin shot him a thumbs-up and staggered to the next cage.

☽

Damn, I hurt. Although he wasn't sure which hurt more, the pain in his rear or the pounding crush of his headache. Devlin winced as the sting in his bottom broke through his dream. He groaned, the dew on the ground beneath him sending shivers through his nude body.

What happened? Flashes of animal sounds, cages rattling and Conrad's booming voice shattered through him. *Dogs in cages. Cats hissing. Howling under the moon. Wanting to be free. Wanting Tala.* He muttered an oath under his breath. Had he and Conrad shifted after letting the animals loose? They must've. Why else would he be outside and naked?

Sunlight heated his back and he curled into a ball, refusing to open his eyes, believing he'd be safe if he just remained quiet. He'd heal if he had enough time.

His mind caught the idea of a woman aiming a shotgun at him while Tala fought for the gun. Had he gotten shot? As if in answer, the throbbing increased in his butt.

Yeah, I've been shot. Shit. My mate shot me. Sure, by accident, but still. Didn't she realize who I was? She'd danced for me, right?

The memory of her call rang again through his head, giving him an ache of an emotional kind. The more times he heard it, the greater became his need for her. Didn't she feel the same way?

The sounds outside his mind grew louder and he snarled, unwilling to allow them entry. *Screw it. Let the world go on without me.*

"Hey, buddy. You all right?"

Aw, crap.

Hoping for any help at all, Devlin sent a wish skyward.

Please, make the voice and the sounds go away. All I want is to lie here and rest until my head deflates to normal size again.

"Did you call the police?"

"No. I called Tala instead."

"What the hell for? You should have called the cops. Did you at least get them locked up?"

Are they going to lock me up? Is Conrad locked up? He thought of his friend captured and thrown into a cage, and silently snarled.

"Yeah, all the dogs are accounted for. But I don't get it. If he wanted to turn them loose, why didn't he take them out the front door instead of letting them out into the animal run? Kind of defeated his purpose, ya know."

"The guy was on a bender. Hell, he probably didn't know which side was up."

Will they just shut the fuck up? He wanted to leave, but he didn't, couldn't, wouldn't move. Not yet. Not until the pain subsided a little.

The two voices argued for a bit longer while Devlin tried to ignore their existence. They could quarrel until the sun exploded for all he cared. That is, until a sharp pain hit his side. Something had poked him. And hard.

"Hey, dude. You're going to have to get up. Like right now." The younger voice seemed more agreeable than the older one, but Devlin didn't care.

"Move your ass, man, or I'll move it for you." The owner of the older voice was definitely less friendly.

Another sting in his side left no doubt which voice was doing the prodding. Devlin flipped over onto his back, whipping his arm out and striking a hard object. The clang of metal hitting stone rewarded his effort. Peeking between puffy eyelids, he glimpsed two pairs of work boots then squeezed his eyes shut.

Aw, double crap.

"Has he said anything yet?"

The sweet lilt wafted over Devlin's sore body, coaxing his eyes open again. Long legs stopped his breath, but his eyes kept moving up their forever length, staying for a moment over her soft rounded stomach, then rising to linger on the generous breasts straining under her shirt. Her name on the plain blue denim shirt was appropriately stitched in gold thread. *Tala Wilde. My Tala.* He let out a shuddered breath, all of his muscles relaxing—except for one.

"Nope. Not a thing." Surly-voiced man wiped his nose on his sleeve. "But he did strike at us."

"Only because you kept stabbing him with the prod." A younger man, his kind eyes meeting Devlin's, pointed at the metal pole lying on the ground near a rock with writing that ordered the reader to *Pee Here.* "Nothing I wouldn't do if someone poked me."

"Ms. Wilde—"

His gaze found her brilliant blue eyes. *Damn, she's beautiful. And more. She's beautiful, suspicious and pissed, too.* But he didn't care how she looked at him. Just as long as she did.

"—we need to call the authorities. This guy's either wacko or waking up from an all-night binge. Or both." Surly leaned closer and sniffed. "From the stink of him, I'd say the bender part's definitely right."

Wilde. What an ideal name for his mate. He hoped her actions—especially in bed—would fit her name.

"I called you instead of the cops because I figured Wilde Veterinary didn't need any bad publicity," Kind Eyes continued even as Surly tried to interrupt. "I mean, do we want to explain how this man, a drunk, got into the clinic? Remember the fuss when the little kid got into the cage with all those flea-ridden kittens? I say we get him out of here before the place opens and clients show up. Besides, he's injured."

"Didn't anyone set the security alarm last night?"

Surly snapped his mouth closed and ducked his head. "I guess someone forgot."

He-he, you mean someone like you? Just thinking about chuckling made his head hurt.

"You mean someone like you?" Tala fisted her hands on her hips.

Devlin stared into her captivating eyes, his breath halting as he waited to hear her voice again. *Does she regret what happened? Does she finally recognize who I am?*

They gazed at each other, neither speaking nor moving. Suddenly, she knelt by his side. "Who are you?

Oh, hell. She doesn't know who I am. Devlin opened his mouth, ready to answer, but the only answer he could give was a croaking sound. *Man, what I wouldn't give for a tall glass of cool water.*

Perfect eyebrows slid toward a perfect upturned nose, making him forget about the water. *She's a vet and takes care of animals.* Although the thought of her caging animals, even if only for a short time, was disturbing, he couldn't help but wonder what it would be like to have her take care of him.

"Do you want me to call a doctor?"

His hand flew to his ass, spreading blood onto his fingers. Shaking his head, he pushed up on his elbows and reached out for her.

She moved with quick ease, surprise more than fear highlighting her features. "Uh, here." She handed him a rag sticking out of her pocket. "Tell me. Do you end up naked in an animal run every time you get drunk?"

Good. She has spirit. He grinned, thankful he'd swallowed the clog in his throat, allowing him to speak. "Not often. Just when I want to meet a beautiful vet."

Her chuckle warmed him more than clothes ever could have. "I haven't heard that pickup line yet. If nothing else, I have to give you points for originality." Her lips curved at the edge in a natural way that could break a man's heart. She kept her eyes locked on him, a dare not quite hidden in the sparkling depths.

"Well, you know. A man does whatever works."

Her gaze slipped to his semi-erect shaft and rested there for several seconds. Faking a cough, he brought her attention back to his face and a flash of heat flickered across her face. *I wonder if the heat spread all the way to the glorious snatch below.*

"Oh, my God."

He glanced at his now fully-extended cock and back to her. "Yeah, I get that a lot from women. Impressive, huh?" She caught his joke and he winked at her, delighting in the blush flowing from her neck into her cheeks. *I bet it does.* "Thanks for noticing."

She blinked twice before lowering her voice, narrowing her eyes and driving her statement home. "You have buckshot in you."

"Yeah." Devlin *humphed* and pushed into a cross-legged position, giving her an even better view of his jewels. He picked up a couple of the pellets that had worked themselves out of his skin. *Silver. No wonder it's taking me so long to heal.* He'd been lucky the hunter had used buckshot. That amount of silver concentrated into one bullet could've killed him. "Damn weekend hunters." He pointed at his ass. "This makes a good argument for gun control, don't ya think?"

Her mouth worked as though she'd tried to say something, but couldn't. At last, she finally got words out. "You're the man Bobby Lee saw outside the apartment, aren't you?" Her eyelashes fluttered, captivating him. "About your dog... I'm so sorry. I didn't mean to... I hope he's okay." Her cheeks flamed. "If you'll send me the vet bill, I'll pay for his care. You *were* there with a w—uh, dog, right?"

"Are you asking or telling me?"

"What?" She frowned, confused at his question for a moment, then dismissed it. "Tell me why."

"Why what?"

"Why were you outside my home?"

He studied her. She hadn't called him. At least, not on purpose. Damn, she didn't even know what he was, much less what they meant to each other. His heart sank. She hadn't recognized him when he was in wolf form either. A knot in his gut formed, letting fear take over. This was going to be more difficult than he had imagined. He'd known from her scent that she was human, but he'd thought, dared to hope, she knew about shifters. About him. But at least she was attracted to him and she had called him. She just didn't know why yet.

Would she believe him when he told her the truth? Or would she laugh and call him crazy? The hard ball in his stomach tightened.

When he started to give her an explanation—a lie—she raised her hand and placed it against his chest. A sizzle of hot flame scorched through him. Her mouth, opened to speak, remained opened. Ocean-colored eyes widened in surprise.

Good. She'd felt it, too. He ran his tongue over his lips and saw her tremble. *Just wait, Tala. It gets better. All you have to do is give us a chance.* He pushed the worry away. Somehow he'd make her believe. Then she'd come to him, like in his dreams.

She swallowed, recovering from her stunned silence. "Uh, never mind. I don't want to know. You just stay away from me." Her glare sent icy chills down his spine, not from fear, but from the hurt her words caused him.

Before he could respond, she bolted from him, wheeling toward the white building behind her. Throwing one final confused look at him, she shouted orders at the two men left gawking at her. "Robert, give the man some of the old work clothes in the back room, then show him out—" her smirk parted her lips in unintended invitation, "—the *rear* entrance."

☾

Dance on the Wilde Side

Tala hopped onto a barstool in her tiny kitchen and turned on the small television sitting on the counter. She took a bite of cereal and let her thoughts wander again—as they had most of the night until she'd finally fallen asleep—to the mystifying, gorgeous man who'd watched her dance, then broken into her clinic.

Of course she didn't believe Bobby Lee's story of the man changing into a wolf. How could she? Her neighbor must've been hysterical. The intruder had a dog with him and Bobby Lee had gotten confused. She frowned, remembering the large creature she'd watched running into the woods. *That was one big dog.* And when the animal's eyes had locked onto hers, she'd known he was no ordinary canine.

She plopped her spoon into the bowl. Who'd have figured on someone watching her the one and only time she'd let loose and left the curtains open? Still, if she had to have a Peeping Tom, then at least her Tom was a doozy. A hunk to the extreme. Built without an ounce of body fat on him.

Seeing him lying on the ground in the animal run had stunned her, but not enough to keep her from taking stock of his remarkable physique. Once she'd laid eyes on that hunky bod of his, all her fear had left her body, leaping out of the way of her fast-moving lust. His long, strong legs had snatched her breath from her and she'd nearly fainted from the sight of his ripped, toned body.

In fact, if her two employees hadn't been there, she'd have given in to the heat coursing through her at the sight of his delicious form curled on the ground. Hell, if she'd had her way, she'd have ridden him even while pets and owners looked on.

She shivered with delight and imagined straddling him, the sun beating on her naked back. But the heat from above was no match for the heat underneath her. She pressed her legs together, capturing his lean torso between them.

Placing her palms on his stone-like pecs, she wiggled against him, covering his shaft with her freely-flowing juices. He grabbed her breasts with both hands, kneading them, rubbing his thumbs over her tits. She laid her head back, letting the sun beat down on her face as she covered his hands with hers, encouraging him to squeeze harder. Running her tongue over her upper lip, she hoped he was watching her. When she finally looked down, he was. His heated gaze raked over her. "How do you want it, wolf man?"

He growled, using his animal-speak instead of words. Yet his meaning was clear enough. Fangs slipped over his lips before his tongue followed in their path.

I want him to bite me. On my tits, my belly and between my legs. Hell, especially between my legs. "Oh, is that the way it is?" She laughed, happy that he wanted a taste. She slinked forward, leaving a trail of her wetness across his stomach and chest. She'd have left more of the trail over his chin, but he didn't wait for her. He clutched her thighs, lifting her as easily as he would have a piece of steak, and crammed his mouth against her pussy. She yelped in surprise and delight, clutching her tits as he had done. "That's it, wolfie. Make me come."

Mewing sounds of delight, she listened to him lapping her juices from her. Her body tightened and she tried to relax, wanting to enjoy the rush of ecstasy coursing through her. "Suck on me, wolfie. Suck me dry."

He moaned, breathing air onto her aching clit and then reversed it by drawing her nub into his mouth. He swept his tongue over her sensitive bud, making her tremble. Gripping her ass like a man holding on for his life, he kept her to him, merciless in his attack. Quake after orgasmic quake racked her body until she was sure she had nothing left. Suddenly, he moved, slipping a little lower to pierce her pussy with his tongue. Darting his tongue in and out, he tongue-fucked her, deeper and longer than she could have imagined. She squirmed, wanting more, yet needing to get away if only for a moment's reprieve. But he was relentless. She cried out, dropping forward, her breasts jiggling, catching his attention. Gasping for air and fighting to hold herself up, she watched his eyes change, the intense glow of brown morphing into brilliant amber.

The tension grew stronger, stronger until she feared she'd black out. The whirlwind of lust channeled up from her abdomen, along her spine to wind around her heart. The next climax, stronger than all the others, took her unaware and she inhaled, exhaling only when the shudders had subsided.

Again he lifted her, this time pushing her over his head. She crawled forward, confused by his abrupt move.

"Stay."

He flipped his body over in one smooth movement to land on his knees. His hard cock bounced, teasing her with his pre-come shining on the tip. She swallowed and wondered if he'd fit inside her. *He's going to be tight.* She licked her lips. *But tight is good.*

Without warning, he pulled her ass to press against his cock, pushed her to her elbows and lifted her bottom. Spreading her bottom, he plunged into her. She screamed, her own hot cream easing the pain of his penetration.

Crack!

The loud noise interrupted her fantasy, blasting the tantalizing image from her mind and dragging her back to reality. Another gunshot brought her gaze to the television screen where a scene straight out of a police drama played out. The words scrolling at the bottom of the screen, however, proved that what she was seeing was real. "Oh shit. The news." Angrily, Tala punched the *Off* button on the remote, snagged her coffee mug, and hopped off the barstool. "Damn it all to hell and back."

Frustrated, she forced herself to get on with the day. What good would it do to fantasize about a man she'd never see again? Crossing over to the sliding glass door, she yanked open the curtains, flooding the apartment with sunlight and, with any luck, driving all images of the naked man from her mind.

What she saw made her drop her mug, splashing coffee

onto the window, the carpet and her jeans. Yet even the burn from the coffee couldn't drag her gaze away from the figure lying on her lounge.

Her fantasy man lay curled on his side with his back to her. At first, the impressive distance between the tips of his shoulders caught her attention, and she swallowed against the tightness closing her throat. Long black hair glistened in the morning light and she held her breath, her fingers itching to touch the silkiness.

The denim shirt he wore lay open, half of the material draping over his back to expose the right side of his firm torso. His jeans, pulled down to cradle his ass, were open at the top, exposing the top portion of his buttocks. One arm curled under his head for a pillow while the other stretched out across his side.

My fantasy man is sleeping on my lounge chair. How cool is that? Perplexed at her ridiculous thought, she reached for the lock on the glass door and paused. This was the third time he'd shown up where she was. *This time I should call the police, right?* Yet something rooted her to the spot.

He looks so peaceful. Loveable even. Like a puppy taking a nap. An incredibly sexy puppy taking a nap. A puppy with blood running down his tight buns.

She gasped. *Oh, my God, is that where I shot him? But wait, I shot the dog, right?* She swallowed and tried to grasp the thought just out of reach, but couldn't. *By accident. But the dog, not the man. Right? Not that it made it much better.* Shaking the disturbing idea away, she made her decision and unlocked the door.

Why hadn't he gotten medical help? Guilt slammed into her. She should've helped him yesterday when she'd had the chance. After all... Sliding the door wide, she went to him, falling to her knees in front of him. She studied his tanned face, her gaze skimming over his slightly parted lips, and watched the steady rise and fall of his Herculean-muscled chest. *Wow, talk about a Greek god.*

For a second, she forgot about his wound—until he released a low moan. His moan galvanized her and she ran through her first aid training. *Hey, it's a dirty job, but someone's got to do it.* She smothered a smile.

Taking care not to touch any of the bloody wounds, she slipped his jeans out of the way and examined the injured areas, biting her lip to keep from making a sound. She'd need to remove his jeans to get a good look at his wound.

"Don't draw your own blood on my account. I've think I've spilled enough for the both of us."

Startled, she jerked backward. His warm brown eyes ran over her body, coming to rest on her face. Apprehension settled in her gut, yet her body wouldn't budge, providing time for her concern for him to overwhelm her fear for herself. "Are you all right?"

At his raised eyebrows, she coughed out a nervous titter, glanced at his injury, and returned to those beautiful eyes. "Sorry. Dumb question." Gazing into his eyes froze her brain, wiping it clean of any ideas. Or at least, any helpful ideas. Instead, lust-filled ideas filled her head and drenched her panties. "Uh…um…"

He smiled, a slow, easy stretching of his mouth, and she studied him, entranced by his rugged square jaw. She tried to rise, shaken by the jolt of desire racing through her body.

His large hand wrapped around her wrist, keeping her on her knees. "No. Don't be afraid."

She should be afraid. The only sane thing she could do was to be afraid. She had a stalker. A stalker who had already peeped into her apartment, shown up at her work—naked—and had come to her home again. Yet fear couldn't raise its ugly head while her hormones raced like missiles through her body. She swore she could come any second now. "What are you doing here? Is your dog okay? Are you okay?"

He closed his eyes, flattening his thick lashes against his

bronze skin. When he opened them again, she could see the awkwardness that he felt. "Well, obviously, I came to see you. And, uh, yeah, the dog's fine." A frown creased his broad forehead. "I didn't mean to spy on you the other night."

She cocked an eyebrow at him and inclined her head. "Uh-huh. And I suppose you've got some property in Brooklyn to sell me?"

His grin, a wide okay-you-caught-me grin, lit hot coals in her stomach. "Okay, I did watch. But I couldn't help myself. I came by and I happened to see you. What man could resist watching a sexy woman dance?"

The man possessed a charm all his own. Besides being a hunk, he knew how to flatter. Should she believe his watching her had been unplanned? God knows she'd yearned to hear those words from a handsome stranger.

He winced and brought her attention back to his wound. Ashamed for allowing her mind to wander, she again tried to rise. Again, he stopped her.

"You need medical attention. Why didn't you get help before now? I'll get a towel or something to help stop the blood."

"No. I'm okay." He lifted up on his elbow and started to get off the lounge.

Shaking her head, she pushed on his chest, her hands sliding under his open shirt. A shock like that of an electric current rocked her, zapped her mind offline, rendering it unable to comprehend anything except her screaming libido. *Holy shit! If touching his chest is like that, what would touching him* there *be like?*

She wasn't certain, but minutes could've passed before she was able to function normally again. She mentally regrouped and forced him down. "You're not going anywhere. You're— Uh, you're—"

"I'm what?"

His tongue slipped over his upper lip, ratcheting up the burn between her thighs. She copied his gesture with her tongue while her fingers explored the sensation of smooth skin over hardened biceps. If she died from electrocution, then so be it. His jaw dropped, parting his mouth, and she fought the urge to thrust her tongue inside.

His voice swept over her, making her breathe in deeply as if she could capture the richness of his tone by smell. Mesmerized, she watched his lips move again.

"I'm what?"

His thick eyebrows lifted in question, prompting her to break free of his spell. Snatching her hands away, she cleared her throat and croaked out her answer. "Oh...uh, you're hurt. Wounded. Shot in the tail."

He blinked at her and plunged those wonderfully masculine eyebrows toward his nose. "In my tail?" Twisting to see his rear, he touched the bloodied area gingerly and turned to her. "No. You shot me in the ass."

"That's what I said." She stared at him, trying to understand the difference. "Wait. I shot *you*?"

The quizzical expression stayed on his face. "You said I got shot in the tail. Trust me." Pointing at his bottom, he spoke in a clipped tone, punctuating each word as if she didn't understand English. "*This* is not my *tail*."

Tala glanced from his face, to his butt, and back to his face. *What the hell does it matter what we call his rump? He said I shot him. But I shot the dog. Had some of the buckshot hit him, too? But I didn't even see him.* Confused, she decided to shelve that discussion for later. *Later?*

"Okay. Whatever you say. But your ass—" she added quotes for emphasis, "—has buckshot in it and requires a doctor. I'll call for an ambulance." *And the police while I'm at it. Yep, Tala, it's time to start thinking again.*

She rose, slapping away his hand—and ignoring the urge to grab it and tug his magnificent chest against hers. With an exasperated sigh, she darted into her apartment. She'd reached the coffee table, scooped up her cell phone and thumbed the number nine into the phone before his hand clamped over hers. "Hey!"

He tugged the phone from her and held up both hands above his head. "Please. Let me explain."

Alarm sliced through her, cold and mean. In one swift motion, she scurried into the kitchen area, putting the counter between them. Her breathing quickened and she struggled to keep the panic at bay, allowing her to think. *What the hell is the matter with me, letting lust overtake common sense? Will he pull a psycho and slice me up? Not if I can help it, he won't!*

She wrenched a drawer open, grabbed a paring knife and pointed it at her hunk-turned-intruder. "Don't come any closer. I'll cut you. I swear I will."

His eyes twinkled at her and he chuckled. Lowering his hands, he nodded at the knife and spoke in a soft, placating tone. "Seriously? What do you think you're going to do with the cute little knife? I'd think you'd have better luck if you called for Billy Bob instead."

"Bobby Lee."

"Whatever."

Irritation at the truth of his words tempered her fear, yet she wouldn't give in. "I'll gouge out your eyes if you come any closer. Stay away from me." She jabbed the knife at him, hoping the gesture would make the knife appear more threatening. "And give me back my phone."

Yet when he attempted to move toward her, offering her phone, she jumped and waved the knife again. "Stop! Don't get any closer!"

"I'm giving you the phone like you told me to do."

Again the truth of his words rankled her. Why the hell had she left the sliding door open for him to follow her inside? Who knew he had the strength to follow her? "Never mind. Just put it down on the coffee table and get the hell out."

He put down the phone as she directed but stayed rooted to his spot. "If you'll let me explain—"

"I told you to get out."

He sighed and flipped his sleek hair behind his ears. "I'll leave. But only after you promise to listen to me."

She fidgeted, unsure what she could do to force him out. How had she gotten into this mess? Trapped in her own apartment with a stranger. How stupid could she be? She ran through several crazy ideas of escape, none of which had a chance in hell of working, and finally gave in. "You'll leave once I've listened to you? You promise?"

He drew himself to his full height and nodded. "I promise."

No one would come if she yelled. Her neighbors were all at work. And the likelihood of getting past him was slim to none. What else could she do except mollify him until she could figure a way out of this situation? "Go ahead."

He nodded and smiled at her. A smile she—God help her—trusted.

"Let's start from the beginning. I'm Devlin Cannon."

She gaped at him and stammered until the words finally sorted themselves out in her mouth. "I—I don't want to know your name."

"Why not?"

When she didn't respond, he continued. "Okay, we'll do it your way. I told you the truth. I never planned on spying on you." He chuckled a deep sexy sound. "I just got lucky."

She blew out a puff of air and tried to concentrate. But his broad shoulders beckoned to her, making her wish she could run her hands under his shirt again. Or maybe past his unbuttoned jeans...

"Nonetheless, I did watch you. I wish I could say I'm sorry I did, but I'd be lying. You're a gorgeous woman and I enjoyed watching you."

Although his declaration whetted a need she'd never had filled, she couldn't let him get away with... With what? Admitting that he'd spied on her? Complimenting her? She

51

couldn't decide whether to feel flattered or angry. Choosing the safer option, she let her anger grow. She took a deep breath and got ready to wail on him. But he beat her to the punch.

Holding up one hand, he tipped his head. "I know, I know. I shouldn't have. Watch, I mean. I'm sorry. But I'll never say I'm sorry I enjoyed every minute of the show." She glowered at him. "But, hey, I got paid back, didn't I? You and Annie Oakley from downstairs shot me with a load of buckshot. Silver buckshot, too." He sported his engaging grin. "And in the ass."

What did it matter if the buckshot was silver or gold or whatever the hell buckshot is made out of? Still, he is wounded and he has such a nice voice. Tala caught herself leaning on the counter, relaxing to the sound of his voice. She jolted up, renewing her defensive position. "Right. In the ass." *Why is he so obsessed with what we call his tush?* "We've established that fact. But since your wound doesn't appear life-threatening, you can get out and leave me alone. Forget what I said about listening to you or helping you. I'm not helping some nutcase who gets drunk and winds up in my animal run."

"Oh, come on. Like you've never gotten drunk and done something stupid. Everyone has at one time or another. Admit it. You're probably a wild animal with a little drink in you. Am I right?"

Her mind flashed to the night she'd gotten on all fours and howled in front of Carly. With pictures to prove it. "What I do is none of your business. Anyway, like I said. Forget I offered."

He moved quickly, scaring her, making her jostle from foot to foot. "Don't move. Unless you're leaving."

He ignored her, crossing over to look at some of the pictures on her walls. "You like wolves." Turning in a slow circle, he stared at all the posters. "A lot."

She frowned, thrown by this change of conversation. "Never mind my interests. The door's over there."

"Yeah, I know."

She got ready to run as he studied the poster of a wolf

pack. Did he think he could get her to loosen up by commenting on her love for wolves? Was his interest real or fake? Glancing at the picture he was studying, he caught her unprepared again when he whipped around to face her.

His eyes snared hers, drawing her into them, holding her to him. Her chest tightened in excitement and her nipples rose in anticipation. Licking his lips, he rolled his shoulders, opening his shirt to expose his rock-hard abs, and she waited for him to speak. Instead, he tilted his head up and howled, sending shivers sprinting down her spine.

She stepped back a couple of steps and gawked at him. "What the hell are you doing?" *He howled. Just like the man in my fantasies.*

His glorious grin, somehow wolfish, returned. "I'm howling for my mate."

Oh, my God. "You howled? You mean, like a wolf?" *Like the animal-man of my dreams.*

The vision of her raising her head to the moon, howling until her throat hurt, flashed through her mind. She blushed, the heat coursing up her neck and into her cheeks. *No! This is not the same thing at all.*

"Right. Like a wolf." His gaze hammered into hers. "Ever done any howling?"

Her blush heated her cheeks, but she shook her head, determined never to admit what she'd done the other night. "Of course not."

"Oh, but I think you have."

How could he know? Her throat closed, keeping her from an admission of guilt. "You're wrong." Tala swallowed and dropped her gaze. Her heart pounded against her chest, making breathing more difficult. He couldn't know. Unless he'd seen her outside the bar. Stunned, she brought her gaze to his and held on. *Who is this guy? Will he hurt me?*

Still playing the role of mind-reader, he answered her. "Don't worry. I'd never hurt you."

She had to get him out. Now. "I'm going to tell you one more time. Leave."

Ignoring her yet again, he pointed at a poster of a wolf and his mate. "Wolves mate for life, you know."

"What? What's that got to do with anything?" Thrown, she stammered and tried to sort out the emotions whirling inside her. How did he keep her from yelling? Why wasn't she screaming for help? Not that anyone would answer. But he didn't know that, so maybe it was worth a try. Yet why was help the last thing she really wanted? She lifted the little knife and slashed through the air. "Look. I'm warning you one last time. Get the hell out."

Answering her demands at last, he turned toward the door, paused and grinned at her.

Right before he collapsed to the floor.

Chapter Three

What the hell?

Tala let out a cry as her intruder hit the floor with a resounding *thud*. She stepped forward out of instinct, wanting to help him, and then stopped, realizing the possibility of a trap. Undecided on how to react, she bounced back and forth on the balls of her feet. "Oh, damn. What do I do now?"

Eyeing her phone on the coffee table near him, she bit her lip, gathered her courage, and made a quick dash to retrieve it. With her phone in hand, she scampered behind the counter again and punched the first button. The man on the floor moaned and she paused. Something about the sound bothered her.

"What'd you say?" Setting the phone down, she leaned over the counter. "Devlin? Was that your name? Do you hear me?" She scowled as much at herself as at the man. "Of course he can't hear you, dimwit. He's hurt and unconscious."

The little voice in her head scolded her, phasing out some of the lingering fear. *Quit talking to yourself. You know he's out cold which is why you should call the cops and escape while you can.*

Yeah, silently talking to yourself is so much better than talking to yourself out loud. Not. She paused, squinting at the lump on her floor. He rolled from his side onto his back, causing her to nervously prance on her feet. *Then why aren't you calling?*

Devlin moaned again and this time her instinct sent her feet off and running before her brain could stop them. Crossing the distance in strides, she fell to the floor beside him, ignoring the warning shouts in her head. *Don't be a crazy woman. Don't be stupid. Run, Tala.*

"Damn it all to hell and back. I don't know why I'm helping you. But right after I do, I'm hiring the best psychiatrist in the city. For me."

She reached out and placed the tips of her fingers alongside his throat, ignoring the jolt of attraction whipping through her fingers all the way to the vee between her legs. His eyelids fluttered a second, making her yank her hand away. Cursing under her breath, she reached out again and pressed harder against his jugular vein. "Good. Your pulse is strong." Her palm slid down his neck as she'd done so many times before when comforting injured animals. But her eyes grew wide at the bulge in his crotch. "Looks like something else is strong, too."

"Only because you touched me." He opened his eyes and winked at her. "Caught you looking again."

"Holy shit!" Tala scrambled backwards, landing on her bottom. Her nails dug into the carpet behind her as she supported herself on her palms. "Quit surprising me." *Move, Tala. Now. Before he gets up.* But her body wouldn't respond. Not while entranced by those chocolate eyes.

Devlin pulled her deeper inside those eyes. Her irritation melted away into their depths, soothed away by their soft gleam.

"Sorry. I didn't mean to." The gleam shifted into a wicked spark. "Not much anyway."

This man is dangerous. In good and bad ways. "Yeah. Right." She wasn't certain if her remark was meant for his words or her thoughts. Her attraction to him ratcheted up to the next level. Who knew she could go so high? "You freaked me out when you fainted."

Devlin elbowed his back off the floor and let out a groan. "Men don't faint. Men pass out."

"Uh, sorry, Mr. Macho. Call it what you will, but out like a light is out like a light." *Unless he'd faked it?*

He shook his head, his straight black hair sifting over his shoulders. For a moment, Tala imagined his face transforming into the face in her dreams. His dancing dark eyes morphed into amber jewels while his jaw changed, elongating, and his teeth grew longer. Somewhat afraid to, yet too curious not to, she sucked in a short breath, steadied her nerves and reached out.

The touch of Devlin's grip on her outstretched hand startled her out of her trance. His fingertips caressed hers, launching rockets of shivers through her hand and into her arm. Yet the shivers were nothing compared to the tremors he evoked when he laced his fingers through hers.

"Are you all right?"

His question was little more than a whisper, yet the concern in his tone blared in her ears. She tilted her head and wondered how this stranger could cause so many reactions within her. She whispered in response, surprised to find her voice working. "Me? Sure. I'm not the one with buckshot in my ass. But are you?"

The expression in his eyes socked her in the gut with its sincerity. "I'm doing much better since I met you."

Damn it all to hell and back. The man knew how to lay it on. And she knew how to lap it up. Like a dog after a treat. Not that she'd ever let him know.

"Okay, then. Since you're okay, you can leave." She hurried to her feet and backpedaled away from him. He watched her as though not understanding her wariness, and pushed himself to a standing position.

His arm muscles flexed with his movement and she couldn't recall when she'd seen such a delectable sight. How would those arms feel wrapped around her? Pulling her body against his? Her ass to his shaft? She swallowed, trying to push the idea of him naked in her bed out of her mind. To her surprise, however, the expression on his face returned her to the present.

What was with this guy? His look, so sad yet determined, hurt yet forgiving, awakened all the yearning in her soul. Here was a kindred spirit. A man who knew what loneliness was. A man who ached for the touch of that one special person.

Get a grip, Tala. You're letting your dreams run wild. And dreams rarely come true.

She'd managed to convince herself of the truth behind her words when Devlin rose, turned and started for the door. He stumbled and clutched the end of her sofa to steady himself, making her sigh, a mixture of relief and disappointment.

"Hey! You're definitely not okay." She was with him, seconds after his stumble, slinging his arm over her shoulder and steering him toward her bedroom. "You need a doctor. Lie down and I'll call for an ambulance."

"Damn silver," he muttered. His tone, however, grew even harsher and his head fell forward. "No. No ambulance. No doctor. You have to promise."

"But—"

"No! Promise. Or let me leave. That's what you want anyway." He shifted their bodies, weaving them away from the bedroom toward the front door.

Tala shoved against him, at once keeping him upright and helping him stagger toward the bedroom. "No way. You need me." She grappled to hold his weight, led him over to the bed and pushed him on top of it. His weight catapulted her along with him, his strong hands gripping her, pulling her to him. Somehow, someway, they flipped, putting her under him as they landed on the soft mattress.

His body pinned hers to the bed and their noses touched, reminding her of two canines greeting each other. A sly grin lifted his mouth and he positioned his arms along the side of her head.

For a moment, she knew pure delight as the bulge in his pants pushed against the cleft in hers, fitting as though made for her. *Only* her. "Uh, I think you should get off me."

His eyes changed, adding golden flakes to their deep richness. "Uh, can't."

She gritted her teeth and ignored the fact that he'd mimicked her. "And why not?"

Devlin feathered his fingers along her neck, tickling her like a puppy playing with her, and she had to squelch her nervous giggle. Her head shouted at her to struggle against him, but other parts of her were out to win the argument.

"I might pass out again." At her quizzical expression, he added with a mock somber face, "You know. If I stood up too fast."

Most of her—aside from her head—wanted nothing more than to keep his hard body on top of her. "I think we can risk it. Now get off me." She grabbed him by the hair and pulled.

"Ow! Yes, ma'am." He lifted up on his forearms and paused to stare at her. "But I need to do this first." With a spark of mischief in his eyes, he tilted his head and licked her.

She inhaled a quick breath as the rough texture of his tongue swiped along her collarbone. Yet instead of being disgusted by the gesture, hot juices burst unchecked between her legs and quivers raced from the moistness into her stomach. *He made me come with a lick! And not even by licking me down there.*

With a low growl, he pushed away from her, falling onto his back. She stayed where she was for a second, unable to force her body to move. At last, common sense—*thank you, brain of mine*—came back and she leapt from the bed, dashing several feet away before daring to confront him. "I don't let any hurt being, animal or man, go uncared for. So be quiet and lie there. Now, stay!" Why did she want to treat him like a dog? She cringed at the warning look he shot her. "You know what I mean."

He ran his hands through the silky strands of hair covering his face, then kept his arms stretched over his head. "Okay. Anything you say."

Narrowing her eyes at him, she studied his features for any telltale signs of deception and found none. "Good. I'll be right back."

Tala darted into the adjoining bathroom, opened the cabinet and dug around for anything she could use to tend his wound. Why in the world had she let this stranger, this dangerously sexy man, into her apartment? And to top it off, now he was in her bed.

Finding nothing useful in the cabinet, she flung the doors open to the storage area below the sink and sifted through the bottles, boxes and other containers. She always rooted for the underdog, but this time she'd gone too far. Who knew what this man really wanted? He could harm or even kill her. Still, if he'd wanted to do that, he'd had plenty of time and chances.

Her hand came to rest on top of a box of bandages and she paused. *I know he wouldn't hurt me. I know I'm safer with him than with anyone else. Besides, I owe him for shooting his dog. Or him. Or maybe both?* She grabbed a bottle of antiseptic and a couple of towels, then sprinted back into her bedroom.

"Oh, my God." In the short span of time she'd spent in the bathroom, Devlin had gotten undressed and pulled the covers down on the bed. He lay, exposing all his glory, with the comforter kicked to the foot of the bed, his hands folded on his chest, and his legs flung wide.

"What the hell are you doing?"

"I'm ready for my physical, doc."

If her mouth flapped any wider, he'd get a hook and reel her in. Determined not to laugh, Devlin cupped his hands behind his neck and cocked his head at her. "What's wrong? Cat get your tongue? Mean, sneaky creatures, those felines."

"What?"

Someone needed to put her out of her misery. And who better than him? "Um, I figured you'd want to get a good look at my wound, so I got undressed." The fabric of her sheets felt good against the stinging in his bottom and he could tell his wounds were quickly mending. If the buckshot hadn't been made with silver it wouldn't have taken him this long. Plus, the slowly healing wounds had given his "passing out" a realistic touch.

She finally managed to close her mouth. "You did?"

"Which are you asking about? Figuring you'd want to look at my wound? Or getting undressed?" The way she perused his body, he could almost see the smoke coming off her. She wanted him. Of that much he was certain. Her stare fell to his sizeable manhood and he had to bite the inside of his mouth to keep from grinning. Of course, a man had the right to have a little fun. Concentrating, he willed his dick to jerk.

"Oh, my God."

"You sure say that a lot."

"Are you frickin' kidding me?"

Funny she should say so, since he was. But he'd never admit it. "About what?"

He saw the frustration flash through her and decided the time for jokes was over. "Never mind." He rolled onto his side to place his buttocks toward her then peeked over his shoulder. "I'm hurting. Do you think you could patch me up and get me something for the pain? Like maybe some liquor?"

She jumped in response as if startled out of a deep sleep. "Uh, I don't think so. In fact, I'm wondering why I'm not calling the police."

"You know you won't because you know I'm not a threat. Because you know something is going on between us."

"Nothing's going on between us."

He stared at her, intent on letting her know where he stood.

"Are you sure?"

She returned his stare, her eyebrows diving toward her cute little nose. Her mouth moved to the side in an odd little quirk, but she remained quiet, soaking in his words. At last she came to the bedside, unrolling the bandage. She lifted the covers over his legs, pausing for a moment when she reached his thigh.

He caught her trying to get another look at his... *Oh boy...* Snapping his fingers, he jolted her back to attention and pulled the sheet over the front of his hips, leaving only his bottom exposed.

She coughed, a nervous and excited cough, and drew the chair closest to the bed under her. Placing her materials on top of the sheet, she cleared her throat again and gingerly touched his wound. "I don't understand why the wounds kept bleeding all this time. At least you aren't bleeding any longer."

Because my body pushes out the pellets and reopens the wounds. Hopefully, they're all out now. But he opted for a safer answer. "After seeing your clean white sheets, I wouldn't dare." He'd have liked to watch her expression, but kept facing the windows. No use in pressing his luck. "By the way, don't you think we should get introduced officially since you're going to cop a feel of my rock-hard butt?"

"Obviously your ego wasn't injured."

Had he heard her chuckle?

"My name's Tala."

"Tala. Yeah, I remember as much from seeing you on television. Your name fits you. And your last name was...?" He knew her last name, but wanted her to say it, knowing it would sound sensual coming from her lips.

"Wilde." She paused. "But you would've known that from the commercial. And from the name on the animal hospital."

"Oh, yeah. Right." He stretched around to grin at her. "Does your last name fit you, too?"

"What do you mean?"

Returning his gaze to the windows, he grinned, knowing she couldn't see him, and gave her some time to think about his meaning. She came to the correct understanding soon enough.

"None of your damn business."

"Hey, I just asked a simple question."

"Somehow I don't think any of your questions are simple."

He started to ask her what *she* meant when he heard the amazement in her voice. Instead, he sought out her pretty eyes again. *They're the same color of blue as the sky in our mountains.*

"Okay, this is weird. You were bleeding on the balcony. I know you were because I saw the blood. And, come to think of it, I don't remember any blood drops on my carpet. This wound is already healing over."

Should he explain now? Or wait until after he'd finished explaining everything else first? "Um, yeah. I'm a fast healer." *Faster when the bullets aren't made of silver. Damn silver.*

"I'll say."

She flinched when she added the antiseptic to the injury, yet he didn't move. She'd flinched because she'd expected him to flinch. Obviously, she had a lot to learn about him.

"So, you understand about the other night, right?" He held his breath, hoping he'd get the answer he wanted. Her hand grazed the skin around his wound, perking up his nerve endings. Maybe she wasn't even aware of her action, but he'd bet all his claws she wanted to touch him. To absorb his texture. To enjoy the feel of his skin against her skin. He knew because he couldn't wait to touch her, smell her, taste her.

"I'm not sure. I guess so. But didn't you think watching me dance was a bit, you know, weird?"

"Weird? No. Not unless I'm not supposed to like women. Which I do. In fact, I love women. Ow!"

"Sorry. Guess I applied too much pressure. By accident, of course."

Yeah, right. She sure has a lot of accidents. Or had she done it because she didn't like what he'd said about loving women? *Other* women? "Besides, I thought your dance was for me." He heard a ripping sound as she tore off a piece of the tape. She continued to work with a quiet rhythm and he listened to the sounds behind him.

"Why would you think such a thing?"

"You mean you weren't? You really didn't realize I was outside?" Again, her fingers played over his buttocks, sending a spark of heat rushing to his groin.

"How would I have known you were outside? Do you think I make a habit of dancing for voyeurs?"

She hadn't known he was there which meant she hadn't sensed him. But she'd called for him, right?

She dabbed at his wound, bringing him out of his thoughts. "Trust me. I'm a vet. Not a stripper."

He gripped the sheet and grappled with the irritation flooding through him. His earlier suspicions were correct. She hadn't realized he'd come for her. And from her questions about his "dog", she didn't realize what he was, either. He would have to change her and tell her the truth. Or vice versa.

He frowned. Then why had she let him—a total stranger—into her home? He'd assumed it was her instinct, their destiny, putting her off her guard. Along with a little acting on his part, of course. "I didn't think you were."

"Good. Because I wouldn't want you to think I put myself on display for men."

So she's worried about what I think of her. She may not be aware that he was a shifter and she was his mate, but she was definitely drawn to him. "So what do you do as a vet?" Shit, he could barely spit out the word *vet*. Why couldn't she have been a teacher, a secretary, a garbage man—someone that didn't put animals in cages?

"Oh, you know. The usual stuff. But along with running my own practice, I also work as a consulting veterinarian at the zoo. Plus, I educate the public about various animals. I take care of the animals and do tours with civic and school groups. And I do the public service messages like the one you probably saw. *Tala's Animal Facts*."

"Oh. Sure." Like he'd ever forget anything about her. He sighed a small measure of relief. At least it sounded like she didn't do anything distasteful working with animals. "What about wolves?"

She pressed the bandage to his rear and applied tape to hold it in place. "What about them?"

Her touch on his skin was like a flame to kindling. Rather than putting out the fire, all he wanted to do was build the flames higher. "Do you do anything with the wolves at the zoo?"

Her hand slid along the curve of his bottom in a gentle caress. Enjoying the sensation of her stroke, he flexed and envisioned her hand stroking another part of his anatomy. He closed his eyes, imagining her hand wrapped around his blood-swollen cock, moving up and down until she lowered her head and slid her tongue over the oozing slit on the tip. He moaned, letting the velvety sound of her voice drift over him.

"Actually, I helped design the wolf habitat."

The vision of her sucking him off splintered apart and he opened his eyes. He grumbled at the thought of caged wolves. "Habitat? Is that vet lingo for cage?" Once she became his mate, she'd have to stop caging animals. "Well, is it?"

"Look. I love wolves. And we treat our wolves with the best care, love and attention we can. What's your problem, anyway?"

Take it easy. She doesn't understand. Not yet.

Turning his head away, he struggled to level his tone. "No problem. I just figured with all the wolf posters you have, you'd rather see wolves running free instead of cooped up in some manmade habitat." He tried, but he couldn't keep from sounding out invisible quotes around the nasty word.

"I would. But their home at the zoo is the next best thing. Besides, they're safe at the zoo. You know. Safe from hunters."

"Safe, but not fully alive. Not able to live their lives as nature intended."

An edge to her tone carried her anger to him. In fact, he could almost see her lips thinning out, pressed tightly together. "The wolves at the zoo are happy."

"How do you know? Have you ever asked them?"

"I'm supposed to ask a wolf if he's happy? Now you're just being silly."

A rustling noise had him flipping to see her gathering her materials and rising to her feet. "Hey, don't get mad. I'm carrying on a discussion, is all."

"I'm not mad." She stepped away a few feet, paused, then faced him. "Okay, maybe a little mad."

"Well, you shouldn't be."

Those big blue eyes grabbed him and threatened to rip out his heart. Hugging the bandage roll, tape and antiseptic to herself, she glowered at him. And he almost wished he'd kept his mouth closed about the wolves.

"How about this? When I'm better, you promise to take me on a tour of the zoo." He leveled his best smile at her. "Convert me." *Unless I change you first.*

"Why don't you get some rest so you can be on your way soon?" She blinked, started to shake her head, and blinked again. "Okay. I'll take you to the zoo."

Now there's something I never thought I'd hear my future mate say. But Devlin nodded at her anyway and plastered on a contented expression.

Shit.

☾

"Did I hear the shower?" Tala peeked into the bedroom, expecting to see Devlin resting in her bed. Wanting to see Devlin in her bed.

Seeing the covers in disarray, she crossed over to the rumpled mess. She brushed aside the disappointment, started smoothing out the sheets and found his discarded bandage. *Damn, I'll have to redo his bandage.* Was he in the shower? Grasping the pillow, she picked up his aroma and sniffed. *He smells like forest, sunshine and testosterone. Or at least, what I think those things should smell like.*

She frowned and forced the intoxicating bouquet out of her head. *Holy crap. In a few short hours, I've taken in a stranger, fixed his wound*—she cringed, remembering how he'd gotten shot—*and given him my bed. I've done some stupid things in the past, but this one tops them all. What the hell am I thinking?*

If she had a brain in her head, she'd call the police right this second. But was it too late? After all, how would she explain taking him in, playing nurse and putting him in her bed? Not to mention that they'd find him in her shower.

The sound of running water beckoned her. Answering the summons, she tiptoed to the bathroom, peeked around the opened door and froze.

Even with the clear glass of the shower stall fogged over, she could still see enough to stun her into silence. Yet, although she wasn't moving on the outside, her insides were a jumble of butterflies and skyrockets. *Could anyone ever get used to seeing such a magnificent piece of animal? Animal?* She wondered about her choice of word, but the sight of him bending over to scrub his legs tossed the errant thought out of her brain. Although she knew she shouldn't stand there peeping, she couldn't help but enjoy the sight. Devlin was a damned Greek god. An Adonis come to life. A capital M. A. N.

Strong runner's legs covered with dark hair drew her gaze upward to his groin. His shaft was extended, ready, as if knowing she would find him. Did this guy always have a hard-on? Would it get even bigger? Was that even humanly possible?

She tilted her head to examine him and let her tongue trace the backs of her front teeth. What would it feel like to take him into her mouth? She released her breath slowly and imagined. *I bet his come is sweet. And salty. And everything a man should taste like.* She gulped, already savoring him. Forcing her gaze away from his shaft, she slid upward over the curly hair.

A six-pack—*hell, an eight-pack*—abdomen rippled with every movement. And his chest. Good God, his chest overwhelmed her. Mountain-like pecs dominated the broad expanse while his brown nipples stood guard. She moaned, letting her need break free within her.

"Tala?"

She croaked out an answer, unsure if she could count on her voice. "Yeah."

The shower door slid open a few inches, letting the water splash onto the bath mat. "Come."

Had any other man commanded her the same way, she would have blasted him with expletives and thrown him out the door. Out of her apartment. Yet the words this man, this stranger, this god spoke to her didn't evoke such a reaction. Instead, her crotch grew wet, her pulse quickened and her pelvic muscles tightened in automatic response.

Hell, yes, she'd come. In every way possible.

She moved without thinking about her actions, wanting to obey him, needing to obey him. And when her brain finally started to object, she shut it down without a qualm.

Crazy? Yes, what she was about to do was crazy. But she didn't care. She'd already trespassed into the Looney Red Zone by letting him in her home. Why not go all the way into Insanity Land?

Besides, she couldn't *not* go to him. Not with his huge beautiful cock calling to her. Not when all a woman's fantasies stood billowed in steam and hot water. She may be crazy to go to him, but she'd be crazier not to. She could almost hear her friends chanting, "You go, girl!"

Devlin held out his hand, dripping more water to the floor, and she reached out to place her palm in his. Spray from the showerhead hit her, soaking her hair and plastering her shirt to her breasts. The dusting of dark hair covering his chest drew her gaze and she lifted her hand to comb her fingers through it.

The heat from his gaze grabbed her, taking what little control she had left and throwing it away. She felt his eyes sear into her, race down her spine and into her crotch. Without removing a stitch of her clothing, she felt more naked than she ever had.

"I want you, Tala Wilde."

She was surprised to find that she could only nod. Speech was now an impossibility.

He groaned and bent his head. His warm tongue slid along her neck until reaching her ear. Nibbling at her lobe, he slipped his fingers under her shirt and drew the soaked clothing over her head. Her bra followed her shirt to the shower floor. Water coursed down her naked back, down the crack between her jeans and skin.

He smiled, full of knowledge and power. "I love the waterfalls."

Confused, she followed his look. The water flowing over her breasts found their way to the ends, the tips of her nipples forming two small waterfalls. *Catch the water, Devlin. Catch and drink it.*

Instead, he fingered the top of her jeans and unbuttoned them. Pulling on each side, he dropped her jeans and panties to the tile floor in one easy motion.

Unashamed as never before, she watched him take all of her in. Had anyone ever looked at her the way he did? *Never.* And somehow she knew no one ever would. She waited, arms at her side, for him to do what he wished with her.

He placed his hands on her shoulders and leaned in again. Her abdomen tightened, readying for him. His tongue slipped from between his lips and she opened her mouth, wanting him inside. Instead, his tongue skimmed along her lips, spreading the taste of him, wild and natural, over her skin.

Oh. Please. And still she couldn't speak.

And yet, somehow, he must have heard her plea because he lowered his head again, this time pushing his tongue into her mouth. His hand gripped the back of her neck, keeping her mouth to his so he could play within, soaking up her juices. She sighed, reveling in his touch, wanting so much more. When his tongue raced to the corner of her mouth, hers followed his, not letting him go, wanting him back inside her mouth. Sucking. Rolling her tongue around his. *If this is all he ever gives me, it will be enough.*

Nibbling at the fullness of her bottom lip, he ran his hands down her arms and pulled her to him.

Or maybe not. No, I want more.

A shudder, a joy ripped through her. He was the one she'd dreamed of, waited for. She'd thought it the first second she'd seen him and now she knew for certain. Whoever this stranger was, he was the one she was meant to love.

Their bodies pressed together, leaving no room for the water to separate them. He shifted, pressing his leg between hers, his crotch against the crease between her stomach and her leg, opening her to rub his leg against her clit. She pushed back, moving side to side for more friction. Strong hands took her ass, spreading her cheeks, running his fingers between the cleft. *Give me more.*

"I want you, Tala." His voice, husky with need, made her ache. "I want you every way I can take you."

At last, she found her own voice. "Then take me every way."

Devlin licked her again, this time around the edge of her ear. That simple gesture ignited the explosion building in her gut and she had to have him. Not daring to take the real prize yet, she skated her fingers over his hard chest, stopping momentarily to play in the swirl of dark wet hair. And rubbed harder against him.

His mouth traced a trail down her neck, nipping as he went along, each nip sharper than the last. She tilted her head, giving him access to her throat, and was rewarded with a low rumble against her skin. The sound, so primal, drew her own primitive emotions out of hiding. She clutched him, wanting him to hurry, yet enjoying the way he teased her.

Arching her back, she welcomed his mouth on her breast. First he licked, drinking in the water. Then he sucked on her skin as though swallowing more water off her. Soft murmurs drifted up to her, but she couldn't understand the muffled words. She did, however, understand their meaning. At last, he latched on to her tit, rolling his tongue over her taut bud, not taking his mouth off her. Harder he suckled her and she felt the tug on the nub between her legs.

"Oh, Devlin." She wanted to say more. *Fuck me. Stay with me. I need you. Don't ever leave me.* But the words wouldn't come.

While he nipped at the bud on her breast, he lessened the pressure of his leg against her clit, giving room for his fingers to find the slit between her folds. She opened wider. Using his fingers as he had his leg, he stroked her, captured her clit between his fingers and squeezed. The exquisite pain zapped into her, increasing her pants.

"Ooh." Yet the soft sigh of her release didn't last long. She dug her fingernails into his shoulders, aware that she'd make marks, happy that she'd leave scratches. She wanted to leave her mark on him, letting the world know he was hers.

After the last shiver rushed through her, she gasped as he entered her, his two fingers darting inside her, out of her, bringing the sticky moisture with them. Continuing the delicious torment, he rubbed his thumb against her, bearing down on her throbbing bud, and continuing to plunge into her. Her own wetness flushed the running water away from her clit, tracking it down the inside of her legs. Her knees weakened and she clung to him for support.

Holding her breast in one hand, he growled, his forehead finding the curve of her neck. Vaguely she realized he was watching what he was doing to her and she bent her head to watch, too. He rubbed, moving his fingers up and down, making small, hard circles around her snatch. Each rub brought more moisture flooding from her, rushing her climax through her, over and over again.

When the pressure abruptly ceased, she tensed and uttered a cry of protest.

He chuckled, sending a waft of warm air across her chest. "Don't worry. I'm not finished yet."

Relieved, she wrapped her arms around his neck, trusting him to meet her desire. Their eyes locked, but she lowered hers. She couldn't blatantly ask for what she wanted.

Thankfully, he understood her silent request and, with a sinful grin, he brought her hands to her sides. "You want me to taste you and I will."

Sliding his tongue over her breasts, then flicking it at each peaked tit, he knelt before her. She pushed her hands against the sides of the shower and watched in fascination, barely daring to breathe lest he stop. He feathered kisses along the soft mound of her stomach, teasing her, ratcheting up her anticipation until she was sure she'd explode.

"Spread wider."

She did as he demanded, ready to experience his tongue on another spot of her body. Instead, Devlin slid his tongue in the crease between her leg and her crotch, tormenting her in more than one excruciatingly delirious way. He took his time, moving slowly over the sensitive skin on the inside of her leg. Biting, sucking, he inched closer.

She groaned, almost a growl in her frustration.

His laugh tickled her while, at the same time, teasing her. "What's the matter, Tala?"

"You know what."

He glanced up, his eyes speckled with amber. "Don't you like what I'm doing?"

"No." She gritted her teeth. "I mean, yes." She let out another half-growl. "You know what I mean."

With a wicked smile, he ran his hands up the insides of her legs and stopped, pressing his thumbs at the creases. "Yeah, sugar. I do." He lifted her right leg to place it on the built-in shower seat. With another smile, he wrapped an arm under each leg, gripping her buttocks, and brought her closer.

She knew he could never be close enough for her. She wanted him inside her. To be a part of her. Joined with her.

With a sudden move, he parted her lips and raked his tongue over her clit. She inhaled sharply and flattened her palms against the walls. He lavished her, melting her soft sighs into loud moans, and licked her in harder and harder strokes, sending shudders throughout her body.

This is what it's like to be ravished. Taken and loving every minute.

She licked her lips, catching the droplets of water there, and reached down to part her other lips. He buried his face between her legs and drank like a man who hadn't enjoyed his favorite drink in years. Listening to his lapping, sucking sounds, she burst open again and struggled to stay on her feet, tremors shaking her from head to toe.

Oh! Devlin definitely knows how to please a woman. He knows exactly how long to lick. Exactly how long to bite. Exactly how long to devour. Oh. OH!

With every orgasm, he increased his onslaught, attacking her swollen nub with renewed enthusiasm. Each time, she couldn't understand why her body didn't tear apart with the almost unbearable desire, and each time he brought her to an even higher realm of pleasure.

Tala closed her eyes and allowed him to shoulder her weight. She had no choice. He'd taken all her strength. Instead, she tracked her fingers through his wet hair and held on for all she was worth. "Dev—oh, hell, please. Please. Don't stop."

Unbelievably, he intensified his attack, using his teeth to

shoot sparks of delightful agony into her crotch. Wonderful, excruciating pain alternated with the jolt of his tongue swiping across her clit, making her pussy clench and release with each stroke. She tensed, barely able to get enough air into her lungs, when suddenly he stopped.

"No!" She looked down at his wet, lust-filled face. "Don't stop. You can't stop. Not now."

He ran his tongue over his upper lip, dragging her juices into his mouth. "You taste great. But I don't want to hog all the fun." Water slipped along the valleys and mountains of his chest, highlighting every wondrous curve. "Aren't you wanting something tasty, too?"

Oh. "Definitely." She held up her hand to catch the spray, then stuck her finger in the air and ran her tongue along its length. "And I'm not talking about water, either." Carefully, he released her, sliding his body up hers to hold her against him and exchange places.

Sitting on the shower seat, he held up his cock—as if it couldn't stand straight without his support!—and wiggled it at her. Longer, wider than before, he had the biggest dick she'd ever seen. Thick, long and pulsing with life. Curved slightly at the end, it glistened with water droplets and more. Blood coursed along the veins, exuding power. She swallowed, scanned it from the hooded tip, along its vein-covered shaft down to the base and imagined how she'd swallow his come.

"Take a picture. It'll last longer."

She laughed. "If I had a camera right now, I'd do just that and send it to all my girlfriends. They'd die of envy."

He cupped the large balls hanging underneath his cock with one hand and reached for her with the other hand. "I'm waiting, Tala. Do you still want a drink?"

"Hell, yeah I do. I'm thirsty as hell." She laughed, knelt between his muscular thighs and ran her hands along his legs, channeling the black hair through her fingers. Spray from the shower covered him, running in rivulets along the creases of his flat stomach, around the curves of his thighs and along his shaft, to drip from his balls. Without using her hands, she reached out with her tongue and touched the tip of his cock. He jumped, taking a quick breath in. *Yum. Sweet, hot and salty. And male. Very male.* Exactly as she'd imagined he'd taste. But she'd only taken a taste. Now she wanted more.

He was already breathing heavily as he took her wet hair and moved it out of the way behind her shoulders. Leaning in, she watched his enraptured face and blew on the mushroomed top. He moaned and took her by the neck. "Quit teasing me."

"Turnaround is fair play."

Again, she leaned forward, bracing herself on his legs. But this time, she opened her mouth and took in the top of him. He gasped and clutched her hair. *Take your time. Make him growl for it.*

"Oh, shit. Tala. God."

She watched, delighting when his amber-flecked eyes clouded over in heat. Scooting closer, she fondled his balls with one hand and took his dick in the other. His shaft twitched, echoing the delight in his expression.

"Tell me to suck you, Devlin. I want you to tell me."

He did growl then, and she had to suppress a smile. "You know I do."

She flicked the end of his cock with her tongue and licked her lips. "I want to hear the words. Come on. Tell me."

He tracked his hands in her hair and gripped her. Bending to look closely into her face, he enunciated the words, making himself crystal clear. "Suck me, Tala. Drain me dry. Suck the skin off my dick and make me howl for more."

Howl? But at his fierce expression, the question was quickly forgotten. She took him in with one quick motion, closing her eyes to concentrate on what she wanted, what he wanted from her. Running her tongue first clockwise, then the other way, she continued to suck on him, tugging all the drink she could from his faucet. He growled again, slipped lower on the seat toward her, opened his legs wider, driving his dick farther into her mouth.

Unprepared, she nearly choked. When she released him, he exhaled as though he'd been holding his breath to keep her sucking. She took in a deep breath and steadied herself for more. She looked up, saw how his jaw worked in horniness, and slid him back into her mouth, taking as much as she could of him.

"Holy shit!" Devlin let go of her shoulders to knead her breasts, rubbing his thumbs over and over her tender nipples. "Tala. My Tala. You've got— Oh, holy shit!"

Determined to bring him to near-climax, she gripped him tighter, pulling him into her mouth with all the strength she could. *Pull. Release. Pull. Release.* The chant continued in her mind and she wanted nothing more than to worship at this shrine for the rest of her life.

"Damn, but you're good."

Wanting to please him even more, she changed to a different rhythm. Slowly, she inched him into her mouth until his cock's tip pushed at the back of her throat. Then, just as slowly, she moved off him, taking her time, hearing the rewards of her efforts in his moans.

"Oh, shit. Tala. Stop. I'm going to come."

Before she could utter a reply, he pulled her away from his cock, bent forward and grabbed the back of her head, crushing her mouth with his. Her tongue wrestled with his and a small cry escaped her, but the desire was too strong to fight. She could taste her juices mixing with his and dragged on his tongue, wanting every drop. Dizzy with desire, she laced her fingers behind his head and held on.

To her surprise, the kiss ended too soon. He broke away and, tugging at the hair on the nape of her neck, stood to take her along with him. He kissed her quickly again and turned her to face the shower wall. Her head fell forward to rest on the tile as his hands massaged her breasts, plying her nipples so they ached in pleasurable agony. But nothing compared to the delight of his cock rubbing the indent between her butt cheeks.

"Tala, tell me you want me to fuck you."

She growled, a sound similar to those he'd made, and answered the only way she could. "Hell, yes, I want you to fuck me."

"You'd better tell me what you want me to do or I'll do it the way I want. And I want to fuck you rough."

A sliver of fear spiked somewhere deep inside her. Could she trust him not to hurt her? Could she trust herself not to let him? Her answer came to her, swift and certain. Yes. She could.

She moaned, long and hard, a moan of frustration, of lust, of heat. "I want you to fuck me the way you want. I want it rough."

He exhaled a low, tortured sound that renewed her waves of hunger. "I want to take you from behind. I want to ram into you."

"Do it, Devlin."

He stepped back with her, pushing her between the shoulders so she'd place her hands on the tile ledge below the glass. He ran a hand along the slit between her legs to find her throbbing bud and she opened her buns for him. His shaft found its target and he rammed inside her, shocking her, thrilling her with the intensity of his move.

Oh, wow. He's so big. She bit her lip, hurting with each thrust, yet loving the pain. Instead of begging him to pull out, she wanted to beg him to never stop.

She bent lower, spreading her legs wider. With one long push he shoved inside her again, bumping her against the shower wall. His resulting groan pleased her in some primal way, and her body rocked along with the pounding of his dick inside her. Together their bodies moved, water cascading off them as if they were one form, the heat rising from their bodies rising with the steam.

"Fuck me hard. Please, Devlin, fuck me hard."

He gripped her ass tighter, increased his speed, pumping into her faster, deeper, longer. She closed her eyes and made the walls wrapped around him clench and unclench with each of his moves. He filled her completely, so tightly that she nearly cried. The sweet wetness that was hers mixed with the water and ran down her legs. Her hair, hanging down both sides of her face, shielded her from the shower spray. She found her fuzzy patch, opened the folds and rubbed her hand agonizingly over her throbbing nub. Her legs shook, weakened by his thrusts and the many orgasms that rolled through her.

She realized she'd wanted this from the moment she'd first seen him in the animal pen. From the second she'd laid eyes on him, she'd wanted him and she'd had to have him. No matter what.

Her panting breath echoed his. His movements made hers. Together, they became one, fucked as one. When his body tensed, she was ready and clenched the muscles of her cave tighter than even before, wanting to drag every bit of manhood out of him.

"Argh! Tala."

Her final release came when he called her name. Shockwaves rippled through her frame, traveling into his until he pulled away from her to roar his climax.

Warm come struck her lower back and she threw her head back, enjoying the feel of his seed against her body. Groaning from his release, he beat his cock against her rump, the tip of it landing in the crease between her butt cheeks, until every ounce was gone.

She slowly, carefully turned to him again, wanting to see his face. A quiet satisfaction permeated him, and she smiled, knowing she'd given him that satisfaction. The water ran down their bodies, cleansing their come from each other and he pressed against her. Holding onto him, she couldn't help but enjoy the quivers still moving along his arms and back. Especially since they matched her own. She slid her hands down the rugged surface of his torso, stopping to rest on his buttocks. "Want to go again?"

He laughed and bent to place his forehead against hers. The gentle, loving gesture nearly brought her to tears.

"Woman, ya gotta give me a little time."

"Will ten minutes be enough?"

They shared a laugh until he took her face in his palms and stared into her eyes. Mirth twitched the sides of his mouth. "You got it."

"Yeah, right. Who are you? Superman?"

"In my own way." He wiggled his eyebrows at her. "Without the cape, of course."

Chuckling at his joke, she skimmed her fingers down the curve of his ass, running over the smooth skin. *What the hell?* Her heart gained speed with what she knew couldn't be true, yet she explored farther, searching for his injury. *What happened to his wound?* The area where his rough wound should be was gone, replaced by smooth skin.

How the hell...?

Chapter Four

"What happened to your wound?"

Devlin ran his hand along her jawline then licked around the rim of her ear. "Wound?" He sniffed, enjoying the intriguing scent of her skin mixed with their bodily fluids. Not to mention the soft sleekness of her toned body. She was now his even though he hadn't marked her yet.

She pushed him away, positioning him so she could see his back. "Your gunshot wound. It feels different."

He looked at where she pointed. It took a moment before he realized what she wanted. He bowed his head, letting his wet hair fall, hiding his face. How would he explain this to her? Was now the time to tell her everything? Or should he wait and tell her about his kind, his pack, their destiny later, after they'd had more time together?

She ran her hands over his ass again, making his dick twitch in response. But another session of lovemaking would have to wait. *Lovemaking.* A satisfied, happy glow flowed over him. As a healthy strong male, he'd had lots of sex in his lifetime, but he'd never thought of any of those encounters as making love.

"Your wound looks like it's healed. How can that be?" She stared at him and he tried to reply, but couldn't think of the right words to say.

When he didn't answer her, she pushed open the door. He clutched her arm, but she jerked it out of his grasp, hurriedly stepping out of the shower to grab the towel.

"Tala, wait a sec." Devlin flipped off the spray and followed Tala, but she'd already exited the bathroom. Without bothering to get another towel, he rushed after her.

He found her in the living room, towel wrapped around her, pacing back and forth in front of the balcony doors. She muttered a few choice words at him and slapped at his hands when he reached for her.

"This doesn't make sense. How could you heal so quickly?" She paused a moment, looking to him for an answer. "Well?"

Was she simply thrown by what she'd seen? Or pissed off? He studied her, trying to decide but ended up distracted by the flare of her nostrils and the heat coloring her face. He fought back the urge to throw her on the sofa and take her again. It was a good thing the woman he loved looked sexy as hell when she was angry because she'd probably get angry at him a lot in the future. "If you'll settle down, I'll try to explain."

Instead, she resumed her trek back and forth across the floor. "Explain how? What I saw can't be. What can you possibly tell me? That you're some kind of engineered human with fantastic healing powers? This isn't some sci-fi movie. This is reality and everything has a logical answer." She stopped and glared at him. "Explain how your wound healed so fast."

"I can't." What could he tell her? To her, his existence was more on the lines of the sci-fi movie she'd mentioned. He raised his eyebrows, opening his eyes wide in a beats-the-hell-outta-me expression.

"What do you mean, you can't? You just said you could."

True, he had. But when it came down to it, was he ready? Was she? He couldn't risk losing her. "Maybe the wound wasn't so bad to begin with. Maybe you're a really good vet, er, nurse. I don't know." The air conditioner blew cold air on his wet body, making him shiver. He hated lying to her but what else could he do?

She considered his explanations but her frown deepened.

At last, she shook her head, dismissing his lame reasons, and he got ready for another barrage of questions. Yet none came.

"You're a really weird man." She narrowed her eyes at him and he squirmed.

Still, what could he say? "If you say so."

She gawked at him, thrown by his lighthearted answer, and laughed.

God, how he loved the sound of her laughter. Who knew laughter could sound so erotic? Goose bumps of desire popped out along his arms.

"Well, gee. As long as you agree with me." She tossed him another exasperated expression. "You better go get dressed. At least then you won't be a naked weird man."

Flashing a mischievous grin, he inwardly sighed a breath of relief, saluted her and marched toward the hallway. Yet before he left the room, he turned back to look at her and caught her peering at his behind. "Hey, Tala. I may be weird, but you like what you see, right?"

When she laughed harder this time, he bent over, shot her the moon and wiggled his butt at her. A pillow hit him square in the rear as he dashed from the room.

☾

Devlin punched a button on his phone to end his call. "Sorry for the interruption. Just needed to check in with my right-hand man. He's handling business while we, uh, get more acquainted." He stepped into place next to her, cutting the length of his stride to keep pace with her shorter one.

"If you need to work—" She didn't want him to leave, but she understood the demands of business.

"Nope, it's fine. Conrad can handle things." He snapped the phone closed. "See? Phone's off so we won't be interrupted again." He shoved it into his pocket and looked around. "Nice place. For a zoo."

Tala searched his face for the sneer she'd heard in his voice. When she couldn't find any, she gave him the benefit of the doubt. "Yes, it is. I'm proud of our natural habitats for the animals. And, of course, our education department is topnotch." Maybe she shouldn't brag, but she wanted him know how much she loved her work and her accomplishments.

Why she cared about his approval, she didn't know. But she did. She still wondered about his wound, but there was just something about the guy that called to her, kept her wanting to find out more. And she'd been more than a little excited when he'd asked her to show him the zoo. Besides, she hadn't anything better to do on her day off.

Yeah, right. That's the reason you're playing tour guide with a man you just met. A man you just had sex with. Super-duper sex, that is.

He pointed at one of her promotional photographs hanging on a wall. "And you're the poster child for the zoo and its good deeds?"

"You know I do some promotional spots for the zoo. Nothing big. Just local stuff."

The crease of his forehead left her wondering if he did approve. The thought of his possible disapproval tightened her neck muscles.

"One thing about the picture, Tala."

"What's that?" She planted her feet apart, ready to defend her work.

"The photograph doesn't do you justice."

His words flowed over her, easing her suspicion, while giving her a major case of get-him-in-bed-right-now-itis. "Thanks."

She tilted her head, trying to discern Devlin's expression as he scanned the area around him. Yet she couldn't tell anything. His features remained unmoving, fixed in an emotionless, noncommittal mask.

"Okay. We've seen the giraffes, the predators and the

felines. Which, judging by your reaction, I gather you don't like cats."

"You got that right."

She waited for more of an explanation, but kept on when she didn't get one. He was definitely more of a dog person. "Okay, then. Let's go see the arctic wolves."

She'd gone a yard or so ahead of him before she realized he hadn't followed her. "What is it, Devlin?" A strange expression flickered across his face, making her wish she could read his mind. But the look was soon gone and the unreadable mask fell back into place.

"Nothing. Let's go."

Tala sighed, leading him down the path that led to the wolf exhibit. A wintry wilderness spanned out before them and she couldn't help but take pride in the layout. "See? I realize it's not as good as the real thing, but we've tried to create as close a natural environment for our wolves as possible." She pointed at her favorite animal. "See the big male sitting on top of the outcrop? That's Shahkan. Isn't he gorgeous?"

The pristine white of the male's fur struck a brilliant contrast to the dark gray of the rock. Lifting his head, Shahkan sniffed the air, acknowledging their presence. His cold eyes noted Tala's existence, flicking over her in one quick moment to settle on Devlin, where his gaze stayed glued for several minutes.

Devlin's grunt brought her attention back to him. The disgust on his face was unmistakable. He loathed what he saw.

"What's the matter? Don't you like wolves, either?"

His answer came on the heels of a snarl. "Of course I do. But after seeing this, I'm wondering if you do."

"What're you talking about? I adore wolves. Can't you see how much I care by the home we've made for them?" The vexation rising up in her had her almost spitting saliva with her words. *How dare he question my love of wolves. Of any animals. Including dumb human animals like him.*

He remained stoic, arms folded, repugnance oozing from every pore. "If you loved them, you'd set them free."

Tala choked, stunned by his answer. "They're here to help their species survive. They're here to help educate humans about them. They're here because I do care."

"If you say so."

For one brief moment, she thought about taking a swing at him. Damn it all to hell and back, how she'd love to wipe that sneer off his face. But she was smart enough to know her punch wouldn't faze him, much less change his opinion. Instead, she returned his glare with all the intensity she could muster. "Yeah. I do say so. I'm the expert here, remember?"

His dark eyes locked onto her and she froze. Something about the gleam in his eyes challenged her assertion, almost as though he considered himself the expert and not her. The idea, of course, was ridiculous, but she couldn't shake it. Could he know more than she thought? "Devlin, you've never said. What do you do for a living?"

The corners of his lips tipped upward, recognizing her probe. "I have various financial interests dealing with imports and exports."

"Anything to do with animals?"

"In my business dealings? Not the way you mean." He squinted at her and smiled a big toothy grin. "But I've known some wolves in my time."

"Really? Of the four-legged or two-legged variety?"

His throaty laugh rang out and a few of the wolves moved together to stare at him. "Both."

She searched his face and saw the humor there. "Is that what you are, Devlin?"

This time he faced her, confronting her. "I'm both." *Now what did that mean?* Spinning on his heel, he strode away from her before she could respond to his strange answer.

"Wait a sec." She sprinted after him, catching him by the

arm to twirl him around. "How can you be both?"

"Remind me to show you sometime."

They paused, glaring at each other. His features closed up, drawing inward, letting his eyes do all the talking, all the arguing. She hardened her own face and stance, ready to stand her ground. Ready for anything he could throw at her.

Making something that sounded like a low growl, he grabbed her and crushed his lips to hers.

She'd been ready for anything except that.

His taste, already so familiar yet still so different, took over her mouth and she welcomed the invasion. She opened her mouth wider, wanting more of him, and he complied. He thrust his tongue inside, wrestling with hers. First sucking on her tongue, he then whipped his around and around hers.

Almost as quickly as he'd kissed her, he took his mouth from hers. A breeze floated over her lips, chilling the heat from them. But he didn't leave her for long.

Leaning in, he nibbled at the curve of her trembling mouth, tickling her with his tongue. Where he'd been hard before, he was now soft. Where he'd taken before, now he asked. She whimpered, answering him, needing him to give more. He pulled her bottom lip with his teeth and touched the aching skin with his tongue.

And again his mouth crushed to hers.

This time, she felt an urgency equaling her own. His tongue forced its way through her lips, into her mouth, running over the soft curve of her cheek. Amazingly, his kiss deepened, growing more insistent with each touch of his tongue.

If he hadn't lifted her off her feet, his kiss would have.

Let him take me into the woods surrounding the path. Hell, just let him take me.

As though reading her mind again, he carried her off the path, still kissing her. Branches brushed against her arms, scratching her, but she didn't care. She gasped, keeping her eyes closed, and clung to him.

Adding small teasing bites to the assault on her lips, he lowered her to her feet in the small bare space among a cluster of dense bushes. She panted, trying to catch her breath, loving the lust coursing through her. Keeping his hand on her lower back, he popped the button on her jeans and tugged the zipper down, letting them fall to her ankles.

She found his zipper, but he snatched her hand away.

"No. Just enjoy."

She couldn't nod, couldn't speak. And lost her breath when he sank to his knees in front of her.

Keeping her eyes closed, she gripped his shoulders and held on. *Please, oh, please.* No other words would form. She could no longer think beyond that simple plea.

His warm breath through her thin panties startled her and she giggled. His heat continued to flow over her, tingling the hair under the material. *Please, oh, please.* Echoing the refrain again, she waited, stilling her body, readying for what she knew was coming. And again he surprised her.

Instead of kissing her on her other lips, he placed one finger of each hand along the top of her panties and skimmed them outward from her belly. She groaned, wanting him to rush, but unable to say anything to urge him on. Instead, she pushed her hips forward, egging him to quit tempting her and lick her.

He chuckled and kept running his fingers along the rim.

After an agonizing wait, his fingers finally met in the middle again—right over her mound.

She moaned again and opened her eyes. Amber eyes twinkled up at her above a grin so mischievous she had to laugh. He grinned wider and lifted one eyebrow.

"Spread your legs."

She licked her lips in the same instant he licked his and felt the wetness gush between her legs. She spread her legs, ready to submit to his wishes and her desire.

Long teeth—*the better to eat you with, my dear*—flashed before gripping the delicate panties and ripping them off. She inhaled and, for the first time, wondered if anyone could hear them. Yet even if someone could, she wouldn't stop him.

He lifted his gaze to her, her panties in his mouth, and flung them away.

He's such an animal. An excitement hotter than she'd ever known swirled in her stomach.

He rubbed his thumbs against her clit and the burning she'd first felt was nothing to the flame scorching through her pussy and into her abdomen. She squirmed, but he stayed with her, never letting the toe-curling pleasure end. The soft breeze wafting around them met the hot wetness dampening her inner thighs and she shivered. Continuing to rotate his thumbs over her clit, he slid his tongue into the crease between her leg and mound.

She mewed, knowing he was teasing her and loving every second of it. Again, she silently begged. But for what? To continue the delightful torture? Or to end the teasing and bring her to the final major climax? If he'd asked her to choose, she couldn't have done it. She dug her fingernails into his shoulders, determined to take everything he gave.

His kisses included nibbling now, splitting her attention between what his mouth did and what his thumbs did. Suddenly, he wrapped one hand around her leg and thrust two fingers into her pussy, keeping his thumb on her aching nub. And still the kisses continued.

She tracked her fingers through the hair at the nape of his neck and let her head fall back. Moaning, she forgot everything except the kisses, his fingers plunging in and out of her wet-slickened channel, and his thumb making hard circles over her clit. Climax after climax vibrated from her center.

Had anyone ever finger-fucked her like this? If someone had, she couldn't remember it. And she would have remembered.

His tongue slid over to join his thumb and she looked down between her tits to watch him eat her. His eyes were open, staring up at her as he swiped his tongue over his thumb, over her hot bud. With a grin, he used his teeth to tug on the skin around her clit. A whirlwind of lust raked into her and she cried out, clamping a hand over her mouth to muffle the sound.

"Tell me you like it, Tala." His warm breath tickled the damp area.

"Oh, hell."

"Tell me. Say the words."

"I can't."

He paused, only for a second, before resuming the finger-fuck.

She gazed down at him and smiled. "I can't. I don't just like it. I frickin' love it."

"Then you're going to go ape-shit for this." His chuckle was short, followed by the press of his mouth on her clit.

She stared at him, wanting to see everything thing he did to her, wanting to see him as she came.

Sucking on her, licking on her, fucking her with his fingers, he stormed her pussy. His hand squeezed her buttock, holding her as close as he could get her. Using his teeth, he sent sharp, short flashes of wonderful pain through her throbbing clit that arced outward in lightning bolts of pleasure. "Oh-oh! I'm going to…"

In answer, he increased the pressure, sucking longer, driving deeper.

Her body tightened, her vaginal walls clutching tightly around his fingers. With another cry no hand could smother, she released, the climax striking her, sending tremors to weaken her legs.

She collapsed on top of him, weak and panting. "Holy shit."

He gently helped her to the ground and wrapped his arms

around her. She snuggled her head under his chin. She smelled her own juices on his breath and sighed. *I could lie against him all day. For the rest of my life.* The idea of spending her life with Devlin shocked her, then pleased her. But would he feel the same way?

Devlin sat up, ramrod straight. "Do you hear that?"

She sat up alongside him, frantically pulling her jeans on and finger-combing her hair. Had someone heard them? How would she explain what they'd done to the zoo's administrators? "Hear what?" she whispered.

"Her. Did you hear her?" Speaking at a normal level, Devlin didn't seem worried about anyone hearing them. But she couldn't mistake the anxiety in his tone. He hurried to his feet, taking her along with him. "There she goes again." He tilted his head to the side, listening. Still gripping her arm, he broke through the branches and back onto the trail. "She's hurt."

Tala did a one-eighty, trying to spot something out of the ordinary. But the crowd around them kept walking, laughing and enjoying the zoo. *At least no one appears to have heard us.* "Who's hurt? Who are you talking about?"

Making a noise that sounded eerily like a wolf's warning growl, Devlin took off sprinting down the path leading to a small building. Tala ran after him, trying to keep up. Following on his heels, she burst into the building to find George Groggins, a new employee, standing outside a small holding cage. With exclamations of glee, he stabbed a metal pole through the bars of the cage, jabbing, prodding the injured wolf cowering in a corner. The animal was trapped, unable to move with her wounded leg, defenseless against the attack.

"George!" Her shout brought the stubby man around, his beaming face freezing in shock. He recognized her and instantly his features melted together, transforming to show the affable exterior she'd come to expect.

George opened his mouth to speak, but choked on his words as Devlin's hands wrapped around his throat.

The gurgling sounds coming from George's mouth encouraged Devlin to squeeze harder. Placing what little of his hands he could get around Devlin's large wrists, the rotund man fought for his life. Tala shouted to let the man go, but Devlin ignored her. Instead, instinct kicked in and his primary thought was to destroy the enemy of the injured she-wolf. With the animal inside him clawing at the surface, trying to get free, he spread his lips wide and snarled.

George's eyes bugged open, beseeching Tala. She seized one of Devlin's arms and pulled at him, but his hands remained locked firmly around George's throat. He wouldn't let this slimeball of a human hurt any wolf if he could stop him. And he could definitely stop him. For good, if necessary.

Tala hung from his arm, but still he didn't, wouldn't let go. His focus stayed on George and his power grew stronger with each second.

Landing on her feet, Tala left them and, although he wanted to see where she'd gone, Devlin kept his eyes on his prey. She'd return. He was sure of it. And then, once he'd dealt with this bastard, he'd explain everything to her. This time he'd have to.

"Devlin, let him go!" She stood behind him and tugged on his shoulders.

He heard the plea, the panic in her voice, yet wouldn't let her dissuade him. "No. This jackal should pay for what he did."

"He will, Devlin. I promise. Now let him go."

Shaking his head in refusal, Devlin opened his mouth wider, allowing his sharp fangs to peek through. He felt his animal grow even stronger, nearer to breaking loose. George, unable to cry, managed a strangled whimper and kicked his feet wildly, trying to break Devlin's hold on him. To stop George's kicking, Devlin bent his head and laid the points of his teeth against the man's neck, pressing just hard enough to make an indentation, but not deep enough to draw blood.

Pain hit him between his shoulder blades, zapping his transformation back to full human form. Loosening his grip on George, he whirled toward Tala.

"Shit!" His angry glare fell to the iron rod in Tala's hand and disbelief flowed through him like icy water through a winter's creek. "You struck me?" Shudders racked his body, but he managed to stay upright even while George's limp body slumped to the floor beside him. "Were you trying to hurt me? Why?"

She lowered the rod, her mouth gaping. "Wow. Most guys would have dropped like a sack of dog food. But you're still standing. Amazing."

"Not that I care for the comparison, but thanks a lot. Wanna try another whack? Maybe this time you can take my head off."

"Don't be so dramatic. I only hit you a little." At his probing glare, she changed her tune. "Okay, maybe more than a little. But you're a big, tough guy and can take it. Obviously. Don't be such a wuss."

He took a shaky step toward her, but stopped when she pointed at George.

"Oh, shit, Devlin. I think you killed him."

With the ache between his shoulders already starting to ebb, Devlin bent to examine his victim. "No, I didn't. The little coward fainted, is all." Snarling his disgust, he strode over to the cage where the she-wolf lay on her side, unmoving. Squatting next to the cage, he examined the wolf, murmuring soft words of comfort.

He turned to see Tala holding George's head in her lap and his stomach lurched. "He doesn't deserve your sympathy. She does." A caustic laugh brought his true feelings out. "Hell, *I* do for you hitting me."

Tala stared at him, her face unreadable. But Devlin didn't have time to sort out her emotions. "Key. Where's the key to this cage?"

Without saying a word, Tala nodded to a pegboard on the wall closest to him. He returned her nod and retrieved the key. Turning the lock, he opened the door and stepped into the cage.

"Devlin, no! You can't go in there. She's wounded and dangerous."

A great sadness crept over Devlin. Could she not see that the man was the dangerous one? Stupid brutality was always more dangerous than the instinct of self-preservation. Yet instead of speaking his thoughts out loud, he chose a different method of teaching her. "No, I don't think so. Trust me."

Kneeling beside the female wolf, Devlin ran his hands over her long muscled body. He blew out a breath of relief when he didn't find any broken bones other than her bandaged leg. Placing both hands on her, he gently stroked her, giving her the best form of treatment he knew how to give. "The asshole didn't break any of her bones. But he beat her up a lot. She'll have bruises on most of her body."

George groaned and Tala laid his head on the floor to move away from him. "That's incredible. She must be horribly injured to let a human run his hands over her without sedation."

"Call the police," George croaked. Even the wolf tried to lift her head at the sound of his voice. "Call the police."

"To come and lock you up, George?"

Devlin, elated at the vehemence in Tala's tone, grinned at her. George struggled to a sitting position and pulled his shirt away from his neck. "That freak bit me."

"I don't see any bite marks. Or blood." Still, Tala checked with Devlin. And although a smile covered her features, he noticed the glint of worry, distrust and confusion in her eyes. "You bit him?"

Devlin puffed a bit of air out the side of his mouth and rolled his eyes. "Of course not. The man's an idiot as well as an animal abuser. The only person I'd ever bite is you."

He swallowed a chuckle at the pink zipping up her neck and into her cheeks. Coughing, she confronted the human slug.

"Okay, George. I'll call the police. And when they get here, you tell them Devlin bit you and I'll tell them about your mistreatment of the animals." At his surprised expression, she added, "Yeah, that's right. I've had my suspicions before now. More than one animal has turned up hurt. So, Georgie. Still want me to call the police?"

Cursing at them, George scrambled to his feet and staggered to the door. "Your boyfriend's a freak. You'd better watch out."

"I'll do that. Oh, and Georgie?"

When she had his full attention, she let him have it. "Rest assured I'll be telling the director about this. Consider yourself fired. Get the hell outta my zoo."

George tossed more threats and curses at them, then stumbled outside.

"Way to go, Tala. Although I'd like to have finished him off for good."

"I was afraid you had." Tala crossed over to him and knelt on the other side of the wolf. "How is she?"

He raised his head to gaze into her worried eyes. "She'll be fine. In time."

Tala nodded and reached out to touch her. But when she got too close, the she-wolf raised her head, bared her fangs and growled. "Easy, girl. I won't hurt you. I guess she doesn't let just anyone touch her. But you certainly have a way with her. Or is that true for all females?" Tala's blue eyes twinkled at him, her next question reaching her eyes well before it reached her lips. "You're really something with her. So tell me. Why do you have the magic touch? Are you a vet?"

He choked at the thought and hid his wince. Wanting to keep his answer as far from the truth as possible, he glanced back at the wolf. "I guess she realizes I'm her knight in not-so-shining armor."

She smiled, although a frown creased her forehead. "I guess we can consider your helping her as passing your luck on."

He tilted his head at her. "Huh?"

"You know. I helped you. Now you're helping her. Passing it on."

Understanding, he drew his hand over the wolf's head. The tired animal closed her eyes, giving total control to him.

"Just incredible. If you ever want a job at the zoo, just let me know. I'll put in a good word for you."

He knew she'd meant the offer as a compliment, but he didn't care. "No thanks. I'd rather be an animal than take care of one."

"Oh, you're an animal, all right. The perfect mix of man and beast."

Startled at her close description of him, he caught her hand and held it. "Yeah, I am."

She blushed, but met his gaze straight on. "Perfect? Or part man and beast?"

He squeezed her hand and let go. "Both."

A smile brightened her face but was quickly replaced by a quizzical expression. He knew she wanted to say something but had changed her mind. Instead, she retrieved her cell phone from her pocket, flipped it opened and punched a number.

"Floyd? It's Tala. Send a couple of men over to the containment building to take the she-wolf to the veterinary office. Oh, and call the director to tell him I just fired George Groggins." She listened for a moment before responding. "Yeah, I know I don't really have the authority, but once John hears why I canned him, he'll make it official."

Devlin took a deep breath and relaxed. He'd dodged a bullet from any further questions about wolves. Or so he thought.

"Devlin? How'd you know she was a female? Even before you came into the building?"

☾

What the hell went on in there? Conrad watched from a safe distance, his body hidden by the bushes and trees surrounding the area near the wolf habitat, as a short, balding man stumbled from the building. Although the chubby man didn't appear injured, the choice words he used about Devlin left no doubt that he'd run into him.

What's Devlin doing at a damn zoo, anyway? Hell, he'll do almost anything for a good female, but go to the zoo? Even if she's a vet, she couldn't have gotten him here without a fight. Unless she's promised him a helluva a lot of outrageous sex. He licked his lips. *Yep, that has to be it. But damn it, if Devlin had only left his phone on, I wouldn't have had to track him down in this awful place. Still, it's a good thing he mentioned where he was.*

Conrad had finally located Devlin and the human female—*Tala Wilde*—when the cry of a she-wolf had ripped through the air. Before Conrad could stop him, Devlin had charged into a small building. After a lot of commotion, the small human had left and Devlin and Tala remained inside. *What can they be doing? Why don't they come out?* It worried him that he hadn't heard anything in a while.

Conrad lifted his nose to sniff the air and resisted the urge to shift to wolf form. The way his luck was running lately, he'd get snatched up by some industrious zoo employee and thrown in the habitat with those other poor bastards. Or, worse, a wolf-shifters' nightmare: snagged by the dogcatcher. No, better to wait and see.

Where are they anyway? Should I take a chance and sneak over to the building's windows for a look inside? Or should I sit tight and wait them out? Shit, how I hate this.

Conrad's stomach rumbled, reminding him that he'd last eaten over five hours ago. That was way too long for a big guy like him to go without sustenance. He sniffed, this time not hunting for Devlin's scent, but for food. Wishing he could follow the tempting smells coming from the antelope habitat, he scanned the area for man-made food. A hot dog vendor's cart sat several paces away and he frowned. What an insulting name for a food. But it would be better than nothing.

He parted the bushes to step through when another scent hit him so hard he had to grip the branches to stay steady on his feet. An odor, so disgusting and repulsive it caused his empty stomach to roll over, assaulted his nostrils. Something foul was close. Very close.

Ducking back behind the bushes, he allowed his inner animal to transform part of him. His eyes shifted, narrowed and changed. Sliding his gaze around the open area in front of him, he searched for the owner of the stench. And found it.

A disheveled man scratched himself and motioned to three other men. *Shifter hunters!* Although the sightseeing public didn't see the difference between themselves and these men, Conrad did. Even their smell, their skin taking on the subtle smell of gun metal and silver, set them apart from other humans. The way the men held their bodies—alert, tense and ready to spring into action—shot warning signals through him. The walkie-talkies fastened to their belts blinked on and off. If he knew anything at all about these men, he knew they secreted weapons of various descriptions on their bodies. Each man studied his surroundings, checking out both visitor and zoo employee.

These scumbags crawled out of their holes every once in a while, making life miserable for the shifters who lived in the city. Unknown to the general population, this group of humans knew about the shifters and made it their mission in life to eradicate the werewolves. Thankfully, the hunters' skills were limited and they rarely found a shifter. But sometimes, like a year ago when they'd run across Sammy Chow of the Chow Pack, they killed.

Conrad shifted a little more, careful to contain his instinct to shift all the way. Although hunters could smell a shifter even in human form, going all wolf made his scent stronger. Still, he allowed his ears to change, wanting to pick up the men's conversation.

"Shit. I know I smelled werewolf a moment ago." The tallest of the four men kept turning in a circle, scoping out everything around him. "It was here for a good five minutes before I lost it."

The burly, box-shaped man nodded. "I know, Carl. I got the same impression. A shifter is near, men, so keep on the alert."

The two other men grunted and pulled away from Carl and the burly man. One of them walked up to the arctic wolf exhibit, raised his hands with an imaginary rifle and pretended to shoot the big male snarling at him from the rocks.

"Skanland, we're close. Damn it, I want another shifter. A year's too long to go without a kill."

The boxy man he'd called Skanland shook his head. "Yeah, I know. But remember, I want some fun with this one first. We capture it and *then* we kill it."

Conrad ground his teeth together, refraining from growling and drawing their attention. He stooped lower behind the bushes. Too bad he couldn't go into a full shift and rid the world of a few of them right here and now. But there were too many innocents around.

Did Devlin know the hunters were around? How would he and the woman get past them?

The hair on Conrad's neck stood at attention. As soon as Devlin exited the building, the hunters would pick up his scent and attack. He had to do something to help his friend. But what?

Chapter Five

Conrad stretched out his neck, hoping to hear more of the hunters' conversation. Maybe, just maybe, if he found out what they had planned, he could come up with a way to help Devlin without him ending up as a trophy mounted over their fireplace.

Two men dressed in khaki pants and shirts emblazoned with the zoo's insignia passed by the hunters, heading for the small building beside the wolf habitat. The man in front pushed open the door of the building and called to those inside. "Tala, what's the problem?" The rest of his words drifted away as the door slammed shut behind them.

Carl, the hunter closest to the building, whipped his head toward the opening. "In there, Skanland. I smelled shifter coming from in there. Faint, but there."

Skanland nodded and moved closer, dropping his voice lower. "Yeah, I smelled it, too. One of them is nearby."

Carl motioned to the other two men. "It's about time. Let's go get him." He slid his hand underneath his shirt and lumbered forward until Skanland's grip on his arm brought him up short.

"No. I told you. I want this one alive." Glancing at the zoo visitors swarming around them, Skanland added, "Besides, it's too busy here. We wouldn't want to make a scene." His grin sported discolored teeth made even uglier by the shine of a golden tooth.

"So what'll we do?"

Crooking his finger at the others, Skanland brought them into a huddle. "We wait. He's gotta come out sooner or later and then we'll follow him. Plus, this way, we can make sure how many we're dealing with. From the smell, I figure it's only one, but a big one. Or maybe two. But you never know until you see their hairy asses."

The other hunters chuckled their agreement. Skanland led them to a nearby picnic shelter and they settled into their places to wait. They were too far for even Conrad's sensitive hearing to pick up their words, but still close enough to watch.

Should I try and make it inside the building to warn Devlin? No, then we'll all be trapped. He curled his lip in disgust. Why couldn't these humans leave them alone? As far as he knew, no shifter had ever done them any harm, except in self-defense. But that didn't seem to matter to the hunters. He couldn't remember a time when the hunters hadn't wanted shifters dead.

Can I take all four of them? Conrad sized up the men and decided he might have a chance. Four against one weren't the best odds, but he'd had worse.

Hunters were a predictable bunch, which was why he never expected them to do what they did. After waiting only a few minutes, they regrouped into a tight group and strode away from the building and their intended prey. Conrad frowned, unable to fathom their actions. And try as he might, he couldn't believe their departure was a good thing. Something was up.

Devlin and Tala exited the building the same moment he made his decision. From the daffy smile on Devlin's face, he guessed they knew nothing about the hunters. "Shit. Talk about a dog in heat."

Devlin's eyes drifted toward the bushes where he was hiding and Conrad ducked. Since the hunters might be watching Devlin, he'd better stay out of sight, but close by so he could help if needed. If the hunters planned on jumping Devlin, he could give the hunters a surprise of their own. Meanwhile, business would have to wait.

Conrad kept low to the shrubs outlining the path Devlin and Tala followed away from the wolf area. He stayed a few yards behind the couple and paused whenever Devlin turned around to scan his surroundings. His friend could sense his presence, but hadn't seen him.

The sun was starting to set beyond the horizon by the time they left the park. Purple and blues painted the sky as Devlin and Tala walked through the parking lot. Trailing them, Conrad ducked behind cars, keeping them within earshot, all the while on the lookout for the hunters.

"You can't find your own car?"

"Not a word, Devlin. I don't normally park in the public lot. I did today so you could see the park entrance. My reserved space is in the employee lot, so I'm not used to having to hunt for my car."

Devlin's soft chuckle matched Conrad's. *She's a spirited one, all right.*

A dark shadow darted by him. He searched the rows of vehicles and the hair on his neck stood erect in alarm. Another dark shape stumbled between a van and a motorcycle, bumped into a fender, and plopped onto his rump with a grunt.

Hunters! But clumsy ones. This could be fun, after all.

Devlin spun around at the hunter's groan and Conrad ducked once more. Both he and the bumbling hunter froze until Tala started pulling Devlin along with her again.

"Psst!"

The hunter jolted, startled at Conrad's hiss, his mouth falling wide to gawk at him. Wiggling his fingers in a small wave, Conrad closed his hand, leaving his middle finger extended. The hunter, dumbfounded, continued to gape at him.

"Aw, hell. Looks like I didn't get the brightest one of the bunch. And that's saying a lot." Deciding the man needed more coaxing, Conrad snarled and quickly discarded his clothing.

Still the man remained motionless.

"What do you not get about a naked man, dude?" When the possible misunderstanding of his question struck him, Conrad cringed, hastening to clarify. "Now hold up. It's not what you're thinking. I meant…a naked man about to shift, you idiot."

Without hesitating, he dropped to all fours and changed. Reddish-blond fur covered his body while his ears elongated and claws scraped blacktop. Growling, he tensed his legs and flung his body at the not-so-bright hunter.

☾

A nerve-splitting howl startled Tala, sending her spinning toward the sound. "What the hell?" Two shapes rolled against the side of a jeep, setting off its alarm system, striking with a force strong enough to dislodge a hubcap and propel the sphere straight toward her.

Devlin grabbed her arm and yanked her out of the way of the vehicle's airborne missile and into his arms. His eyes, that strange mix of brown and gold, held her until another cry—definitely human this time—broke their connection. One of the dark shapes scampered underneath a car and Tala stooped, hoping to see where it'd gone. "Did you see that?"

Had she really seen what she thought she'd seen? She bent lower to get a clearer view, but the shape was gone.

Two khaki-clad men raced in pursuit of the fleeing form, pausing to grab the first man and haul him to his feet. "Why'd you let him get away?"

The first man shook them loose. "It ain't my fault. I ain't used to seeing another man get naked."

Tala crooked her head, wondering if she'd heard him correctly. *A naked man in the zoo parking lot?* Devlin had ended up naked in her clinic's animal pen. For a second, she worried that he'd gone commando.

Devlin caught her suspicious glance. "Oh, come on. Tell me

you didn't think they were talking about me. Besides, we've been together all day."

She made a face and turned just in time to see the men dash between the rows of cars. Several yards away, one of the men stopped and stared at Devlin as if only now noticing them. He pointed at Devlin but before he could say anything, the others reversed their course to snatch him along with them.

"Come on. We need to get out of here." Devlin jerked her arm, breaking for the opposite direction.

She wrenched her arm free and whirled on him. "No! I want to see what's going on. Don't you?" She stared at him, confused by his lack of curiosity, when suddenly his face changed, its shape contorting, almost as if his jaw had extended before her eyes. *It must be the excitement.* She shook her head, denying what she'd seen. "I want to know what I saw. 'Cause if I didn't know better, I'd swear I saw a wolf. I saw a man wrestling with a wolf." *But if the man wrestled a wolf, why did he mention a naked man? Naked men and wrestling wolves? Oh, come on.*

"A wolf?" Devlin glanced in the direction the men had run and shook his head. "What color was the— Never mind. I'm sure he, uh, the man is fine. Besides, they're long gone."

"But I need to tell zoo security about this." Tala turned back toward the zoo entrance.

"Tala!"

She found herself stunned by his gaze. His eyes, more yellow than brown now, trapped her, cementing her feet to the ground. Her breath shortened, quickening to match the pace of her pounding heartbeat. "Yes?" Suddenly the image of him kneeling at her feet, his tongue sliding over her naked skin, rocked her, weakening her knees again. She couldn't believe she'd had a climax in the middle of the zoo. But she was damn glad she had.

"Tala!"

"I loved it." Hell, yes, she'd loved every minute of their tryst in the bushes.

"What?" Devlin cocked his head to the side, confusion written across his face. Again he stretched out his hand to her. "Let's go."

Once she realized what she'd said, she shook her head and tried to regain her composure. *Earth to Tala. You're out of the bushes and in a parking lot with a wild wolf.* Yet when she looked at Devlin, she wasn't sure which wild wolf she meant. This time, however, she took his hand.

Leading her, Devlin sprinted away, weaving in and out between the rows of cars. Tala fought to keep up, her long legs lengthening to match his stride. Her breath scratched through her throat.

With unerring accuracy, Devlin brought them to her sports car, grabbed the keys from her and punched the button to unlock the doors. He swung her into the passenger's seat, then jogged to the driver's side and slid into place. Shooting her a disgruntled look, he turned the ignition and pulled out of the parking spot without another glance.

"I don't understand you. Why don't you want to find out what's going on? Especially with a wolf involved. And how'd you know where my car was? Not to mention letting me walk around hunting for it and looking like a dummy."

Devlin grunted, and scanned the lot, worry flickering across his features, then shook his head. "No time. Not our problem." He tossed her a smirk. "Didn't ask."

"What's with the stilted speech? Don't care. Me, Jane. You, Tarzan?"

He shook his head and kept his sight glued to the outside. "Home, Tala. Now." Lifting both eyebrows, he added, "Clear enough?"

"Yeah, clear. Very bossy, but clear. And, by the way, I don't take well to anyone bossing—"

Devlin stomped on the brake pedal, sending her flying forward. Her hands, held up to protect herself, rammed against the dashboard as her gaze locked onto the hood of her car. A very large golden red wolf crouched on the shiny blue surface.

Her mouth fell open and she grabbed Devlin by the arm. Yet even while she tugged on him, Devlin ignored her, scowling at the wolf. The wolf and Devlin stared at each other. Then, in the same moment, both Devlin and the wolf cocked their heads at each other and lifted one eyebrow in a what-the-hell-are-you-doing-here gesture.

Unable to believe what she'd seen, Tala whispered, "Did you see him? He copied you. You two did the same thing."

But again, Devlin didn't answer. Man and wolf concentrated on each other for several seconds more before the wolf tensed, muscles rippling in preparation. Baring his fangs, the wolf flicked his tail in a defiant swish.

"Go home. Now."

"Go home? Are you kidding? He's not a dog, you know. You might as well ask him to fetch your slippers." Yet she'd swear she saw understanding in the wolf's eyes.

"Get them!"

Devlin, Tala, and the wolf turned in sync to see the three men joined by a fourth. All of them rushed through a line of vehicles toward their car, guns drawn and ready.

Tala's adrenalin kicked into high gear, sending her into flight mode. Devlin was right. This was no time to ask questions. At least, not until she understood what this was about. As though reading her thoughts, the wolf sprang away from the car, raking claw marks across her hood, and landing on the roof of a nearby sedan.

"Hey, my car!"

The damage on her car was forgotten, however, when the wolf lifted a front paw to cover his mouth, almost as if saying, "Oops. Sorry."

Tala blinked, squinted at him but by then he'd lowered his paw and hunkered down into a low crouch. The sedan's roof bent under his weight, creaking in protest when he bounded to yet another vehicle. She strained to follow the wolf's path.

Devlin rammed the accelerator pedal to the floor, lurching her against the seat.

She checked the side mirror to see the men stop in their tracks, shout angry slurs at them, and rotate as a group to continue the way the wolf had fled.

"Oh, my God. Is this amazing or what? I told you I saw a wolf." Tala reached into her pocket, flipped open her cell phone and dialed. "He's not one of ours, either. So huge. So amazing. And did you see his unusual coloring? God, he was beautiful."

"I wouldn't call him beautiful. Average, maybe."

What'd he say? She stared at Devlin, not believing the tone in his voice. "Shit, Devlin. You actually sound jealous. Of a wolf." Whether it was about a wolf or not, his being jealous was hot. And making her hotter by the second.

What was it about this man that made her react so differently than she ever had to any other man? What was it about this man that made her constantly think of throwing him to the ground and fucking him until they both fell apart exhausted?

Devlin ignored her, concentrating on wheeling her car around the parking lot. The car swerved, barely missing collisions with the parked vehicles on each row. She gasped and grappled for the strap above her. A low rumble sounded from deep inside Devlin and the warmth flowing between her legs doubled in intensity.

For Pete's sake, girl. There's a time and place. Get your mind off the sex. She ignored the protest her body launched, determined to stay in control. "Damn it all to hell and back, Devlin. Watch where you're going."

"I am."

The strain in his voice shot her in the gut with apprehension, cooling the burn in her abdomen. He hadn't appeared this nervous before they'd gotten in the car when the men were almost upon them. So why now?

After several rings, she heard a man's voice on the other

end of the line and pressed her phone to her ear. "Jim, it's Tala. You're never going to believe this. There's a wolf. A big, beautiful wolf in the parking lot." She laughed, astounded she could do so. "No, I'm not kidding. He's huge and gorgeous with unusual golden-red fur. Get some men out to the lot, but not before you notify the authorities. Some jackasses are trying to hunt him down and I get the impression they're not concerned about who might get hurt in the process."

She listened to the disbelief in Jim's voice, but didn't let him finish. "I don't know where he came from. Maybe someone's pet got too big. Or more likely, he's down from the mountains."

Devlin yanked the car to the left, inches from a head-on crash with a lamppost.

Gritting her teeth, she clutched the armrest for support and silently sent up a prayer. "Shit, Devlin, watch out!"

Devlin fixed her with an expression loaded with worry. "Trust me. He's not someone's pet."

"I'm more worried about your driving than the wolf, you maniac." She covered the phone. "How do you know, anyway?"

"I just do. Trust me on this one."

"What? Yeah, Jim. I'm here. Huh? No. Just a friend. Now get going before someone gets hurt or the wolf gets away." She clicked off the phone as another swerve swept her against the door.

Devlin spotted the exit and whooped, whipping the car out of the lot and onto the road running parallel to the zoo. The car banked off the side of the road, spinning its wheels in the gravel and rocking Tala against the door. "Hey, come on! Are you trying to kill us? Slow down."

Devlin looked down at his foot and eased up on the gas pedal. A truck's horn blared, jerking their heads up toward an oncoming eighteen-wheeler.

"Shit! Devlin!" Tala fell sideways and grabbed the steering wheel. The car careened to the right and onto the shoulder of the road. Gravel, dirt and debris struck the car and windshield, tearing a cry from her throat. "Hit the brake!"

Instead, Devlin slammed his boot down on the accelerator, sending the car fishtailing along the side of the road. She screamed, losing her grip on the steering wheel.

"The brake, Devlin. The brake. The other one!" Tala bounced in her seat and braced for the inevitable crash.

Devlin's jaw slammed tight and he thrust his foot onto the brake. Jerking forward, Tala's head whipped back and forth, catching her tongue between her teeth. Blood squirted into her mouth but she held fast to the dashboard and handgrip. At last, the car came to a stop.

Anger broke through her fear. "Where'd you learn to drive? The Indy 500?"

He grumbled at her through clenched teeth. "I'm doing the best I can." Shooting her an odd look, he added, "Considering."

"Considering what?"

"Considering I've never driven a car before."

Tala didn't know whether to laugh or to cry. But for damn sure, she'd get him out of the driver's seat. They'd gotten lucky this time. Usually the road leading to the zoo was filled with motorists, but today, only a few cars had sped by them, honking their horns in warning.

"Are you seriously telling me you've never driven before?"

Devlin, in typical macho-male style, glared at her and returned to staring out at the road. "Not officially. I never had a need to drive."

"How can you not have a need to drive?" Who *was* this guy? *First he howls like a wolf, then he comforts a wild wolf. Then, to top it off, he ends up driving my car when he doesn't know how.* She swallowed, thankful that the bleeding had stopped. She ran the possible scenarios through her mind. Was he from another country? One where owning and driving a car wasn't the norm? Was he Amish? Perhaps independently wealthy with a chauffeur? Yeah, he had the air of a man who answered to no one. But, even with a paid driver, why wouldn't

Dance on the Wilde Side

he have learned to drive?

"But you managed to get us on the road. You almost killed us a few times, but you knew enough to get us out of the parking lot."

"I watched you drive to the zoo. It didn't look too difficult."

Tala wondered if the day could get any stranger. "Oh, right. It's a cinch. No need for any actual lessons."

"Look. Don't make this a big deal. You can drive if you want." Devlin swung open his door, pushed his massive body out of the car and strode to the passenger's side.

Blowing out a huge breath of relief, Tala climbed over the console and into the driver's seat. "Gee, thanks. I believe I will."

She switched on the engine, waited for her hands to stop shaking, and pulled onto the road. Picking up her ringing phone, she hoped her jangled nerves wouldn't show in her voice. "Tala here."

Devlin kept his head averted, looking out the window, obviously hoping to avoid her inevitable questions. Unfortunately, Jim did nothing to soothe her uneasiness. "You didn't find anything? No wolf? No men? But how?" She noted the disbelief registering in his words. "And nobody else saw or heard anything?"

After Jim's explanation, Tala shut her phone and slid it back into her pocket. Even though Devlin didn't act interested, she decided he needed to hear the news. "The head of security said they canvassed the entire lot and came up empty. No men and no wolf. Only a couple of dented and scratched cars. They're continuing to check out the rest of the zoo, but nothing so far."

He kept his head turned away from her.

"Well, I have the claw marks on my hood to prove I'm not insane. And you, of course." *As evidence. But on the other hand, maybe he was the crazy one...*

Devlin shifted to face her, an odd expression covering his features. "You're not insane." He smirked. "And neither am I."

Now it was her turn to avoid a face-to-face talk. She kept her eyes on the road before them, fighting to keep from asking him questions.

"Still, I wouldn't go spreading the story around if I were you. Those marks on your hood are just that. Scratches, not necessarily claw marks."

Tala stretched her neck to get a better look at the long lines running half the length of her hood. "Yeah, I guess I can't prove they came from wolf claws. Or claws of any kind." She wouldn't want any reporters to get wind of the story, anyway. "The media would have a field day with a large wolf that can mimic people's gestures. Besides, I wouldn't want anyone to panic over this. Visitors might stay away from the zoo."

Devlin slumped down in the seat, the stress oozing out of his body in almost tangible waves. But why would he worry about this?

Tala made a mental note to call Jim once they got home. She needed to make sure the authorities kept an eye out for the animal. Not to mention the weapon-wielding men.

☾

They arrived at her apartment after a quiet, strained ride home. Tala stalked around her car, noting the damage to the hood as well as other scratches and dents. Devlin distanced himself from her curse-filled mutterings, deciding the best course of action was to keep his mouth shut until she finished her tirade. He didn't blame her, of course, but he didn't see the need to be close enough to get singed from her scorching wrath. Instead, he waited for her to finish and silently followed her up the steps into her apartment.

"I could use something to eat."

Tala shot him a you've-got-some-nerve look but headed into the small kitchen anyway. In rapid-fire motion, she dove into the cupboards and refrigerator, putting a loaf of bread and sandwich meat onto the counter beside him.

"Just so you'll understand. I'm not your waitress or your cook." She stopped, hands on her hips, ready for action. "In fact, I'm not sure what I am. Or what we are. Or even what *you* are."

Figuring silence was beneficial to his health, Devlin shoved one of the sandwiches he'd made into his mouth. Maybe if he kept his mouth full she wouldn't expect him to answer. If he was lucky, her hurricane rant would blow itself out soon.

"I have this problem with taking in strays. Especially injured strays. Besides, I felt kind of guilty about... Well, you know what." She eyed him, suspicion oozing from her. "But you're better now. In fact, I still haven't figured out how you healed so fast. So why are you still hanging around? And why am I letting you?"

Devlin lowered his head, letting his hair fall in front of his face. Next to her dropping the subject, he hoped his passive behavior would keep her talking without expecting any responses. Fortunately for him, it did.

"I'll tell you why. Because I'm a sap, that's why. A grade-A, prime-beef, stupid-ass sap. A sucker for a hurt soul and a helluva great—"

At her abrupt stop, Devlin glanced up and caught the expression on her face. Grinning, he finished the sentence for her. "A helluva great lover?"

She blushed. This tough, independent, liberated, sexually-free woman blushed. And he loved the color on her.

"Never mind. And don't go finishing my sentences for me."

She tried to move past him, but he caught her around the waist and pulled her to him. "I don't think you want me to 'never mind'. In fact, I think you want me to mind a lot." He nuzzled her earlobe and she rewarded him with a shuddering sigh.

Slipping his tongue inside her ear, he ran his hand along her spine to slide under the clasps of her bra. He moved his other hand up the front, pulling her T-shirt along with him. In one smooth motion, shirt and bra fell to the floor.

"Devlin."

"Don't tell me to stop."

She leaned her head to one side, letting his mouth travel from her ear to her throat. He lingered there, feathering light kisses into the hollow of her throat, and she laid her head back. Blowing his breath against her skin, he felt the tremor shudder through her.

"Devlin."

"Shh." He couldn't let her go now, not even if she asked him. Nipping at her collarbone, he fondled her breast, playing with the firm tip of her nipple, the heat from her radiating into his palm. She trembled under his touch again. He loved her reactions to his touch.

"Dev-lin."

He nipped at her shoulder, making a small red mark on her skin, and smiled. Soon he'd mark her. Soon she'd be his and all the world would know it. "What, Tala?"

She took his hand, breaking his grip on her. "Bedroom. Now."

"Whatever you say."

He followed her to the bed, then thrust her around to face him and dove at her breast with his mouth. The hunger inside him grew stronger, driving all rational thought from him. The animal, eager to make her his, urged him on.

Take her. Make her mine. Now.

Sucking her tit into his mouth, he played his tongue over the strong softness there while he stripped her of her jeans. She smelled so sweet yet so wild. Wilder than she knew. Holding her nipple between his teeth, he ran his tongue back and forth across the taut tip.

A different kind of force surged through him. Not the power of the beast within him wanting to break through, but a strength he'd never experienced. A drive so much greater than any other. A yearning so much more consuming. An intensity he could only get from his mate, his female, his Tala.

While he fondled her bottom, she made quick work of his clothes, and soon they stood together, naked in the dimming light filtering through the curtains on the window.

He growled, lifted her, then tossed her on the bed. She laughed in delight as he fell on top of her. Supporting her breasts, he stuck his head between them. Eyes closed, he allowed the soft fullness of her to envelop him, and he soaked in the sweet aroma of her warm skin. Could a man ever tire of her smell? No. Never.

Tala laced her fingers through his hair, encouraging him to stay between her voluptuous globes. Moving his hands away, she took hold of her breasts and rubbed them across his cheeks in opposite directions. He sighed, happy to remain between them forever.

She moaned as he caressed both nubs and she spread her legs wide for him, strengthening his desire for her.

"Take me, Devlin."

He gazed up at her. "Not yet." With a wicked grin, he ran his tongue in the space between her breasts, lapping at her skin, wetting every inch between the luscious mounds. "I want to play first." Pushing up, he straddled her and moved forward, placing his legs on either side of her chest. Her eyes widened as she realized what he wanted.

He placed his swollen cock between her tits and coaxed her to squeeze her breasts together with her hand, enclosing his dick between them. She pushed them against his cock, then ran her tongue over her lips, nearly driving him crazy for the want of her.

"Fuck my tits."

Her eyes, gleaming with desire, took his breath away. Slowly, he began to move, taking his time, luxuriating in the feel of her smooth warm skin against him. Her gaze fell from his to watch the tip of his shaft poking out from between her breasts, then disappearing between their mountains. Her mouth parted, letting the end of her tongue dart out to catch the top of his oozing mushroom tip. Those slight touches whirled a hurricane of lust from his crotch into his gut. The delicious sensation tore him apart and made him ache for her to take all of him inside her mouth.

"Tala, my Tala."

His words pleased her—he could see it on her face—and she lifted her head to try and take him into her mouth. *Yes!* He pushed again, putting his dick inches from her face, daring her, daring himself to take the risk.

"Be careful. You're liable to make me come."

"Yum. Yum." The sinful smile crossing her features nearly made him explode.

"No, sugar, we don't want that. I want to fuck you both ways." He increased his speed, all while holding back, keeping himself from letting go. The sensation of feeling his cock slide along the sides of her tits was incredible. The moist end of her tongue tantalizing him added amazing to the incredible. It was almost as good as having her hot pussy wrapped around him.

His hands gripped her tits, her rigid nipples rubbing against his palms as he slid back and forth. Her flat stomach massaged his balls, making him throb even harder.

"Are you sure?"

He laughed, looked into her expectant face and gave the idea another thought. But he knew what he really wanted. "No. But I think if I'm going to last that long, I'm going to have to switch." She groaned and he almost reconsidered.

He struggled to keep the animal inside from showing in his eyes, on his face. But oh, how the animal wanted his mate! "Don't worry. I'm going to make you scream, Tala." He gently brushed a strand of hair away from her face. "I want you to scream my name."

A raw rumble rolled in his throat and he moved to lie on

top of her again, to rub against her and luxuriate in the feel of her. The heat in her expression drove the animal inside him wild and he thrust his hands into her long hair, securing her head in place. His tongue attacked her mouth, wanting to possess all her tastes, all her essence. As he rubbed, she whimpered, a whimper of need and urgency, pushing him to the edge of reason.

"Are you ready to scream, Tala?"

Her eyes narrowed, but she nodded, her panted breaths making her breasts bounce to their rhythm. "We'll see who screams first."

Ah, a challenge. And just the type of challenge I love. Grabbing her hands, he pulled her arms above her head and held them with one hand. She paused, motionless, as a flicker of alarm crossed her face.

He ignored the hurt her look gave him. "Tala. You know you can trust me. Still, if you want me to stop..." *Don't make me stop.*

"Yeah, I know. But can you trust me?" An answering determination sparkled in her eyes and she bucked, trying to break free of his hold. The harder she fought, the tighter he held her, the brighter the shine in her eyes became.

An amused delight pumped his blood faster. "So you want to play rough, huh?"

She gritted her teeth and bucked, trying to throw him from her, a grin spreading over her beautiful face. At the sight of her sweating and fighting against him, the power of the animal within him rose, threatening his tenuous hold. Fangs grew and he battled to keep from shifting. "Damn, woman, you're strong."

"Not sure you can handle me? Come on, Devlin. Show me what you've got."

He renewed his hold on her and, using his other hand, guided his shaft between her folds, just far enough to torment her. "Do you want me, Tala?"

She giggled. "Do you want me, Devlin?"

They laughed together this time and he knew he'd met his match in more than one way. His lips came down on hers and he tasted the muskiness of his pre-come. His abdomen tightened with the taste and the smell, and the wolf inside roared his need. Holding himself, he moved his cock against her clit, working it around her, over her.

She tensed, the passion showing on her face.

"Scream for me, Tala."

"No." She panted the word, adding evidence to what he already knew. The corners of her mouth tipped upward, beckoning him to kiss them. "Make—" *pant*, "—me."

He dragged his tongue over those taunting lips, nibbling and sucking. He rubbed his dick against her, harder, enjoying the wetness spreading between her legs and onto him. "Don't mind if I do."

Pushing her legs farther apart with his own, he moved onto his knees and braced against her. Her face lit up with anticipation. God, how he loved her expressions. He lifted her legs, positioned his dick and slammed into her. She grunted from the impact and wrapped her legs around him.

"Oh, damn, Devlin. Fuck me." Wild eyes met his, demanding more from him.

He found her nipple and sucked, matching his sucks to the pounding he gave her, his hips lunging faster with each thrust. She arched to meet him, urging him to take her, possess her. Her pussy enclosed him, wrapping her hot wetness around him, tightening every time he drove into her, releasing when he slid back out.

She's so tight. So wet. She feels so good, so hot, so…mine. He closed his eyes, fighting against the inevitable, trying to make the sweet ecstasy last.

At least until he won the challenge. "Scream my name, Tala. Scream it so everyone will hear you."

She squirmed, trying to break free of his hand holding hers. Soft mews of lust murmured from her, thrilling him more than he could have imagined.

"Scream my name."

Just as he was sure he couldn't hold on much longer, he heard her whisper.

"Devlin."

He opened his eyes and almost lost his grip on what little control he had left. The look of desire, want, need…of love…in her eyes stirred him to the core. He couldn't imagine his life without her. "Louder. Don't just say my name. Shout it like you mean it."

She panted, gasping with each lunge as they rocked together on the bed. "Devlin." She said it louder, with meaning.

"More." He let go of her arms and parted her folds to pinch her clit. She jerked, another orgasm racking her body. "Scream."

Throwing her head back, she flattened her hands on his chest and cried his name. "Devlin!"

He rammed into her stronger than ever before and she cried out at the force of his thrust. They scooted to the headboard, bumping her head against the wood. But she didn't complain.

He bent over her and took a breast in his hand, still inside her, never wanting to leave her. "God, that's a beautiful sound. Do it again, Tala."

"Devlin!" She screamed his name louder, longer, digging her nails into his back, fixing his body to hers. "Devlin!"

The exhilaration flowing through him found its way to his heart and he couldn't resist any longer. His physical control was no match for the emotions bursting inside him. At last he gave in and climaxed with a howl ripping from his throat. Fighting the animal within him no longer, he lowered his head, opened his jaws and sank his fangs into her shoulder.

Chapter Six

"Ow! Shit!"

The strength she'd shown earlier was nothing in comparison to the strength she now used to toss him off her. Scrambling from the bed, she stumbled backwards until she struck the dresser. She sank to the floor and leaned her throbbing shoulder against the solid oak. "Ow! Damn it all to hell and back. You bit me!"

Devlin rose up on one elbow, blinked at her as if trying to focus, and swung off the bed. "Tala, let me explain." His amber eyes slowly gained more brown.

Tala gripped her shoulder, blood oozing onto her hand. "Are you nuts? What do you think you are? Some kind of animal? You bit me!" She grabbed an old T-shirt from the dresser and stuck it on top of the wound.

"You said that twice already."

She scowled at him, his remark stoking the volcano threatening to erupt from within her. *If he thinks I'm angry now...*

He winced. "I know. I'm sorry. I should've prepared—"

"Get away from me." She attempted to calm the mix of pain, shock and—God help her—lust trying to overwhelm her brain, but couldn't. "Why the hell did you bite me?" *Does it really matter?* She gave the question a moment's thought. *Yeah, the why does matter.*

"I didn't mean to. I just got carried away in the moment."

Pushing his hair away from his remorseful face, he beseeched her. "Tala, please, listen to me."

He inched nearer until she stuck out a hand to stop him. "Please listen? What next? 'Please let me go for the jugular this time?' Would you like me to lie still while you finish the job?" Keeping her eyes glued on him, she grasped the furniture and hauled herself to her feet. *I can't believe it. This guy bit me!* Gritting at the pain, she snatched up her robe in the process, and headed for the bathroom.

Devlin started to follow her but she would have none of it. "Oh, no you don't. You stay where you are. Or get the hell out. But don't you dare follow me." She thrust her finger at him in a threatening jab and stalked into the bathroom, slamming the door behind her.

Tala fell against the door and tried to catch both her breath and her sanity. *What the hell just happened? One minute I'm getting laid and laid good. Okay, laid great. And in the next, I've got teeth in me. Had their rough play gotten out of hand?* She crossed over to the sink to stare into the small oval mirror above the basin and frowned at her white complexion. *Sure, I've had rough sex before and even a little biting, but this is wild. Too wild.* With two fingers, she gently removed the robe and blood-reddened shirt to examine the injured area. Two major holes flanked a row of smaller indentations with similar marks in another semi-circle below. *Looks like an animal bit me.*

Reaching for a washcloth, she wet the soft cotton under the faucet and gingerly dabbed at the gashes. The sting shot down her shoulder and into her arm. *I will not cry. I will not cry.*

"Tala? Are you all right? Do you need my help?"

Is he kidding? "Never mind. I'll take care of myself."

Tala continued cleaning the area until the bleeding finally slowed down. She fumbled through her medicine cabinet, located the rubbing alcohol and poured some onto the cloth. Inhaling a long one, she held her breath and placed the alcohol-soaked material on her shoulder. A quick yelp escaped her before she could stop it.

"Tala, please. Let me help you."

She ignored Devlin's knock on the door as well as his words. Tears came to her eyes, and she stuffed the bathrobe's collar into her mouth to stifle her cry. Gripping her robe with all her strength, she waited for the pain to lessen.

"Tala, are you all right? Answer me or I'm going to break down the door."

Oh no, he didn't! She'd thought she was angry before. But the fury boiling over in her now put her previous ire to shame. *How dare he threaten me! First, he tears up my car, then he bites me like some caveman—or more like a sabertooth tiger—and now he has the nerve to threaten to break down my door?*

"Devlin, back off or I'm going to bite your balls off." *Crap, would he think that sounds as sexy as I do?* Her mind was on kinky sex when she'd just been bitten. Was she as crazy as he was? She threw the blood-soaked cloth to the floor, grabbed the bandages from the medicine cabinet and plastered on a quick bandage.

"I'm worried about you, babe."

A red stain spread across the bandage. Enough was enough. She'd put herself in danger with this stranger long enough. Determined, she swung open the door.

She registered Devlin's surprised expression as she charged at him, relishing the fact that he moved as fast as he could to get away from her. He'd gotten dressed in the meantime, and his shirt flew open in his attempt to get out of her way. But she kept at him, punching her finger into the middle of his solid chest.

"I told you to back off and I meant what I said. And don't call me babe. I'm no one's babe. Especially not yours."

Devlin's startled look transformed into deep furrows on his brow. "Will you stop acting like I beat you up? I realize I screwed up but, after all, it's only a bite." He widened his stance, a fortified front to withstand her furious attack.

"A bite? *Only* a bite?" Tala laid one hand on her bandage and the other fisted on her hips. "You drew blood. Who the hell draws blood while having sex? When I wanted to play rough in the sack I didn't have bloodshed in mind."

The gleam in Devlin's eyes slowed her down, and uneasiness rippled through her shaking frame. How could he stand there and act like what he'd done was no big deal? Even if he did look sexy as hell. Even if part of her wanted to jump his bones again.

Tala sucked in a big gulp of air and tried to steady herself. Hell, for a second there, she'd wanted to bite him back.

"I didn't mean to bite you." At least he had the decency to look contrite. "Okay, maybe I did. A little. Besides, we were making love. Not having sex."

Man, how I'd love to smack him. Making love? Is that what he thinks? "Love hurts, is that what you think? Are you one of those guys?"

"No. But I wasn't the only one wanting the rough stuff. You did, too."

She ground her teeth together and resolved to keep his butt on the line. "Don't try to change the subject."

Devlin's big brown eyes met hers and his eyebrows—such masculine, heart-stopping eyebrows—lifted in an imploring manner. Almost the way the she-wolf had looked at him earlier. As if asking for help. As if asking for understanding from a kindred soul. An *aw* went down from her brain and straight into her heart. Why was she such a pushover for this guy?

Devlin reached around her and tried to draw her into his arms. For a second, the temptation to snuggle against his broad chest almost broke her determination, but she stepped back, keeping clear of him.

"I don't think it was an accident." She peered at him, knowing in her gut something else was at the bottom of what he'd done. "It was more."

He let his arms fall to his side, not following her as she

moved away from him. "Okay. You want the truth? Well, here it is. I wanted to mark you."

"Mark me?" What the hell did he mean? "Like branding a cow?

Devlin stammered, opened his mouth several times to speak and then closed his mouth, his lips forming a tight line across his face. Had he started to tell her something? Perhaps the real and total truth? She studied his face for some meaning behind his actions and saw him mentally shut down.

"Uh, of course not. I wanted to mark you as in..."

"As in what?" She took a step closer to him, hoping he'd come out and say what he found so difficult to say. "Just tell me."

"As in giving you a hickey."

Tala jerked in stunned response. "A hickey? You bit me trying to give me a hickey?"

Devlin tucked his head, averting his face from hers. "Yeah, I know. It was a stupid thing to do. I guess I just lost control when I started to give you a, you know, and got a little too excited."

She couldn't help it. She had to laugh. "What are you? Thirteen? Since when do grown men give hickeys?"

He shot her an exasperated expression, one filled with anger, embarrassment and frustration. "Can we get off this subject?"

"No. If you're going to give me a hickey like some stupid teenager, then I want to know we're going steady." *Okay, where the hell had that come from? One minute I'm determined to throw him out and then in the next I want him to proclaim his love for me.*

"Steady? So, like, does that mean you'll go to the prom with me?" Devlin's expression was priceless, taking away some of her steam.

But not enough of it. "It was a joke." *Sort of.* "Where the hell were you raised, Devlin? You can barely drive a car, you still give hickeys and you have an uncanny way with wolves. Were you raised by a pack of wolves or something? By nature-loving hippies? What gives?"

His features hardened, vanishing the twinkle in his eye, and he spit his words at her. "Look, I've had enough. I messed up and I apologized. Now get over it."

The volcano boiling within her finally let loose, exploding in a rage. She hissed between her clenched teeth, "Get out, Devlin. Get the hell out of my home."

His jaw worked and he glowered at her, but he didn't budge an inch. "You're making a bigger deal of this than you should. Grow up, Tala."

"You're telling *me* to grow up?" Whirling, she marched to her front door. As she knew he would, Devlin followed on her heels. Thrusting the door wide open, she shouted and pointed into the hallway. "I said, get the hell out of my home!"

Devlin snarled at her—a snarl that weakened her knees—strode out into the hallway and stormed by Mrs. Puwoty, scaring the poor old lady. The octogenarian screeched in fright, clutching her hands to her chest in her bumbling attempt to sidestep him.

The instant he'd left, an ache greater than she'd ever known assaulted Tala, leaving her chest tight and her body shaking in the aftermath. Trying to put on a brave front for Mrs. Puwoty, Tala attempted a small, tight smile, nodded at the older woman and closed the door.

☾

Devlin entered the quaint shopping district and tucked his head, not wanting to make eye contact with the people strolling from store to store. He walked on, ignoring the sounds around him until his rage calmed to a low simmer. Yet still he couldn't figure out who made him the angriest: Tala or himself.

He let the tension roll out of him with a low growl that sent a young woman carrying an infant scurrying to the other side of the street. She and her baby let out plaintive wails. *Great. Now I'm scaring young mothers and babies. What next, Dev, terrorizing school kids?*

How had he lost control of the situation? Should he have told Tala the truth? Should he have told her he'd marked her as his mate?

He'd been ready to do just that but her anger had thrown him. He shook his head and started to growl again, but stopped when he caught the anxious expression of an old man who stood rooted to one spot, warily watching him. Instead, Devlin spread his lips in what he hoped passed for a reassuring smile and waved. *Crap. Add giving old men heart attacks to my list.*

Had Tala thrown him out for good? If so, how would he get back into her life? Although rage permeated his body, another more dangerous feeling lay just below the surface. Heartache. His heart was in pain. He'd heard others talk about heartache but had never really believed it possible, chalking it up to overemotional fools. But now he knew. This kind of emotional hurt made getting physically injured seem like a skinned knee.

"Devlin."

His friend's familiar voice brought him to a standstill. *Conrad.* He swept the darkening street around him and picked out a black shape resting against a light pole. Striding over, he grabbed him, enveloping him in a bear hug.

"Thank God you're okay." He put the big man at arm's length and ran his gaze up and down his body, checking for anything out of place. "I see you escaped the hunters in one piece."

Conrad's echoing grin dropped at the question. "Well, duh. Since when are four inept hunters a match for me? In fact, I had a great time playing with them."

"Just as long as you're okay." Devlin cupped Conrad's cheek in his palm and nodded. He kept nodding as a diversion, giving him time to he draw back his arm. He socked his friend in the nose, knocking him to the ground.

"What the fuck?" Conrad lay on the ground, holding his hand over his bleeding nose. "Why'd you do that?"

"Why the hell are you following me? And why the fuck are you out messing with hunters when you're supposed to be handling business for me while I tend to a personal matter? Shit, Conrad, I count on you to do what I say. When you don't, you're going to suffer the consequences." Devlin's pitch was deep and threatening, too angry to worry about the people staring at them.

Several people scurried away from them. Conrad hollered after them, as though they were worried for his safety, instead of fleeing for their own lives, "No, no, everyone. Not to worry. I'm fine." He pushed himself to his feet, calling to the few remaining onlookers. "Just a minor squabble is all. No problem."

Devlin growled at him, clenching his fists to keep from striking him again.

"You didn't have to hit me, you know. We could've just talked like civilized men." Conrad still pinched his nose even though the bleeding had already stopped.

"Yeah, but it wouldn't have felt as good."

"Oh, so funny, dude. Not." Conrad eyed him. "Seems to me you're angry about something other than my scoping out you and your female." He hooked his arm around Devlin's shoulder and led him toward a hole-in-the-wall bar. "First of all, if you'd leave your damn phone on, I wouldn't have to track you down. I wanted your input on an important business matter."

Devlin scowled and knew he'd jumped to the wrong conclusion. But that didn't mean he was going to apologize. "What kind of important—"

"Never mind now. I handled it. And as far as the hunters were concerned, dude, they were after you. I was just keeping your hide off some jerk hunter's wall."

Devlin started to protest, but Conrad dragged him inside

the bar. The awful combination of tobacco, human body odors and liquor hit Devlin's sensitive nose and he coughed, trying to rid himself of the stench. "Me? It looked like they were after your sorry butt. Not mine."

"Ah, well, mine would make the more handsome trophy. But that's where you're wrong." Conrad slid onto a barstool and motioned for Devlin to do the same. "Those scumbags wanted to ambush you and your lady friend. Fortunately for both of you, I sidetracked them." He drew the bartender's attention. "Two draft beers."

Devlin waited for the bartender to set their drinks in front of them before questioning his friend. "So the hunters were after me. How'd they pick up my tail? Er, trail?"

The big man choked on his laugh. "How do they ever pick up a trail? Sheer luck most of the time. But the point is, they know we're here. Both of us." He dragged a long swig from his glass, winked at a neon-red-haired girl sitting at the edge of the counter, and nudged Devlin. "Talk about picking up some tail…"

Devlin sipped his drink, then flipped his phone on. "Yeah, I guess. The trail, not the tail. How did you know where to find me tonight?"

Conrad raised his glass at the girl, who was joined by two girlfriends. "Don't look now, D-man, but there's a trio of honeys at three o'clock."

Devlin glanced at the girls, noted the caked-on makeup. Their obvious attempt to look more sophisticated and attractive had failed, and he grimaced at their skimpy outfits. Hookers? He studied them closer and came to a different conclusion. Nope, not hookers. Worse. Barflies on the prowl. He accidentally made eye contact with one of them. A redhead. *Damn. I hope she doesn't think anything of it. After Tala why would I want anyone else?* "Answer my question."

His friend puffed out an exaggerated sigh. "No biggie. I looked up her address. You'd think someone like her—you know, on television—would be unlisted, but she's not. So I kind of hung around until you came storming out." He grinned and slugged back his drink. "What happened?"

"That's none of your business." Devlin eyed his friend hard enough to make him turn away.

The redhead, her hair sticking out at all angles, waved at Devlin and ran her tongue over her even redder lips.

Yep, all I need is some bar bimbo after me. Stay away, Red. Devlin groaned, wished he was with Tala, and confronted Conrad again. "So you found me. Now what?"

"I figured you might still need my help after the problem at the zoo." His grin grew wider as the redhead cupped her boobs and jiggled them at them. "Besides, if the mopey expression on your face is any indication, you could use your good ol' buddy right now. What's up? Your female kick you out already?"

Conrad's quick assessment of his situation dropped his mood another ten notches. "Sort of." He frowned, annoyed at the twinkle in his friend's eyes. "But it's only temporary. Once she calms down, she'll forget all about my, um, mistake."

"Um, mistake?" Conrad scooped up a handful of peanuts from the bowl on the bar and tossed them into his mouth. "Oooh, sounds interesting. You must have fucked up big time for her to boot you to the curb this fast. I mean, you two looked rather chummy strolling around the zoo. Like two little puppies in love." To add insult to injury, he broke into a rendition of "Puppy Love". "And they called it puppy luh-uh-uh-uv."

"Cut the American Idol audition." Devlin noted the other customers smiling—laughing—at them and wished for invisibility. "I don't need your help. Other than doing what you're supposed to be doing—handling the business while I take some time off."

Not fazed by Devlin's reaction, Conrad shrugged off his admonishment. "What'd you do to piss her off? You break into the vet clinic butt-naked again and hit on the kitties? Got a feline fetish you haven't told me about?"

Devlin set his drink down on the bar with a loud bang, drawing the bartender's attention. "Never mind."

But Conrad was Conrad which meant he didn't rattle easily. He downed the last of his beer and ordered another one. "So 'fess up? You say something bad about the zoo or vets? I'd imagine she wouldn't like you dissing her work very much."

Devlin frowned. "It was no big deal. I got a little too aggressive in bed. I bit her—"

"You bit her?" Conrad's nonchalant attitude disappeared in a flash. "Did you mark her? Oh, shit, you did, didn't you? So she's the real deal, huh?"

"No, I didn't. I started to, but I restrained myself. Just in time. And yeah, she's the real deal." *No need for him to know just yet that I really did mark her. Not until Tala and I get back together.* Devlin swallowed a gulp of beer and reflected on his predicament.

"Well, don't worry none. She'll cool down. Eventually." Like someone switching on a light, the concern vanished from Conrad and the happy-go-lucky grin was back in place. Cupping his hand around Devlin's neck, Conrad drew him closer and whispered, "How about you and me have a little fun tonight? You know. Before you go getting hooked up with one female for the rest of your life. Better live while you can, dude." He jerked his thumb at the slutty trio and winked at Devlin. "Good thing your wingman is here to help you get laid."

Devlin sneaked another peek at the girls with the wild hair and tight clothes. Maybe before he'd met Tala, but not now. The chunky blonde blew a kiss at him and he hid the cringe he felt. "No thanks. But if you want to, don't mind me."

"Aw, hell, come on. I can't let my best bud down. Consider it an unplanned bachelor party."

He slid off the bar and Devlin caught him by the arm. "No, C. I'm not interested."

"Sure, boss man, no problem. But what's wrong with a little harmless flirting?" Conrad flashed him a wicked sneer and tugged his arm free. He sauntered a few steps toward the women then stopped and turned back. Wrinkling his nose, he sniffed the air. "Damn, Dev. Do you smell something rotten?"

A shadow came out of the crowd, heading straight for Conrad. Devlin's warning growl came too late. A hunter smashed a bottle over the big man's head, buckling his knees and sending him crashing to the floor. Devlin howled and threw himself at the hunter standing over his friend with a jagged bottle in his hand. Other patrons scattered to the sides of the room.

"Argh!" The hunter scrambled backwards to elude Devlin's attack and tripped over his own feet, landing on his back. He flipped onto his hands and knees, and tried to scramble out of reach, one hand still clutching the broken bottle.

Devlin clutched his collar and flung him against the bar, ripping the man's shirt. The man's head lolled to the side.

"Get them!"

Devlin saw two more hunters running toward him and roared his anger. Letting a small part of his power loose, he grabbed each of the men by the neck and lifted them into the air.

"Kill 'em, sweetie!" The Bar Bitch Trio jumped up and down, clapping and cheering.

Devlin held the hunters high and bashed their heads together, delighting in the responding *crack*. Reveling in the force coursing through him, he bobbed a short bow and saluted his fans.

The bartender, apparently used to brawls, stood, arms crossed in a patient yet bored manner. He scowled at Devlin but didn't say a word.

"Don't look now, but another one's headed this way," the redhead warned.

Conrad, recovered and standing beside him, patted Devlin on the shoulder as he rubbed the back of his head. "Shit of an asshole. He really whacked me."

"Good thing you don't use your head for anything important, huh?"

"Very funny. Ha-ha." Conrad rolled his eyes at him, then pointed at a box-shaped hunter winding his way through the throng of bar patrons rushing for the door. "Damn. This one's called Skanland and he's carrying something more deadly than a bottle."

Skanland hurried toward them, his hand stuck inside his leather jacket. His lips curled into a snarl, accenting the thick scar running along the side of his neck. As the hunter drew closer, he pulled out a large handgun and pointed it at Conrad.

Conrad groaned and shook his head. "Well, shit. Why do they always aim for the big guy first?"

"Bigger target." Devlin lurched forward but Skanland darted away. "Don't try it, shifter, or your canine crony here is roadkill."

The animal raged inside Devlin, begging for release, and he scanned the room around him. Too many eyes would witness his transformation if he shifted. Yet he couldn't stop his fangs from lengthening. He opened his jaws in a challenge. "Hunter, you pull the trigger and I'll rip out your bowels." A sneer lifted his lips at the flicker of fear in Skanland's eyes. "I haven't had dinner yet and I'll eat anything. Even hunter guts."

"Now, boys, what's the problem?" Conrad snaked his arm around Devlin's waist. "My sugar daddy here and I were having a little drinkie-poo together when your friends—" he wiggled his wrist to flap his fingers at the unconscious hunters, "—decided to break up our little tête-à-tête. Wasn't that just plain rude?" Sliding away from Devlin, Conrad sashayed a few feet closer to the hunter. "Oh, I get it. Are you wanting to get with us, too? Huh, sweet thang?" He puckered his lips, pouting at the man.

Devlin couldn't help but admire his friend's courage—even if he didn't care much for his humor. "Man, be careful." He widened his eyes, shooting his friend an unmistakable signal. "His finger's already twitching."

The squat hunter took a step back, revulsion written on his face. "What the crap? Keep your queer paws off me, you limp-wristed dogface."

Conrad feigned a shocked expression, clamping his hands over his mouth and puffing up in fake indignation. "I can not believe you just said those mean, horrible things to me. You are a bad, bad, *bad* little man."

"C, don't push it. Hunters are stupid, but Skanland doesn't look that stupid."

Skanland darted his gaze between the two shifters. "Never thought there could be anything worse than a shifter. Now I know there is. A fag shifter."

Conrad *tsked* and shook his index finger at him. "We prefer the word *homosexual*, you uncouth pig. How very un-PC of you."

Devlin shrugged at his friend's see-I-told-you-so expression. "Then again, maybe I'm wrong."

Skanland pressed the muzzle of the gun against Conrad's forehead, pointing his chin at Devlin. "So you know my name, huh? Good. You should know who's going to wipe you and all the other mongrels off the face of the earth." He glared at Devlin. "Listen to your friend, dog breath. When my associates wake up, we're all going to take a little walk outside to my van and head on over to a party at my house. You're gonna love our party favors."

Conrad pushed the gun away and jumped up and down, clapping his hands together. "Yippee! A party. Oh, but wait. I forgot. We've already made plans for the evening."

Devlin caught the direction of Conrad's glance and nodded his understanding. "He's right, friend. No offense, but we'd rather party with them." He looked past Skanland to the person standing behind him.

"Come on, do you think I'd fall for that old trick? I ain't stupid, you know." Skanland rolled his upper lip in scorn at Devlin's unspoken disbelief. "I ain't!"

Devlin tilted his head and shrugged. "If you say so. But my daddy always told me you shouldn't ignore a lady with a stun gun."

Skanland had just enough time to turn around and find the red-haired barfly standing behind him. "Fuck!"

"Bye, bye, jerk face." She rammed the weapon against his neck.

Spasms jerked the hunter's body and he hit the floor face first.

"Talk about in the neck of time." Conrad cocked his head at the redhead, aiming his glorious smile at her. "Get it? *Neck* of time? You, sweetheart, are a lifesaver."

The redhead saluted him and kicked the hunter's gun under the bar. "No problem. I cain't stand to see anyone picked on by bullies. Especially not yummy-looking hunks like you two."

Devlin released a breath he hadn't realized he'd held in check. "And I'm glad you did. Thanks for the assistance."

"No problem." Red's fire-engine lips spread wide and Devlin couldn't help comparing her to the Tasmanian She-Devil. He swallowed, forcing the unsettling image from his head.

"She can't take all the credit. The stun gun's mine." The big-breasted blonde standing next to Red batted her eyes first at Conrad and then Devlin.

"Yeah, but I taught her how to use it, Betty." The last of the trio, a skinny brunette, pushed her way between her friends. "All you did was let Roxy try it out on you."

Betty blinked twice, opened her mouth to speak and came up empty.

What we have here is a lack of brain function. Devlin couldn't believe the absurdity of their conversation. Roxy, aka Red, had used Betty Big Breasts as her guinea pig for stun gun training? "Then we should thank all of you."

"My friend is right. We should thank you. With everything

we have to offer."

Sometimes his friend could charm a worm out of an apple. Although clean breath would charm these girls.

"How about we get out of here?" Roxy and Betty slid into Conrad's welcoming embrace. "I don't want to be around when those guys come to."

The skinny one pouted and gave Devlin a give-me-a-hug face. Succumbing to the moment, he wrapped his arm around her and followed his friend and the other women to the front door. The girls' giggles echoed around the room and Conrad dropped his hands to squeeze their rumps.

Slinging the bar door open, the big man and the girls made a straight arrow to a multicolored Volkswagen Beetle convertible. Devlin tried to release his hold on the other girl, but she kept a death-grip on his waist.

Roxy jumped into the back seat and motioned for Conrad to do the same. "Come on, man. Let's head on over to our place and keep the good times going."

Betty clapped her hands in delight and hopped up and down, turning her huge mammary glands into quivering mountains of flesh. "Ooh, goodie. Playtime with boy toys." She squashed into the back seat next to Conrad and tossed the keys to Devlin's human attachment. "You drive, Trixie. I don't want to miss a minute with my new honey bun." Licking her lips like a fox in a henhouse, she ran her gaze up and down Conrad's body. "I bet he's got a long hard one just ready to make me all hot and happy."

Roxy, however, wasn't about to give up an inch. Especially not an inch of male. "Hey, who said he's yours? I'm the one who saved his cute tush tonight. So I should have dibs on him first."

Conrad wiggled his eyebrows at Devlin and ate up the attention from the two complaining women. "Now, girls, there's no need to fuss. Trust me. My friend and I have more than enough to satisfy all of you." He planted a quick kiss on Roxy's ruby lips.

"Hey!" Betty stuck out her lower lip until he laid a smack on her, too.

"Dev, get a move on." He sent him a wink that said, "Don't worry. It's just a little fun."

Trixie tugged at Devlin. "Yeah, Devvy. Come on. Let's go. You can ride shotgun for me."

Devlin's mind flew into high gear, visualizing a shotgun in the hands of Trixie's backwoods father. The image shook him, racing along his spine to tingle in his feet, urging them to take flight. No way would he risk another load of buckshot in the ass. Taking her arms, he gently pried her away from him. "Sorry, sweetheart, but I'll have to pass."

"There they are!"

The hunters exited the bar and stormed toward them, albeit it on wobbly legs. *Impressive speeds for men recovering from a serious beat-down.* Unfortunately, hunters were notoriously hardheaded and resilient.

Devlin pushed a protesting Trixie around the front of the car and into the driver's seat. "Girls, I suggest you hit the road."

"Get in, man. This is no time to hang around here." Conrad lifted up to reach for Devlin, but Roxy and Betty dragged him back into the seat again.

Devlin snarled at the men moving closer to the car and slammed the car door after Trixie. "Damn it all to hell and back." Hurdling over the door, Devlin landed in the passenger's seat just as Trixie turned over the engine.

"Where'd you pick up that phrase, dude?"

But Devlin didn't have time to answer. Trixie gleefully shouted at the top of her lungs, soon joined by Roxy and Betty, and stomped her foot to the gas pedal. Gravel shot in the air and rained down on the angry men chasing behind them.

"Zero to sixty, sweet man. Zero to sixty." Trixie laughed, her ratted hair holding as hard as a rock against the wind. The crowded Bug flew into traffic. Horns blared and drivers cursed as Devlin held onto the handle and prepared to die. *And Tala thinks my driving is bad.*

Thirty minutes later, after seven near collisions, a couple of incidents of road rage, and one fender-bumping mishap with a stop sign, Trixie pulled into a rundown apartment building's parking lot and swung into a space beneath a metal carport. Shoving the gear into *P*, Trixie shouted for the girls to pile out of the car and take the men along with them.

"Woo-hoo! Testosterone time!"

☾

George hid in a corner of the deli behind a wall of newspaper and spied on Tala Wilde. *Bitch.* He gritted his teeth, hatred searing through him. Her animalistic boyfriend had almost killed him and she'd had the balls to fire him. Hell, she'd done it even when she didn't have the authority to do so.

He rubbed his neck where the bruise still remained, a purplish green reminder of his humiliation at the hands of her wolf-loving companion. But no matter. Revenge would heal all his wounds.

The bitch handed money to the clerk behind the counter and took her sandwich. When she turned his way, he lifted his paper higher, waited a few seconds, then held his breath and peeked around the edge. *Whew. She didn't notice me.* Releasing his pent-up breath, he brought the coffee cup to his lips and was shocked to see his hand shake. *Shit. Get a grip, man.* Placing the cup down before he let it slip through his trembling grasp, he watched the bitch stride from the deli. Although he wanted nothing more than to jump up and hit her, he remained seated, knowing he'd have to bide his time.

Devlin. She'd called her boyfriend Devlin. Remembering Devlin's hands on him wasn't half as scary as remembering the way the man's—the freak's—features had morphed, with long vicious-looking teeth protruding from his mouth. What the hell was he anyway?

Just like before, fear swept through him and he swallowed the bile rising to his throat.

He waited a moment longer before throwing a couple of dollars on the tabletop and lurching out of his chair to hurry through the door. Tala was several yards away, moving at a rapid speed. He frowned and stretched out his stocky legs to keep up with her incredible pace. Since when had she gotten so fast? The way she moved her body had changed, too. Instead of short paces, she flowed along with more fluid, more powerful strides. Although he struggled to keep up, he soon lost sight of her.

Doesn't matter. She'll find out she can't treat me the way she did and not get punished. He licked his lips, the thrill of imagining her cowering before him giving him an added burst of adrenalin. *You're gonna come crawlin' on your knees. It's payback time, bitch.*

Chapter Seven

Tala surveyed the area behind her apartment and chewed on her bottom lip. *Damn him to hell and back. Why do I always get involved with all the offbeat men of the world?*

"Crap." She headed to the kitchen for one last cup of coffee. Just like the last five cups she'd called "the last one". But she'd known she wouldn't get any sleep tonight. Not with her stomach as torn up as her heart.

Where the hell can he be? She scowled at her reflection in the microwave and punched the *Start* button to heat up the coffee. *Well, what do I care, anyway? I'm the one who threw him out. Good riddance.* "Argh!"

Picking up her cup with care—even though she felt more like throwing it—she traced her steps back to the sliding glass door. Leave it to her to get hung up on a man she'd just met. A man she knew nothing about. Or was the mystery, the possible danger, part of his attraction? Maybe, but she could sense there was more to it. He called to her in some unknown, primal way as though they were meant for each other.

She peered into the woods around her home and stared at the moon. To top it off, he had her wishing he was out there, snooping on her again.

She sipped the hot brew and let her mind wander. *What if he's hurt again?* "No, he's fine. Better than fine." But even saying the words out loud didn't make her feel better. She reached up to rub the marks on her neck. *He bit me. How strange is a man who bites a woman? Even if it did turn me on. And stranger yet, who heals as fast as he did?*

The man had more secrets than she liked, but she couldn't rid herself of the memory of him licking along her body, around the curve of her breasts. The place between her legs clenched and she groaned, needing him more than ever. *Better to keep my mind away from sex. At least until he comes back.* She blew out an exasperated sigh. No doubt about it. She wanted him back. Mentally shaking herself, she put her mind on the questions he'd left unanswered.

How *had* Devlin healed so fast? Had she thought the injury was worse than it really had been? She'd seen enough wounds on animals to know his injury wasn't a scratch. Yet, without proper medical help, the wound had closed up and starting scarring over. Even the scars weren't that bad.

So the man heals fast. So what? Healing quickly isn't a bad thing, after all. Unusual, maybe. But biting people? A man who bites while making love? She remembered Devlin's insistence on the term "making love" instead of "having sex" and smiled. *Lots of people do kinky stuff in bed and by some people's standards, biting is pretty tame. Still...*

Tala moved her hand along her neck, massaging out the rigidity in her muscles. The memory of Devlin's tongue on her body sent renewed goose bumps along her arms. *Damn it all to hell and back. He's the best lover I've ever had.*

Wanting him as a lover was one thing. Yet the deeper, stronger urge ripping her heart apart took hold and held on. Devlin was more than just a good lay. Something about him called to her, making her ready to throw all logic aside and follow him anywhere. Even to hell and back.

She renewed her stance at the window. Could she take him in again? Would she let him in her bed again? And even more important, should she let him in her heart forever?

☾

At this point, Devlin was unsure if the Bar Bitch Trio were more of a danger than the hunters. Trixie held on to his arm and pulled him toward her apartment, making his gut churn.

He protested each step of the way, but she dismissed each of his not-so-polite arguments and ignored his not-so-subtle attempts to break free. As they drew closer to her door, he gave up the pretense of civility and jerked his arm out of her grasp. "Look! I'm sorry!"

Conrad, flanked by Betty and Roxy, swiveled around and scowled at him. The girls gaped at his outburst. Cocking his head, the C-man shot him a warning look. "Problem, Dev?"

"Yeah, I've got a problem." The low pitch of his voice laid down a challenge, drawing an invisible line in the sand.

The foursome glared at him, ready to meet his dare. Roxy spoke up, ice dripping from her tone. "So what's your problem? Is Trixie not good enough for you?"

Hunters, where are you when I need you? Right now he wouldn't mind getting shot and mounted on one of their walls. "Uh, sure she is." He smiled at Trixie, the picture of Daddy's Little Girl Gone Wrong with confusion, anger and hope somehow managing to show up under all the heavy makeup. "But I can't be with any woman."

A stunned silence followed his statement. He grimaced. A blind man could see what they were thinking. *Oh, shit.*

Roxy turned to each of her friends before narrowing her eyes at him. "But wasn't the gay thing a gag for the bully?" She stepped back from Conrad, skimming her eyes up and down his body. "Are you telling me you two really are together? And I mean, together-together." Making a circle with her thumb and middle finger, she poked the index finger of her other hand through the hole she'd formed.

Devlin couldn't wait to correct her. "No, no. You don't understand."

Trixie stepped up to him, pressing her skinny frame against

him. "No, sweet man, we understand real good. And I'm sorry if we dragged you along for nothing. We didn't know you was really gay. If we had, we'd have left you alone." An over-plucked eyebrow arched upward. "Unless you don't want to be gay?"

Roxy gave Trixie a slap on the shoulder. "Don't be dumb, bitch. Didn't you see that Dr. Phil show? He cain't choose to be gay or not. He was born girly."

Trixie, however, couldn't give up the dream without a fight. "Are you sure? I mean, I could try and change you. You know, give it a shot to bring you back to the straight and narrow. I mean, I like a dick as good as the next person, but if you try some pussy, you might find out you like it a whole lot better. Have you ever even been with a woman?"

Measuring his shaft against a giant's couldn't have delivered a bigger blow to his self-esteem. "No. Yes. I mean, you've got me all wrong." Devlin bounced his gaze from one girl to the next. Conrad rolled his lips inward, trying to suffocate a laugh. "I swear. I love women. All kinds of women."

Roxy scoffed, "Well, sure you do, hon. Most homos do. You know, to go shopping with. Queers love gal pals."

Unable to hold back any longer, Conrad fell against the wall and clamped a hand over his mouth. But he couldn't stop his body from shaking with humor.

Devlin fought to maintain some shred of dignity. "You're not getting this right. I like women. And I like fucking women." He stood up straighter, trying to puff up his chest as well as his image. "And let me tell you, I've fucked my share of females."

Three pairs of mascara-laden eyes studied him. Ever the brilliant one, Trixie asked the question Devlin could almost see chugging slowly through their tiny brains. "Then I don't get it. If you like women and I'm good enough, why won't you come inside and get it on?"

Bluntness, thy name is Trixie. "I'd love to." *Please, oh, please, let them believe me.* "Except for one thing."

"Yeah? And what would that be?"

"I belong to one woman and one woman alone."

To his utter relief, all three women let out a group "aw". Tears welled up in Trixie's eyes, compassion flooding her face while the other two gathered him into their arms. Conrad, however, let out a long moan.

"Wow. A one-woman man. I ain't never met one of those." Roxy's astonishment at his declaration almost floored him.

"This is so special. Don't worry. Now that we understand, we won't take you away from her." All three women shook their heads, fervent in their commitment.

Devlin raised a questioning eyebrow at Betty. *Maybe Betty Big Boobs should be called Betty Big Heart.*

"Even though we could, you know."

Apparently neither her heart nor her boobs were as big as her ego. Devlin adopted a pious look and nodded, extricating himself from their clutches. "I'm glad you understand." He caught his friend's eye and shot him a silent message. "But C-man, on the other hand, is a lady's dream come true. A regular sex machine in bed."

The women dropped Devlin's arms faster than lead weights off the side of a punctured hot air balloon and scooted over to Conrad. Roxy pulled him toward a door with the sign *Hottie Hangout* emblazoned on the front and shoved her friends off him. "Back off, bitches. I saw him first."

Yet Betty wouldn't let Roxy get away with anything—much less with Conrad. "Like I care. He likes blondes best, don't ya, sweetie?"

"But can't we all play with him? I thought we all shared." Trixie opened the door and wiggled her fingers at Devlin. "By-ee, Devvy. Run on home to your lucky woman."

"Ladies, ladies, there's no need to fight over me." Conrad grinned at Devlin. "But I'm afraid I won't be able to join you, either. You see, I'm running the ship while Dev's off courting his true love."

"A ship?" Trixie grabbed onto his shirt. "You mean you've

got a ship? How big is it?" She cuddled against Conrad's chest and batted her eyelashes at him. "Do you have one of those yacht thingies? Are you rich?"

Devlin jumped in before Conrad could respond. "Honey, he's got the biggest ship around."

All the women froze, eyes wide, gaping at each other before simultaneously emitting the same word. "Oooh!"

Conrad laughed. "Good one, man. But what about business?"

Devlin winked at him. "Give me a call in the morning." He gave his friend a good-natured shove toward the door. "*If* you survive." Chuckling, he turned on his heels and slipped into the night.

☾

"Tala."

She'd known it was him. Even before he knocked, she'd known he'd be standing on the other side, and no amount of rational thought could have prevented her from opening the door.

"Devlin."

They stared at each other, sizing each other up. And yet, she wanted him as much as she ever had. More. Still, that didn't mean she didn't want some answers.

Turning on her heel, she dashed into the living room, leaving the door wide open for him to follow. With a yell of frustration, she confronted him. "Now can you explain? Tell me what's going on with you?" *With us.*

She saw the flash in his eyes a second before his face hardened. "I didn't mean to hurt you."

"But you did." She crossed her arms, trying to maintain a stern exterior. "You did hurt me. You bit me. All I want to know is why you did it. The real reason."

"I was hoping you'd know why."

He was as confusing as he was sexy. "Quit playing games with me. How the hell would I know why you bit me?"

He scowled. "You should know it here." He fisted his hand over his heart. "You should instinctively know."

She paused, at first unsure what he meant. Then, slowly, the truth of his words seeped through her. Needing to think without those mesmerizing eyes boring into her, she turned to one of her wolf posters. Yet she didn't see the poster.

An image of Devlin cradling the she-wolf's head in his lap came to her. Anyone who could care for an animal like that wouldn't hurt her on purpose. Another vision of him holding her after they'd shared amazing soul-sharing sex shook her resolve to hold firm, breaking the ice-cold reserve she'd tried so hard to build. Something inside her told her he was right. She *should* know.

"I think I do," she whispered. She sought his eyes, hoping he could see the plea in hers. "I think I do know."

She released pent-up air and unfolded her arms, letting him cross over to her. An ache for him lashed through her abdomen, shooting her libido into overdrive. His hands, stirring and comforting at the same time, rested on her arms. Following her desire, she leaned into him, molding her soft body to his hard one. "I don't know how, but somehow I know it. That we're right."

She laid her head against his chest, seeking to be even closer, and slipped her arms around his torso. His body felt so good, so right, easing the tightness in her chest so she could finally breathe easier. She had been barely breathing the whole time he'd been gone.

He hugged her close and ran his hand down her body, stopping at the slope above her bottom. She smiled and slid her hand along his body to rest in the same place above his rear. *Move lower, Devlin, and I'll do the same.* "So why didn't you explain?"

"I tried, but you weren't ready to listen. You needed time. You may need still more."

"Oh." The tighter he held her, the less she cared about the reason. Memories of their lovemaking sent shivers through her and anything threatening those feelings, their connection, fled her brain. Yearning, hot and fluid, ripped away everything else, making her pulse in anticipation.

Devlin moved his hands into her hair, bringing her gaze to his. "Tala?"

She nodded, sure of his question and her answer. "Yes."

"I would never hurt you. Didn't mean it as something to hurt you." She caught the quick flash of regret on his face. His gaze dove into hers, imploring her, commanding her to believe.

She inhaled a quick breath as tears stung her eyes. She searched his face and found the answer she'd dreamed of. "I know."

"I'm sorry. It won't happen again." Diving into her being, he searched inside her for the truth. "Unless you want me to."

His soft teasing grin settled the massive butterflies fluttering in her stomach, leaving nothing but trust behind. Taking his hand, she led him to the bedroom. Once they'd reached the bed, she turned to him, took his face between her hands and brought his mouth to hers. Her tongue slipped between his lips, seeking his, finding his. As their tongues played, she snaked her hands around his ribcage, bringing his shirt along with her. He shook it off and let the material pile at his feet.

Nibbling at his bottom lip, she flipped open his jeans, pushing down the zipper by yanking the flaps apart. Devlin copied her with her jeans, tugging them off her hips so she could step away from them. The rest of her clothes soon joined the jeans, shrugged to the floor.

Tala pushed him to a sitting position on the bed and dropped to her knees. His excited groan thrilled her almost as much as her eye-level view of his enlarged shaft. Wrapping her palms around him, she licked the underside of his cock, gliding her tongue along the thick trunk until she reached the tip. Devlin grabbed her hair to keep her close, but she resisted, pushing against the bed for support.

With slow precision, she twirled her tongue over his tip until he had to let go of her hair to fall back on the bed. Stroking him first with her hand, she slid her tongue over her fingers, along his trunk and higher to tickle the already oozing head. When he jerked, she cupped his balls, moving her fingers to massage them. He gave a tortured, happy moan. Smiling, she paused, removing her mouth from him.

"No, don't stop."

Pleased by the thickness in his voice, she licked him once, then deep-throated him, driving him as far into her mouth as she could. The crown of his shaft bumped the back of her throat and her saliva washed the pre-come from his skin. She held him in her mouth, dragging all the taste she could get from him, sucking, wrapping her tongue around him. Still cupping his balls, she fingered the curly hair around them. He gasped and clutched at the bedspread.

"Tala. Oh, shit, Tala."

She slipped him out of her mouth, enjoying the soft popping sound it made. "Do you like it, Devlin?"

He growled and reached for her, but she weaved out of his reach. "Uh-uh-uh. This is my turn." Again, she dove onto him, pulling and sucking. When she stopped again, he cried out as she'd intended for him to do. "Sit up, Devlin. I want to watch your face." He followed her directions, urging her to take him into her mouth again. She tilted her head, still tugging on him, to see the ecstasy flow over his face.

He is mine. She worked with her hands and her mouth, and rejoiced at the thought. Giving head to any other man would have felt wrong, dirty, even submissive to her. But not with Devlin. With this act, she'd claim him as her own. For good and bad.

She sighed, letting her warm breath cascade over her hands and down his shaft. He uttered another louder growl. Playing with his balls, squeezing them with just the right amount of pressure, she coaxed more sounds of delight from him. Her tongue explored his dick, starting at the base where his hair tickled her nose and slowly making a clockwise trip around the thick shaft. At last she reached the summit and toyed with the cap, the remaining obstacle before she arrived at the peak of the mountain.

Now all I have to do is plant my flag. The fantasy took flight as she imagined standing on a lava-covered mountaintop, plunging her flagpole into the ground. *I, Tala the Conqueror, hereby proclaim this Mount Devlin.* She giggled, sending short puffs of air along the vein-covered length.

"Oh, damn, Tala. Stop dragging this out. Suck me dry. *Now.*"

His words, along with the act of taking him, made her greedy with power. She pulled off him and heard him gasp in dismay. "Oh, I'll suck you. Don't you worry about that. You just better worry that you can handle me. But first, I want to take a good look."

Taking him in both hands, she smiled and ran a thumb over the weeping end of his cock. Leisurely, she touched the tip of her tongue to one of the blue veins and tracked its course to the end. He moved his ass closer to the edge, obviously wanting her to take him into her mouth again.

"Are you ready, Devlin?" At his nod, she dragged him inside quickly, then slipped him out even faster.

"Oh, shit, yeah!" He brushed her hair over her shoulders. "I'm going to blow my top." Tracking his fingers through her hair, he licked his lips and watched her, waited for her. His unblinking amber eyes dug into her, begging her to take him.

She smiled, considered making him wait longer and decided against it. Besides, the flood between her legs wanted him now. Sending him a special look, she opened her mouth, placing only the oozing head into her mouth.

He growled, impatient and needy.

Slowly, inch by inch, she took him in, playing her tongue along the underside of his cock. He growled again, letting go of her to grip the bedspread. "Oh, damn, that's so…"

She sucked him, taking him into her mouth in an agonizingly slow trek, then reversed her way, inch by inch, until she reached the mushroomed top. Keeping the head in her mouth, she nibbled on the tip, tasting his growing orgasm.

At last, she popped him out and grinned at him. "Good?"

"Hell, no. Not good." He was breathing heavily, his amber eyes now clouded over with unspent lust. "Fucking fantastic."

The growl he made burned through her, sparking her yearning into a searing flame. She had to steady herself, refraining from spreading her legs and ramming his cock into her. *Hang on. Don't stop yet.*

First, she wanted to tease him. She fondled his balls, loving the way he moaned at her touch. Then, without warning, she deep-throated him again, taking him to the back of her throat. He cried out and tightened his hold on her hair.

Ignoring the pain his grip caused her, she sucked harder and harder, dragging her mouth to the end and then diving down on him again. Her tongue went wild, lapping up all the tastes he gave her. Pumping with her hands to match the rhythm of her mouth, she gave her man all the love she held inside her. And waited for his explosion.

Suddenly, he cried out and shoved her away from him. "You're torturing me, woman."

"That's kind of what I was going for." Tala giggled and squeezed her breasts together, knowing they would capture his attention. "Woman, huh?" She arched an eyebrow and shot him an I-don't-know-about-that look. "I guess woman is better than babe. But not by much."

With a grunt, he grabbed her underneath her arms and lifted her, pulling her on top of him. She squealed and scooted with him toward the center of the bed. "So you don't like me calling you woman, either, huh?" He buried his face in the curve of her neck, his chuckle tickling her skin. "Would you prefer 'my queen'? Or how about just plain old beautiful?"

"Nope. I have a name. Use it. And be careful, bud. No more biting. Got it?"

In answer, he slid his tongue along her collarbone and the red gashes remaining from her wounds. Deliberately taking his time, he made his way across her chest until his mouth latched onto her breast, sucking at her tit like a starving man.

Spreading her legs, she guided him inside her. "I need you, Devlin. Big time." Wiggling her eyebrows at him, she added, "And I do mean *big* time."

He growled again. Why did he growl so often? Not that she minded. In fact, she loved his growl. Yet the question went unanswered, her train of thought lost to his cock thrusting into her. Rock hard, his shaft plunged into her cave, digging deeper until he could go no farther. The walls surrounded him, claiming him, holding him to her. She locked her legs around his hips and rode him, forever binding herself to him.

He quickened his pace, ramming into her faster, making his balls bump against her wet slit. Taking her tit in his teeth, he lashed the taut nub with his tongue. His raw growl washed over her again, exciting her, driving her need higher.

She slammed into him, wanting to take all of him. "Oh, Devlin."

He responded, rumbling a low moan against her tit to flow warmly over her breast.

She met each of his thrusts with her own, pulling him to her with her arms and her vagina. Heat, unrestrained, roared inside her and her release escalated, soaring to the sky. Throwing back her head, she let loose with an animal-like scream in the same instant that Devlin turned his head to the side and howled.

☾

"I have never tasted anything so good in my life." Devlin licked the fingers on one hand while balancing the takeout box on his other.

"Hey!" Tala playfully bumped against him.

"Well, almost never." His wicked grin sparked a small fire in her abdomen. "I'm telling you, if mankind never does anything more than invent pizza, he's fulfilled his purpose in this world."

They crossed the restaurant parking lot together with the late afternoon sun warming their backs. Tala giggled. "So forget about world peace, just keep the pizza coming?"

"Give everyone in the world free pizza and you'd have world peace. And solve world hunger at the same time."

Tala laughed and punched the button on her car's remote. *Who'd have thought so much could come in such a short time?* After spending a relaxing day together, she was looking forward to another night of bliss wrapped in Devlin's arms. She slipped her arm in his and greeted his smile with one of her own.

Whether the smell or the flash of movement out of the corner of her eye made her stop, she wasn't sure. Maybe it was both. Yet when she looked at the bushes, she saw nothing out of the ordinary. However, she couldn't mistake the familiar stench.

"I know that smell." Devlin wrinkled his nose in distaste.

She glanced at him, not surprised he'd caught the odor, too. "Yeah. I'm trying to place it, but— Oh, crap."

"What?" Devlin folded her into his arms and scanned the foliage around the pizza parlor's lot. "Did you see something?"

"I thought I did. And I remember what—or who—makes that stink. It's George Groggins' aftershave."

"Who?"

She pulled away from Devlin to search for the ex-employee. "You know. The man who hurt the she-wolf. He must be somewhere close by."

"Not for long."

Was that Devlin's voice? Tala turned to study him closer. His tone was lower than she'd ever heard, meaner, like controlled chaos ready to break free. She'd expected him to react, but was unprepared for what she saw.

Devlin inhaled a quick sharp breath and, without warning, his face changed, contorted, until he didn't look like himself. His jaw altered, shooting outward. His mouth opened, forced wide by his rapidly growing teeth.

Holy shit.

Tala stared at Devlin. *Are those fangs?* Falling backwards, she gawked at him, forgetting about George. *How did any man, anyone, have teeth like that?* Amazed, yet strangely drawn to the sight, she tried to match what she saw with anything logical. She bit down, surprised to find that her own teeth felt too big for her mouth. *I'm losing it. Maybe someone put drugs in the pizza?* She gritted her teeth again, but this time her teeth seemed normal. *Am I drugged?*

A growl rumbled through him as he stalked in a circle, checking out the surrounding vehicles. "Do you see him anywhere?"

"What? Who?"

Devlin, the normal-looking Devlin, met her gaze and in his eyes she saw recognition, acknowledgement.

"You changed a second ago." She paused, giving him time to deny it, but he didn't. "What is with you? What are you hiding? And this time I'm not getting distracted. So spit it out, Devlin. I'd rather know now than find out later." *Before it's too late. But isn't it already too late?*

He inhaled deeply and licked his lips. "You saw, didn't you?"

No. Maybe I don't really want to go there after all. "I don't know what you mean."

Devlin tilted his head and arched an eyebrow. "Yes, you do. You saw my fangs."

He'd said the words. Out loud so he couldn't take them back. "I, uh, I don't know. Maybe. But no. I'm sure I imagined everything." She blurted out a short laugh, hoping to make a joke of what she'd seen. Or what she thought she'd seen. She grasped at straws. "I'm thinking the pizza was doped."

"The food's fine. And no, you didn't imagine anything." He stared at her, molding his gaze to hers. "Tala, I need to tell you about me. *All* about me."

Damn it all to hell and back. I'm successful. I'm strong. I've got everything I need in my life. Except Mr. Right. Damn, I'd take Mr. Not-A-Weirdo right now.

The air around her felt heavier, denser, harder to suck into her lungs, and her breathing quickened. She didn't want this conversation to go on. If it did, they couldn't stay like they were, and everything she'd hoped for might end up lost. "Forget I asked. I don't want to hear this, Devlin. L-let's just go home." She wheeled around and started for her car. "And no, you can't drive."

His hand on her arm brought her around until she stood close to him. The blood rushing through her ears picked up speed and her heart thudded against her ribcage. "Let me go." Yet his eyes of warm chocolate melted into hers, leaving her unable to break free.

"Tala, I know this will be difficult for you to understand and accept. But if you look into your heart, you'll find I'm telling you the truth. You said you knew the truth."

"No." She looked around her and then down at the ground. "I'd rather not. Let's go back to thirty minutes earlier when you crammed two slices of pizza in your mouth. Hell, let me cram two slices in your mouth."

"You have to hear this." His ran his hands up and down her arms. "I'm what people call a werewolf. But we prefer to call ourselves shifters."

She gaped at him, unable to rationalize what he'd said. *I didn't know what I'd expected him to say, but it sure wasn't this.*

She couldn't help herself. She had to let it out. Nothing could control her reaction.

She laughed. Full out, full-throated, hold-the-belly-'cause-it-hurts laughed.

In fact, she couldn't stop laughing. "You're kidding me, right? A werewolf? Holy shit, Devlin, are you saying you change into a wolf during a full moon?"

His gaze zoned in on her, silently forcing her to believe. "I'm serious, Tala."

"You're telling me you're the Wolf Man?" She wrapped her arms around her waist and tears streamed down her face. But she couldn't stop laughing. "So you grow fur and everything? Don't you know most women don't like hairy men?"

"Tala, stop." He reached for her, but she darted out of his grasp.

Whistling, she snapped her fingers. "Here, boy. Oh, wait. I guess wolves don't heel like dogs do, right?"

She continued to giggle. Yet, her chest tightened as if her heart couldn't pump the blood fast enough through its arteries. "And what else, Devlin? Were you going to bite me and change me into a werewolf, too? Recruit another she-wolf for the pack?"

Devlin's gaze locked onto her, his face a cold mask.

I'd be very worried if this weren't so funny. Or is it?

Something flipped over in her belly and settled like a rock in her gut. She was stuck in this insane conversation no matter how loudly she laughed. "Oh, crap. You did bite me." She whirled around, looking at her bottom. "Am I going to grow a tail when the moon comes out? Will I run around in circles chasing my tail? Oh, shit. I just did!" She stopped spinning and dropped her mouth wide in feigned delight. "Does this mean I'll have cubs instead of children? A litter?"

"We need to talk seriously about this, Tala."

"Too bad, Devlin. I don't think there's a full moon tonight so we'll have to wait a few days for a romp under the stars. But, hey, in the meantime, you can pick out which brand of dog food you'd like me to feed you. Or does your appetite run to steaks?" Her voice pitched higher, hysterics pushing aside her restraint. "But here's the good news. We don't even have to cook them. Werewolves prefer their meat rare, right?" *Maybe if I keep talking, he'll stop forcing me to listen.*

"Tala, don't mock me."

All the frantic humor left her, quickly replaced by anger. "Then don't feed me a crock of shit."

He grabbed her hand and held her in place. "I'm not. You need to know who I am. What I am." His gaze bored into her. "In fact, listen to yourself. The real you inside. You already know, Tala. You said so. Just let yourself believe."

"Oh, I do know. I know you're one funny man. But the joke's over, okay?"

Devlin growled, frustration echoing through the grumble.

"And what's with all the growling? Is it part of your act?"

He grabbed her before she could react, slamming his mouth against hers, driving his tongue into her mouth. Strong arms held her and she struggled, making a halfhearted attempt to get away. Yet, although she told herself she wanted to run, her body responded to him, heating up in seconds when he pressed against her.

Devlin trailed kisses down her neck and pulled her shirt aside. He nipped at her skin, licking her between each nip. Giving up any pretense, she slid her hands under his arms and around his broad torso to grip his shirt from behind. She clung to him for a minute before taking his hand from the hollow above her bottom, and placing it over her breast.

Bending his head, he sought out her nipple and bit through the fabric covering the firm bud. "Tala, I have to tell you all of it. You have to understand. You have to let yourself feel it."

The warmth in her panties increased as she grew wet with

desire. She didn't want to know. All she understood was how much she wanted him, lusted for him. "Shut up, Devlin, and take me home."

The shock of him pushing her away left her dazed and unsteady on her feet. "No. Don't stop." Why couldn't he just do as she asked?

Cupping her face between his hands, he forced her to look at him. His hard gaze trapped her, snaring her like a rabbit in a noose. "You're going to hear me out."

Afraid to say anything, afraid to move, she waited, knowing she had no choice but to listen. Her pulse quickened to an impossible rate and fear ran an even race with longing.

"I'm a lycanthrope. A shifter. A werewolf."

"No." She reached for his hands and averted her gaze from his face. *Please don't let him be crazy.* Yet another, stronger emotion reared its head, demanding she pay attention. She did know. The churning in her gut held the truth she didn't want to acknowledge, couldn't acknowledge.

He gripped her harder, forcing her to look at him again. "I'm Devlin Cannon of the Cannon Pack. We've lived in this area for generations, both in the city and in the hills."

"You've got a problem if you think I'm going for this wolf-man thing." She silently begged him, wanting him to tell her everything was a joke. "It's a joke, right? I mean, what I saw…"

His abrupt laugh sounded more like a bark than any sound a human would make. Yet, still she wouldn't, couldn't believe. If she did, everything would change and things were too good right now.

"Tala, I came to the city to find my mate." He kissed her, lightly, lovingly. "I came to find you."

What had he said? Stunned, she waited, hoping she'd misunderstood him. She was his 'mate'?

"I'm telling you the truth. You're my mate, Tala."

Oh, my God.

Tala broke free and stumbled away from him. Whether she'd dredged up enough strength at long last or he'd loosened his hold on her, she didn't know. And didn't care. Her soul ripped apart as the scariest thought of all sank in. *I love him. Even if he's...Even if I'm...* Her mind stalled, refusing to let her deny his words any longer.

She backed away, her heart pounding not from all he'd told her, but from the truth no longer hidden within her. "You were right. I—I do need more time." Without giving him a chance to speak, she dashed for her car.

Chapter Eight

A werewolf. A shifter. The man thinks he's some kind of an animal.

Glancing at the front door, she again wondered where Devlin was, but pushed away the anxiety. She'd asked him to give her time and stay clear of her until she'd calmed down, hadn't she? And he'd return later, no doubt. At least, she hoped he'd return. But when he did, would he still claim to be a werewolf?

You saw him. Don't you believe your own eyes?

The nagging thoughts dug at her, making her try to understand. Her love for him couldn't have let her do anything less.

Damn it all to hell and back. I do love him.

She frowned, then smiled. She'd found him at last, her wolf-like man. She looked at the poster of the pack of wolves and let her mind wander, allowing herself to believe the unbelievable.

The wolves in the picture seemed to move and she fantasized that she was the female. Cubs surrounded her, while the large wolf—Devlin, of course—stood watch over their romping youngsters. Sighing, Tala let the cozy family image play in her mind. *Would Devlin and I have lots of—*

Cubs? I'm thinking of having baby wolves? What in the world is the matter with me? I've gone crazy. Wolf cubs instead of children. Or would they be both? She glanced at the poster again. One of the cubs put on a happy doggy smile, waved, and called to her. "Hi, Mom!"

Tala fell against the back of her couch and shoved a pillow over her face to bury her scream. Yelling for a full minute helped ease the stress building inside her. Slowly, she dared to peek above the cushion, squinting at the poster again. Thankfully, the poster had returned to normal with no talking animals. *I have got to get a grip.*

She threw the pillow against the wall, striking the poster of the male wolf and his mate. Maybe she deserved this. Was her attraction, her love of wolves driving her over the edge? Hadn't she imagined her own teeth lengthening into fangs?

This can not be happening. Girl, you need professional help.

She tunneled her fingers through her hair and scanned the room around her. Wolf pictures, knickknacks and figurines were everywhere. Could Devlin be playing on her obsession? She shook her head. No, he'd been sincere in his declaration. Frustration brought tears and she growled at her lack of control.

Growled? Now I'm growling, too? Like Devlin does?

She spotted her grandfather's picture and paused. Her grandfather shared her passion for wolves, particularly the wolves around the hills of Denver. Could he help?

She rose to go to the mantel and pick up the photo of the small gray-haired man. Her grandfather, Ross Wilde, had told her a fascinating, unbelievable story during her childhood visits to his home outside the city. Hadn't the story included wolves? Wolves as part of a family? Maybe even her family? Yet as hard as she tried, she couldn't fit the pieces of the tale into place. Too many years had passed since she'd last heard the story.

I think it's time to pay Gramps a visit. She reached for her cell phone, punched in the numbers and waited for him to pick up. After several minutes, he answered, his voice bringing a tender glow to her heart.

"Gramps? It's Tala." She smiled into the receiver. A visit

was long overdue, no matter what the reason.

"Tala? Hi, honey. How ya doing, Cookie?"

Her grin stretched wider at the affectionate nickname. "Fine, Gramps." God, how she loved him. She'd forgotten just how much until she'd heard his voice. "Only you can get away with giving me such a cutesy name. I'd sock anyone else who tried."

He chuckled, his tone vibrant and full of life. "Hey, grandfathers can get away with all kinds of shit."

Tala laughed and mimicked her late grandmother. "Watch your mouth, old man. Knock off the swearing, damn you."

He hooted, delighted at her imitation. "Funny how she hated for me to cuss, especially since she could hold her own with the best of them."

Tala couldn't respond. Not with her throat swelling up with emotion.

"Your grandmother would be proud of you, Cookie, just like I am. Just like your parents would be."

Tala eyes watered. The car accident claiming her parents' lives was years ago, but the heartache lived on. "Thanks, Gramps."

A silence fell between them. Lost in thought about her parents, Tala caught only a part of her grandfather's next words.

"...calling about? Not that I'm not happy to hear from you. You should call me more often and drop by anytime you like."

"Funny you should say so because I thought I'd come out for a visit. You know, to catch up on things." *And to ask you about my werewolf lover, Gramps.* She winced at the strange thought. *How the heck am I going to bring the subject up?*

"Hey, terrific! When are you coming?"

"No time like the present. If you're not busy." She pictured him sitting around the big kitchen table with his friends. The smoke from the cigars he refused to give up would fill the room while potato chips and beer cans littered the counters around them. "Or I can wait if you have plans. Have you got a game going later, Gramps?"

"Naw. I wiped the boys out last night. Come on over. Now's as good a time as any."

"Great. I'll head right over."

The "boys" consisted of five men, all Gramps' closest friends, all about the same eighty years of age, all from the same neighborhood. They'd managed to remain close throughout the years. Closer than most people ever got. She frowned. Her grandmother had called them "the Pack". Tala always assumed Granny meant they were like Frank Sinatra's Rat Pack.

But could she have meant something else? Something more like Devlin's pack?

☾

"Hey, Cookie. You're looking hot."

Tala shot Gramps a you-are-such-a-flirt look. "Watch it, old man. You're too old for me."

He laughed and pushed the door wider for her, giving her a chance to glance around. Nothing much had changed in the small neat house. Granted, the neighborhood had grown when the city had expanded to include the outlying areas, but Gramps had resisted selling any of his five acres. Now his house sat on the cul-de-sac surrounded by newer, bigger homes.

"Aw, leave it to you, Gramps." Tala strode into the room and took a cookie out of the box sitting on the coffee table. "Chocolate chip. My favorite. I love how you always have cookies for me."

"Sorry they aren't homemade like your Gran's."

She hugged him, enjoying his familiar aroma. His natural body scent was stronger than she remembered. Sitting with him on the couch, she kept her head down, not yet ready to ask the tough questions.

"So, Cookie. What's up? What's bugging you?"

She looked up to find him eyeing her. "I never could hide anything from you."

He ran a hand over her shoulder, comforting her with his touch, sending waves of reassurance flooding through her. "That's right, so don't even try."

Taking in a large breath, she decided to dive right in. "Do you remember the story you used to tell me when I was a kid? You know. The one about wolves?"

His hand slid from her shoulder at the same moment his smile slid from his face. "Sure. Why?"

"I can't remember all of it. Did it have something to do with…"

"With what?"

"I know this will sound stupid, Gramps. But did it have something to do with werewolves?"

Gramps' gaze met hers and a trickle of apprehension ran down her spine. *Oh, shit, he's going to tell me something I'm not going to like.*

"Cookie, the story isn't just a story. It's about your family." He searched her face. "It's about the pack."

The pack? The butterflies filling her stomach turned into bats. Big, bad, ugly bats. "What do you mean?" Did she really want to hear this? "I thought the Pack was just a name Granny called your poker buddies." She shoved the cookie into her mouth. *Stop asking questions and get the hell outta here.*

Yet she knew she couldn't leave until she'd heard the truth. Indeed, if she were honest with herself, the idea of a pack was intriguing. Intriguing, but scary.

"Yeah, it was. But those buddies were also part of our lives. Part of our heritage." He gave her a comforting smile. "The members of the pack are our kind of people."

"I don't understand. What are you saying?" *You know what*

he's saying.

"Do you remember me telling you about your special ancestors? Remember how I told you they had a gift, a power most other humans didn't have?"

Fear constricted her breathing but she pressed on. "I figured you'd juiced up the story with a bit of fantasy. *Breathe, Tala.* "Gramps, get to the point, okay? You're freaking me out."

A spark glittered in his eyes. "Your ancestors were part of a group of unique individuals." He squeezed her hands, his bushy eyebrows arching at her. "Cookie, you have shifter blood in you."

Suddenly the world tipped at an odd angle, doubling her vision, and she gasped. She gripped his hands and held on, needing strength to stay connected to a sane world, a world of reality. "Do you mean werewolves? Tell me you're making this up."

A strange, sad expression flitted across his features. "No, Cookie. I'm not. We're not fond of that word but, yes, werewolves are what most people call our kind. You come from a proud line of shifters. Trust me on this."

She waited for him to chuckle and say he was pulling her leg. An idea, a way to disprove all this nonsense, came to her. "Then why haven't I ever seen anyone change into a wolf? Why haven't I ever noticed anything odd?"

"First of all, we aren't odd, not then, not now. You've never been aware of our gift because our blood has been diluted with human blood for many years. Most of us have lost the ability to transform."

She grasped at another straw. "So we don't have enough of this so-called shifter blood in us to do us any harm?"

"Harm? To shift is a gift, not something harmful, but your great-great-grandfather was the last one in our family who had the ability."

"Did you ever see him change?"

"It's called shifting. And no, I never did."

"Then you don't know if this is for real and not merely a family legend, do you?"

Gramps took her hands. "Rumors are often filled with more truth than fiction. I know if you'll search your heart, you'll realize I'm telling you the facts. Besides, some of my poker buddies can still shift. And them I've seen."

Could her grandfather and all his friends be delusional? Was this a form of old age dementia? Tala studied her grandfather's earnest expression and knew he had all his mental capacities intact. Unless… "Gramps, doesn't Luther use medicinal marijuana for his glaucoma?"

His laughter echoed around the small room. "So you think we're just a bunch of old farts getting high and imagining we're shifters?"

"Well…" Leave it to Gramps to put her in her place. "At least that would make more sense. This is just so unbelievable."

His laughter died down and he hugged her, comforting her as he'd done all her life. "You've got shifter blood in you, Cookie. If you can't take my word, then look inside yourself for confirmation. You'll instinctively know it and be able to feel it. You'll sense your true self. Be proud of your heritage, Cookie."

When she sighed, he narrowed his eyes, zeroing in on her. "Now I've got a question or two. What brought all this up? Have you howled at the moon lately?"

☾

Devlin still wasn't at the apartment when Tala got home. She'd hoped he'd be there waiting for her. After all, she hadn't told him to get lost or anything. Not permanently, anyway.

She flopped onto the couch. *What the hell is happening to me? Everything changed that night at the club. Could I have conked my head too hard when I fell? But I didn't fall down. I crouched down. Like a four-legged animal. Like a wolf. Damn it all to hell and back, I howled.* Her grandfather's words echoed back to her. *"Have you howled at the moon lately?"*

The only other explanation was even harder to believe. Had she actually summoned her mate? How ridiculous! The urge to scream again crawled up her throat, but she fought it down. *I wish I could forget everything Gramps said and somehow keep from getting pulled into Devlin's fantasy.*

But what if his fantasy is true? What if werewolves—shifters—really exist? She tracked her fingers through her hair and paced over to the desk where her computer rested. *Do I really want to know?* She eyed the screensaver depicting a pack of wolves, her hand poised over the mouse. *I'd be better off knowing the truth, right?*

Slipping into the chair, she steeled her nerves and typed key words into the search criteria. "Here goes nothing." A quick bark of a laugh escaped her. "Or everything."

After an hour of scanning the many websites about lycanthropes, she leaned back in her chair, more confused than ever. Depending on which website she clicked on, Devlin and her grandfather were either making the whole shifter thing up—*no way would Gramps lie to her*—or they really were real werewolves. Or they were just plain insane.

Could Devlin be mentally ill? After all, he'd spied on her and slept on her balcony. Not to mention his little break-in at her clinic. She had to admit his actions weren't exactly average, everyday kind of things to do. Still, her heart wouldn't let her mind accept the insanity explanation.

Some people truly believe they're werewolves. Like Devlin does. Like Gramps does.

Like I do.

Unable to stand the images and facts any longer—much less her errant thoughts—she clicked on the mouse and shut down all the websites. *But if they—we're—not crazy, then how do I explain what I saw? Did I really see Devlin change?* She closed her eyes, picturing Devlin as he'd reacted to the smell of George's aftershave.

I saw fangs. Not teeth. Honest-to-God, sharp-as-a-knife fangs.

Another image of Devlin came, his head shaped differently, grabbing George and coming to the she-wolf's rescue. He'd shifted then, too. She'd dismissed what she'd seen at the time, but could she now?

Shaking her head, she crossed over to stand in front of the mirror. She stared at her image and smiled, stretching her lips to expose her teeth. But they looked like normal, non-lethal teeth. Hooking her thumbs on either side of her mouth, she pulled on her upper lip. *Shape? Normal. Color? Normal. Length? Normal. Nothing canine-like.*

She chuckled. *I'm not insane. I'm just acting stupid.* Rubbing a hand over her neck, she shook her head and dropped her gaze to the table below.

A pure silver bracelet rested in a crystal bowl. Tala fingered the bracelet, moving it around, studying its shiny surface. Silver had always made her vaguely ill. The more silver the object contained, the more ill she became. So if a silver bullet could kill a werewolf, then could a little silver make one sick? Even one with diluted shifter blood?

The absurdity of her question hit her and she whirled around, striding out on the balcony—and away from the bracelet. But she couldn't run from the whisper in her mind. *It's better to know.*

Above her the moon glowed, a brilliant white orb against the dark sky. Glancing around, she checked to make certain no one else was near. What she was about to do was ridiculous and she didn't want an audience. A shiver of anticipation zipped through her as she cleared her throat, lifted her chin toward the sky—and howled.

Her first attempt was weak and breathy. *Hell, I sound more like a sick hyena than a wolf baying at the moon. Pitiful, Tala. Really pitiful.* Setting her feet apart, she fisted her hands on her hips, circled her neck to loosen the muscles, and let out a longer, stronger call. *Better.* A third, more forceful cry followed, this one surprising her. The sound of her last howl carried on the wind, echoing through the air.

Wow. Not bad.

"Mommy, there's a doggy upstairs."

Tala jolted, clamped a hand over her mouth and slinked over to the glass doors.

"No playing with imaginary pets right now, sweetie."

Please don't let Caroline come outside. Tala pressed against the glass, trying to get as close as possible to the building. *And definitely not Bobby Lee with his shotgun.*

"But Mommy. The doggy's crying."

"Good grief, Tracy. First a monkey and now a doggie. You know people can't have pets in our building. Close the patio door and come back inside."

After hearing the door slam shut, Tala moved as quietly as possible—*like a wolf?*— and slipped inside her apartment. Once safely on the couch, she clutched her tummy and burst into a fit of giggles. *Baying at the moon is definitely not my thing.*

Relieved, she flicked on the television to her favorite classic movie channel. The horror film *The Wolf Man* appeared just as the monster began morphing from man to animal. Staring at the transformation, Tala scrutinized the way his body changed in bone structure and appearance. *Granted, it's a movie, but maybe...*

The Wolf Man's face bent and contorted. He jutted out his chin and the length of his jaw expanded. Thrusting her own chin forward, she tried to imagine the pain of such a transformation. *No wonder they always make a lot of noise.*

The Wolf Man hunched over as his clothes shredded across his back and shortened on his arms. Without thinking, she slipped off the couch and crawled over to the television.

Tala copied his conversion step by step. When he wrenched a body part one way, she tried to do the same. When he rumbled one of his growls, she mimicked it with one of her own. Concentrating, she envisioned coarse hair sprouting all over her body, claws striking out from the tips of her fingernails, and ears growing to fur-tipped triangles on her head.

"Grrrr." Tala let the sound roll from the back of her throat and over her tongue. She shook her head when he shook his, ready to feel his anguish when he cried into the night sky. She bared her teeth and could almost, just almost, feel the tips of fangs on her lower lip. Could she be changing?

"Having fun?"

Tala shrieked, pushed up from the floor, stumbled, and landed on her bottom. "Damn it all to hell and back!" She glared at Devlin, too embarrassed to think what to do next.

Devlin's gaze skimmed from her to the television and around to her again. "Are you trying to do what I think you're trying to do?" A wide smirk covered his face and a twinkle came to his eye.

Tala scrambled to her feet. Who did he think he was, making fun of her? "I'm just watching a movie." When she saw his raised eyebrows, she hurried on. "And exercising."

One eyebrow cocked a bit higher, relaying his disbelief. "Ri-ight. Exercising." The bemused expression matched his growing smirk.

Tala tugged at her disheveled shirt and mentally dug in her heels. "It's a new fitness trend sweeping the nation."

"Really?"

She glared at him, miffed by his smugness. "Yeah. Really."

"And what do you call this new workout? Abs of Steel for the Alpha Wolf? Pilates for Predators? Tae Bo for Timber Wolves?"

Okay, so the guy is funny. She stammered, searching her brain for any title halfway plausible. "Um, it's called Maniacal Yoga." *Oh, shit. That name sucks.*

Devlin laughed and crossed his arms over his wide chest.

"Hmm. Kind of a weird name, don't ya think? Even weirder than my guesses."

Unable to stand his you-are-so-full-of-shit stare, Tala huffed at him and strode into the kitchen. She opened the refrigerator door and took her time scanning the contents. Not that she actually wanted food. She just needed time to cool down. "I didn't pick the name, you know."

"Of course not. But you know, from the way you were moving your body and all, I'd swear you were trying to shift."

The cold can of soda she'd pick up slipped through her fingers, but she caught it halfway to the floor. She gawked at the can in her hand. *How the hell?* Since when had her reflexes gotten so fast? Keeping her face turned from him, she worked to keep her voice even. "Don't be ridiculous."

"So you weren't trying to shift?"

She popped the top and took a drink, forcing the liquid past her closed-up throat and down to the bubbling pit in her stomach. "Of course not."

"Good. Because if you ever wanted to shift, it would look like this."

Chapter Nine

Devlin allowed the animal part of him to rise to the surface. Sweet release erupted along with the pain that always accompanied a full transformation. Keeping his eyes on Tala, he willed her to face him. The smell of her apprehension drifted to him, saddening him. Above all else, he didn't want her to fear him.

Stripping off his clothes, he let the change continue. Still, she kept her back to him. "Tala, you have to watch to understand. Watch me. Now." Although spoken in a whisper, his command took hold and she pivoted slowly to face him.

The shock on her face made his heart ache for her. Her eyes, wide and staring like a deer caught in a hunter's scope, scanned him up and down. But he kept on shifting.

"It's okay, Tala." Years of practice had taught him how to speak even while his fangs sharpened and his skull shape morphed. "I'm still Devlin. No matter what form my body is in." Claws grew on both feet and hands and he held up one hand for her inspection.

She struggled to speak, but nothing came out. Leaning against the refrigerator door, she shook her head and gaped.

He stretched, getting used to his other body structure, and she jumped. "I would never hurt you, Tala. Never."

Within seconds, Devlin dropped to all fours, standing before Tala as a large black wolf. A rumble echoed from his chest, the need to howl rushing through him, but he kept his urge under control. Instead, he did something he never expected he would ever do. Dipping his head in a low bow, he offered himself to her.

To pet.

His love for her lanced through his heart and he realized the extent of his emotion. Was this what love did to a person? Here he was, Devlin Cannon, alpha male, bowing to a female. Yet he knew he'd do anything for her to understand and not fear him. Even bow.

With his head lowered, he couldn't see Tala's reaction. He took shallow breaths, trying to make little-to-no sound, afraid he might frighten her more.

When her hand touched the top of his head, he let out a long sigh, releasing his apprehension. He remained motionless, not wanting to scare her from touching him more, and was rewarded when her fingers bent, catching a bit of his fur. She moaned, running her hand down the length of his neck, holding his neck and his hope in her palm. Still stroking him, she petted him as she would a beloved dog.

Devlin raised his head and smiled a wolfish smile. "See? I won't bite you again." His smile widened, a mischievous idea zipping through his mind. "Not unless you want me to."

Tala gazed at him, her eyes meeting his. At long last, she blew out a puff of air that loosened up her whole body. "I...I don't believe this."

"Why not? You saw me shift. You see me now. What more can I do to convince you?" He rose, reaching out to her, claws retracted, to place his paws on her shoulders. She, however, wasn't ready for closeness and yelped, slipping away from him. Trying not to let his disappointment show, he followed her.

"So everything you told me is the truth."

Although her words seemed more like a statement of fact than a question, Devlin answered. "Believe what you see." He studied her, sizing her up. Was she ready for all the facts?

Tala slanted her head and continued to scrutinize him. At

least she appeared calmer than before, even though those icy blue eyes had yet to blink. "And you can speak."

"Shifters aren't dogs. We're people, which means we still remember how to talk like people."

"But I'd think just the physiology of it would make speaking—"

"Stop it. Stop thinking like a vet and believe what you're hearing." Surely she'd believe him now. "Tala, I haven't told you everything."

Anger flashed in her eyes and he smiled. *Ah, there's the feisty female I know and love.* "Hold on. I couldn't tell you before. You'd have freaked out worse than you did just now."

She considered his explanation and accepted it with a curt nod. "Go on, then. Tell me everything now." Her sarcastic laugh bit at him. "But damn it all to hell and back, what more can there be?"

"I tried to tell you before. I came to the city to find my mate. *You're* my mate."

At last Tala blinked, as though he'd surprised her with a snake thrust at her nose. "But why me?" She scanned his body, her forehead creasing in dismay.

How could she not believe him? After everything she'd seen, how could being his mate prove to be the most unbelievable part? "I haven't misled you, have I?"

She shook her head, but looked unconvinced. "But how can I be your mate? I'm human."

He'd opened his mouth to explain how he could change her, make her lycan, when she gasped and clamped a hand over her mouth.

"What, Tala? What's wrong?"

Excitement and a little bit of fear sparkled in her eyes. "My grandfather."

Huh? Her grandfather? "What about him?"

Lacing the fingers of her hands behind her head, she

crossed to sit down on the couch. "My grandfather is a retired zoologist. When you made those wild claims about being a werewolf—"

"Shifter."

"Shifter. I went to see him, to get his opinion and to ask him about the family story he used to tell me."

Tired of trying to maintain an upright position, Devlin dropped to the floor and rubbed up beside her. "Yeah? Go on."

"He said I have shifter blood in me. Diluted through generations of marriages to humans—which is why I don't change—but I have shifter blood, nonetheless."

Rising to place his forepaws beside her on the couch, he issued a low satisfied growl. "I thought you might. Otherwise, I don't think I'd have heard your call. Nor do I think we would've connected so quickly." He gave her a wolfish grin. "If you hadn't instinctively known about yourself, about us, I'd have never made it inside your home."

Tears sprang to her eyes. "Oh, shit, Devlin. Oh, shit. It's all really true." She paused, then swallowed hard. "The dreams."

Was she talking about his dreams of her? But how would she know? "What dreams?"

But she refused to tell him, shaking her head. Perhaps later... Right now he needed to take her in his arms to comfort her, to comfort him. Wanting her body next to his, he began the change back to human.

This time, she watched him closely. Mesmerized, she stood, unmoving, her eyes taking in every change, every detail of the process until he stood before her, naked and ready.

"Uh, Devlin?"

"Yeah?"

"Do you always get an erection when you transform?"

Of all of the questions she could have asked, he hadn't expected that one. Glancing down, he laughed and shook his head. "No and thank goodness. Having a hard-on every time I shifted would cause major complications. And quite a few stares. Even if I say so myself." He chuckled, hoping for one in return. But she acted as though she hadn't even understood his joke.

"So the big bad black wolf is what you always look like?"

Bad? Was she kidding? He frowned at her, unsure of what answer he should give. He opted for humor again. "Only when I'm around beautiful blondes like you and Goldilocks."

This time his joke hit home and she chuckled. Relief flooded through him and he grinned at her, happy to smell her fear leaving her. He was even more thrilled when she accepted his outstretched hand. "Does this mean you'll come home with me to the mountains?"

Her hand squeezed his. "Is that where you live?"

"Yeah, mostly. Although I do come into town for business. When I have to."

"So...you live in a cave? In the woods?"

Her nervous expression was endearing. "In caves. But don't worry. Our caves are quite different from what you mean. You're going to be amazed. We have all the modern comforts of life with none of the hassles of the city. And as for your job, if you still want to keep it, we'll figure something out."

She frowned, conflict covering her face. "No." She released his hand. "I mean, how can I? I don't change. Just because I have a little shifter blood in me, doesn't mean I could live with your people. Or that I'd even want to."

The joy he'd felt evaporated. "No, Tala, you don't understand." He took her hands, unable not to touch her. "You'll change. You have shifter blood in you so it shouldn't take long. All we have to do is bring it out."

"You mean like my sad attempt when you came in?"

"Good. So you admit it. You were trying to shift, huh? But, no. You'll change. Don't worry. When I bit you, I started the conversion."

She moved away, putting both physical and emotional distance between them. He ached to follow her, but knew he'd better not.

"Are you talking about the other day? That wasn't just a hickey gone wrong? You meant to sink your teeth into me? Without asking me?"

Had he told her too much, too soon? Yet, the truth was out and he had to make her understand. "I'm sorry you're upset. But it was a natural thing for me to do. I couldn't control myself."

Her words came out fast and furious. "I don't give a fuck what you think is natural. You had no right, Devlin. No right at all. And then you lied to me about what you'd done. I knew it!"

He cringed at the tears coming to her eyes and prayed they wouldn't fall. He'd hate to see her cry. Ever. But especially because of him. "I'm sorry, but you were so upset, I couldn't tell you the truth. Not then. Tala, you're my mate. My lifelong partner. It's destiny for us to be together. You know that."

"Destiny? What the hell are you talking about? Sure, I agree we're connected in some indefinable way, but..." She shook her head and backed away from him.

He nodded, understanding her denial and hoping she would come to see the reality, the history of it all. "We're meant to mate, Tala. Think about it for a minute. Your ancestors were shifters. Your family is shifter." A memory of his mother, her eyes glowing as she talked about finding his one true mate filled his mind. "Shifters and wolves are alike. We mate for life with the one who was meant for us. Tala, just imagine the future. You, me and a pack of kids."

She stared at him, glanced at the wolf family poster and blanched. His words about a family had sunk in. "A family?"

"Sure, why not?"

"Kids?"

"Uh, yeah. Don't you like kids?"

"Shifter kids?"

He cocked his head at her, trying to understand her thoughts. "Well, kids, really. But yeah, they'll shift like we can."

"Oh, my God."

"Tala, it's all right."

She took another look at the poster. "But I have my friends, my grandfather, my work here. I can't go running off with you to live in the woods." She tunneled her fingers through her hair. "Me live in the woods? This is all so out there. So incredible. I need time…"

Still more time? Granted, this was a lot to comprehend, but how much time did she need? When would she learn to heed her instincts? He sighed, forcing himself to consider her feelings. "Then take the time. We can talk about it all later. Digest everything you've seen and heard first." Still, he couldn't help but add, "You'd love the freedom. I know you would. I could see the freedom in you wanting to break out the night I watched you dance."

A wild race of emotions cascaded over her features. Anger, lust, desire and need came and went until only apprehension remained. "No. I can't."

Frustration held in check far too long roared out of Devlin. "Damn it, we belong together. I know it and you know it. You called to me, Tala, and I came for you." He strode over to her, took her by the shoulders and forced her to look him in the eyes. "I need you and I want you." Putting all his energy behind his determination, he willed her to accept their future together. "And I'm going to have you."

She opened her mouth to speak and he took it as an invitation. Crushing his mouth to hers, he slid a hand behind her neck and held her tightly against him. Her smell, so hot, so spicy, so *her*, filled his nostrils. Drinking in the warm nectar of her, he fought to control the aggressiveness raging through him. She tensed and pushed against his chest.

Devlin jerked away from her, abrupt and wrenching, leaving Tala gasping for air. He wouldn't force her even though the primal urges screaming within him demanded he throw her down and take her as his female. Instead, he picked her up, carrying her like a piece of fragile crystal, and strode into the bedroom.

She tucked her head against his chest and murmured soft indecipherable sounds, shooting his pulse rate higher. With all the tenderness he could manage, he lowered her to her feet.

"Put your faith in what was meant to be, Tala. You're mine and I'm yours."

Keeping his gaze fixed on hers, he slipped his hands under her shirt to lift it off, letting the fabric glide over the curves of her breasts. Freeing her of her bra next, he took her face in his hands and pressed feather-light kisses against her lips. She whimpered, but made no move to stop him.

He unsnapped her jeans, then thumbed them over her lush hips to let them drop to her ankles. With a groan, he broke free of her blue magnetic pools and let his sight skim down her flat stomach, drawn to the lacy white of her panties. God, the sight of her drove him wild. Wilder than the animal inside him had ever been able to be. He thrilled at the silky smoothness of her skin.

Trapping her face between his palms, he dared to find those pools again, dared to make her search within him. He had to make her accept what she already knew in her heart. "Tala, I've waited for you all my life and now that I've found you, I'm not going to let your fear keep us apart." He narrowed his eyes, strengthening his resolve. "I know you've waited for me, too. Maybe you didn't realize it, but you waited nonetheless."

A flash of a realization flickered across her face. But she remained silent.

He lowered to his knees, kissing her as he went, then nipped at the pink rosebud on the front of her chaste white panties and tugged. The material slipped an inch lower, giving him a quick peek at the curly treasure underneath. He slid them another inch and knew he'd reached the end of his patience. He groaned with need and edged the silky material over her pelvis and past her mound. When the lacy material fell to the floor, he paused, drinking in the sight of his desire. Cupping her buttocks, he leaned forward and pressed his face against her. Her scent, a mix of sweet lotion and heat, filled him. He nuzzled his nose into the middle of her hair and breathed deeply.

"Devlin."

The simple act of her saying his name spurred him on. He dragged in one last deep breath, sat back and, with all her clothes gathered at her feet, tapped one ankle, coaxing her away from the pile. She understood and stepped to the bed to sit on the edge.

He ran both hands over the smooth skin of her legs, giving her gentle encouragement to spread them wider. He wasn't sure how much longer he could resist drinking his fill. When she did, he shot her a playful look and lifted her legs over his shoulders.

Tala let out a low contented sigh, lay back on the bedspread and spread her arms over her head. "Devlin?"

"Shh. Let me enjoy taking care of you." This time she'd know they weren't having sex. This time she'd know they were making love.

He lowered his face to her bush and ran his thumbs along the curve of her folds. An excited quiver rippled along her legs. To tease her, he licked the inside of her thigh with a slow, leisurely lap. Startled, she jerked, but he held her firmly in place. Slowly, lovingly, he skimmed up the tender flesh with his teeth, wanting to bite, but resisting the urge. When he made it to the crease at the top of her leg, he pressed his lips to her and sucked. She whimpered and his dick throbbed in response.

Running his tongue over the top of her folds, he caught the sweet flavor that was Tala and tugged her closer. Although he'd hoped to play longer, teasing her until she begged him, he couldn't hold back. He spread her pussy-lips, slipped his tongue inside to fondle and sucked her already wet nub.

"I'll never get tired of tasting you." Tracing the sides of her legs with his fingers, he skimmed his hands over her flat stomach before she grabbed his hands and squeezed. "Easy, Tala, easy." Her moan wrenched the need inside his abdomen free, making his cock grow harder, bigger. "Turn on your side."

She hesitated, then did as he'd asked. Holding both legs over one shoulder, he pushed the fleshy top of her legs apart and jabbed his tongue in her pussy. She gasped, sending his yearning for more higher. Sliding his tongue along, he followed the tangy path from her pussy to her ass. He heard her intake of breath. "I need to taste every inch." When he was certain she was okay, he ran his tongue back and forth, gathering every drop of her delicious come.

Tala was his. Not as a possession or submissive female, but as his mate, his other half, his partner in life. She shivered under the lashings of his tongue, but he stayed focused on the main objective: to make Tala understand they would stay together.

When he couldn't stand any more temptation, when his need for her overrode him, he rose and she growled her displeasure at him for stopping. A smirk crooked the corner of his mouth as he climbed on top of her, placing his knee at the moist cleft between her legs and shoving her farther onto the bed. "I'm glad you liked it. I want you to need me as much as I need you." Falling on top of her to pin her to the bed, he saw the horny gleam in her eyes and knew she did.

"Relax and enjoy." He gathered all of his love and kissed her again, nipping her upper lip with gentle tugs. His tongue took command, swiping the inside of her mouth, wanting all the sensations she had to give. He grasped her breast, rubbed her hard nipple between two fingers, and rumbled his satisfaction into her throat. He nearly lost himself when she moaned back, giving him her warm breath.

Although he'd wanted to take time with her, savoring every touch, every smell, he couldn't. The burn inside him, unleashing the animal within, lashed out, and he knew he didn't have long. He gritted his teeth, silently demanding that he keep control. But when her gaze met his, he nearly conceded the battle. He had to have her, had to feel his shaft surrounded by her hot tight walls. Clutching her ass, he lifted her, positioning his body. He took both her tits, squeezed them, and delighted in the firm roundness.

His wolf knew he was weakened and, before he could stop it, he felt the shift spreading through him, breaking over him. He froze, stunned at its intensity. He squeezed his eyes shut in the struggle to maintain control. He couldn't unleash the animal. Not yet.

When he looked at her again, the brilliance of her sapphire eyes shone against her tanned face. Her blonde hair, spread out around her head, sent an overwhelming ache through him. An ache to bury his hands in her hair and run its silkiness over his body. An ache to grab onto her and never let her go. Reverently, he stroked her breasts, ran his hand along her firm stomach, then back up to pinch her taut nipples.

Damn, she's beautiful. He soaked in the sight of her, struggling to keep from ramming his shaft into her. He couldn't, not until the last possible moment. "Damn, you're beautiful." She gaped at him with a surprised expression, as though she didn't believe him. "Tala, don't you know how beautiful you are? Hasn't anyone told you?"

Tears gathered in her eyes. "Not for a long time." The rest of her words strangled in her throat. She averted her eyes from his, but not before he saw the pain lingering there.

How could such a glorious woman not have experienced her own beauty? Were the men she'd had before him blind? His breathing grew shorter, panting in his need to again keep the wolf at bay for as long as he could.

This time he failed.

Razor-like claws ripped into the covers underneath them and his facial structure began to distort along with the rest of his body. His strength increased, taking over the weak hold he maintained until he raised his massive head to roar his frustration. Yet just as he was about to cry out, her palm cupped his cheek, bringing his hot glare down to her.

The tenderness on her face knocked all the emotion save love from him. He held his breath, stunned and thrilled to see what lay beneath him. No one had ever looked at him like that. She was open to him, all her emotions, all her fear and hopes, all her love on display for him. Only for him.

"I dreamed of you. As a man." A single tear slid down her cheek. "And as a wolf. But I never thought you were real."

Her admission whetted his need and he strained against the power seeking to be set free.

"Stay with me, Devlin. As a man. I need you."

At her plea, his body relaxed, losing the wolf-like characteristics. His claws retracted and his face returned to human form. The animal's power within him lessened and he regained more control. Whenever she needed him, however she needed him, he would be there.

She wrapped herself around him, driving him insane with the silkiness of her inner thighs nestled against his waist. Lifting her, he sat her on top of his legs, curving his cock to nestle against her mound in her curly hair.

"I can't—wait much—longer." He panted the words, surprised he could even speak.

Letting her hair fall between them, blanketing his chest, she wiggled just enough, covering him with her wetness. "Then don't."

He roared his relief and thanks, and drove into her. She gasped and clung to him, her hips moving to match his pounding rhythm. They kept their hold with their gazes, each thrusting against the other with unbridled need. He pumped harder, deeper, closing his eyes to hear the creaking the bed made with every bounce, the squish of their sweaty bodies when they came together then separated, the soft grunts and mews she made.

Pushing her breasts together, he sucked both hard pebbles into his mouth. She cried louder, arching her back to thrust them to him. Every time he tugged on them, she cried louder, yet pushed them at his face. He nibbled, nipped, licked, enjoying the different sounds she made. When she leaned backward, taking them away from him, he nearly shouted in pain. And then rammed his cock into her again. Harder. Higher. Deeper.

"Tell me you're mine, Tala."

She whimpered with need. Her long hair danced around her shoulders.

"Tell me you're mine. Now."

"Devlin."

He held on, wanting to let her come first, wanting her pleasure before his, but needing to hear the words. He pulled her cheeks apart and widened his stance, opening her even wider. She yelped, surprise filtering across her face, before finally determination set in. Clasping his hair, she held on and rode him.

"Damn it, Tala. Say the words. I need to hear you say them."

She clamped her teeth together, circling her hips to grind into him. Staring into his eyes, she finally answered. "I'm yours." She then lifted the corners of her lips in a temptress's smile. "And you're mine."

Those simple words filled him as no lovemaking ever could. Yet he was unprepared for her next words.

"Devlin, mark me again."

He stopped, panting, throbbing, and stared at her, wondering if he'd heard her correctly. "What'd you say?"

The conviction in her expression left no doubt of her words. "Mark me again. Do it." She turned her head to the right, exposing more of her left shoulder in one last silent signal to obey her.

The wolf inside him howled its delight and his release tore through him, stiffening his body even as the surges continued. He cried out in ecstasy and shifted, bringing forth his fangs. Spreading his lips wide, he plunged his teeth into her.

☾

"This is freakin' sinful."

Tala stretched, molding her body to Devlin's naked skin, delighting in the sensation of his strong lean form next to her nude one.

Devlin murmured his agreement and ran his hand along the curves from the top of her shoulder to the bottom of her thigh. His eyes burned with lustful fever even though they'd finished making love only a few minutes earlier.

With his hair spread across his pillow, his other arm supported her head and she nuzzled her nose into his chest. His rich musky scent filled her nostrils, making her feel safe and loved. She closed her eyes, letting all her other senses take him in. "I'm glad I took the time off from work even if we never got out of the house." She sighed, happy and contented for the first time in years.

"*Because* we never got out of the house." Devlin sported his mischievous twinkle and pulled her closer. "I may never let you out of bed again."

"Promise?" Tala batted her eyes at him. "If I had my way, we'd stay in bed forever."

"We can make your wish come true, you know. Come home with me and we'll spend all day, every day, together. Playing in the sun, making love whenever we want, hunting. Doing anything we want."

He kissed her, starting at the fullness of her lips and working outward. His tongue teased her, lightly touching the slight part between her lips, yet never going inside. The easy comfort she'd felt moments before was blown away by the desire gusting through her. Could life get any better than this? She almost forgot what she'd started to say.

"I'm not sure about the hunting thing. All the blood and guts? Yuck." She wrinkled her nose at him. "I couldn't hurt Bambi." *Besides, who'd rather hunt than make love?*

"Believe me. Bambi could hurt you if he wanted to. But you'll get used to hunting. In fact, as soon as you shift the first time, you'll find you'll have a real appetite for tracking down your own food." He rose up, bending over her to nip her on the shoulder.

Tala laughed and pushed him back. "If you say so. But I'd still prefer a four-star hotel with room service." But would she ever shift? Hadn't she tried to morph many times during their self-imposed seclusion and had failed every time?

Devlin noted her turned-down mouth and cleared his throat so she'd pay closer attention to him. "I know what you're thinking."

"Oh, you do, do you?" She playfully slapped his shoulder. "Think you know me so well, huh?"

"Yeah, I do." His palm slid over her cheek, a loving, cherishing gesture. "Don't worry. You'll change when you're ready. So quit worrying about it."

She blew out an aggravated sigh and concentrated on the sexy body next to hers. "Okay. I'll try." She traced a path over his hard pecs, down the firm hills and valley of his six-pack abs and stopped just short of the curly mass below. Devlin had remarkable recuperative powers, but she didn't think even he would be ready to romp again this soon. Wow, how her life had changed since Devlin's appearance! "You know I've got to go into work tomorrow, right?"

Devlin grumbled and flipped onto his side to face her. "Don't. Stay with me instead." His eyes grew darker with worry. "Besides, the hunters I told you about may still be around. I want you here, safe in my arms."

"I can't believe there's this whole other world filled with

shifters and people who hunt them." She shook her head, more concerned for him than for herself. "Besides, why would they care about me? I'm not a shifter. At least, not yet."

He tightened his hold on her as if he'd never let her go. Which, she thought, was not a bad way to live.

"They might use you to get to me."

She envisioned Devlin's bloodied body, cold and lifeless, and a chill passed over her. "I'd never let them use me to hurt you. Or your family."

"You might not have a choice." He dove into her, pulling her down into his dark depths.

Running her fingertip over his full lips, he surprised and thrilled her when he sucked her finger into his mouth. He ran his tongue around the length and a flash of pleasure erupted in her belly. "You're so bad for me, Devlin."

"Yeah, but I'm a good kind of bad." He wiggled his eyebrows at her, mimicking Groucho Marx. "And you love being bad with me."

"True. But someone's got to pay the rent. And I like the idea of having a kept man."

He nuzzled her neck, nipping at the hollow between her collarbones. "You can keep me any way you want."

"And you'd be worth every penny."

He growled, a seriousness replacing his lighthearted manner. "Let me pay. Let me take care of everything."

"No way. I'm an independent woman." With regret, she pulled her finger away from his mouth and studied his face, trying to determine if he'd meant it and saw that he had. "Just how do you get money, anyway? I mean, you said you're in the import-export industry, but you never talk about your business." Like him, she edged up on her elbow and poked him in the chest. "What are you, connected to the Mafia? Don't tell me there's a shifter Mafioso."

He puffed out his cheeks, Marlon Brando style, mimicking

the actor in his *Godfather* portrayal. "People do favors for me. I make them an offer they can't refuse. Capiche?"

She squealed when he hoisted her body on top of his. Gliding his hands down her torso, he clamped onto her ass. "See, woman? You'd better behave or you could end up with a horse's head in your bed."

"Better the head of a horse than the asshole of a wolf."

"Why, you little—" He went in for the attack, tickling her just under the ribs.

"Argh! Quit it!" Tala pinched his nipples, making him yelp in feigned pain. As if she could ever truly hurt him. At last, he stopped tickling her. "No, seriously, Devlin. Tell me the truth. Are you independently wealthy or what?"

"Okay, okay. No need to get violent." He tilted his head, moving one hand through the hair falling forward over her face. "Actually, I have many lucrative investments making very substantial profits. And, due to my incredible business savvy—" he wiggled his eyebrows at her, "—I've got good people who oversee the daily operations so I don't have to. You've heard me on the phone with my friend Conrad, right? He's my right-hand man."

She leaned forward to playfully bite his nipple. "Don't you mean right-paw man?"

"Hey, watch the teeth or I'll have to use mine on you. And mine are bigger."

She arched an eyebrow. "Promises, promises."

He chuckled and raked his finger along her arm. The simple gesture wetted the cleft between her legs. *Devlin only has to touch me to touch me.*

"Working to earn money isn't a necessity. It's not for me and it won't be for you."

Her mouth fell open. "Are you saying you really are independently wealthy?"

Clutching a bunch of her hair, he ran a thumb along the

top of her ear, looking at it as though he'd never seen an ear as beautiful as hers. "Let's just say, money will never be a problem."

"Holy shit, Devlin. Why didn't you tell me?"

"Should I have?" His dark eyes grew grave. "Why? Is money that important to you?"

She tweaked his nipple again for good measure. "I'm not a gold digger, if that's what you're asking. But now that I know you're loaded, I'll definitely let you pay half the frickin' rent."

For a second she was afraid he'd not understood her joke. Then he let loose with a deep, rolling laugh and pulled her to him.

☾

George followed Tala across the street and through the entrance of the zoo. As he was about to approach her, however, a box-shaped man slid out from behind a vendor's stall, placing himself behind her. Two other men joined him, keeping their distance from each other and Tala. But George could see they were together by the unspoken signals they sent each other.

Hmm, seems sweet Tala has more admirers. George slacked off his pace so they wouldn't notice him. *What's going on?*

He trailed the men at a greater distance as they followed Tala. When she entered the building housing her office, they stopped and took up different positions outside. Sliding onto a bench, George picked up a discarded zoo map and pretended to study it.

Why were these men following Tala? He checked them out and noted their similar nondescript beige clothing. They were trying to appear to be typical zoo visitors, but they kept glancing at the door. They'd tracked her for a reason. But why? He got comfortable on the bench and waited.

George checked his watch. Thirty minutes had passed since they'd taken up their various positions. *Come on, guys.*

Make a move. She's not coming out anytime soon.

As if on command, the chunky man signaled to the others and walked away, scooting around the corner of the building housing the restrooms. His companions, however, remained at their posts.

Oh, sure. Go take a leak. Don't worry about keeping your watch. George frowned and squirmed in place. He wasn't the only one needing a break. But he'd be damned if he'd leave and miss anything.

When one of the men glanced in his direction, George whipped the map back in front of his face and ducked his head. *Don't get stupid. Stay alert.*

I wonder what she has that they want. Curiosity made him peek over the edge of the map again. "Five bucks say these guys have something to do with your freaky boyfriend."

"Now there's a bet you'd win."

A smelly rag clamped over his mouth and nose. An arm snaked around his chest, dragging him behind the bushes. Struggling against the unseen attacker, he squealed but the rag muffled the sound. Seconds later, a terrifying darkness swept over him.

Chapter Ten

George struggled against the giant man pinning his arms behind him. "Who the fuck are you guys?"

The squat man who stood in front of him crossed his arms, obviously not in a pleasant mood. "I was gonna ask you the same thing." A long scar, the type of scar a person got after a battle for his life, ran down the side of the man's neck.

"None of your damn business." George scanned the inside of the work shed. Dim light filtered through the cracks in the small wood building and he contemplated shouting for help. Until a strong hand throttled his neck, choking off his air supply.

"Watch how you talk, little man." His tormentor pressed his nose close to his. "I don't take shit from a nobody like you."

The monster of a man let go of George's throat, giving much-needed oxygen to his brain. Once the fuzziness left him, he tried a different approach. Maybe he wasn't a brave man, but he wasn't an idiot, either. He coughed and sputtered out the words. "S-sorry. Didn't know you were so touchy."

The satisfied smirk his captor sported held no warmth. "Like I said. Who are you?"

He rolled his head around, trying to ease some of the pain throbbing at the base of his skull and buying himself time to think. "Name's George. And you?"

"His name's Skanland and I'm Carl."

Skanland struck out in his direction and George braced for

the blow. But the blow zipped by him, instead whacking the brute holding his arms. At least the hit hadn't been meant for him.

"Shut up. I'll do the talking, dumbass."

Carl didn't budge and tightened the grip on George's arms. "Hey, not so rough."

"Why were you watching us?" Skanland fingered a toothpick out of his pocket and propped it in the side of his mouth.

Should he tell them? George studied the man before him. Granted, Skanland didn't appear to be the brightest brick in the wall, but just how stupid was he? Still, he had nothing to gain by telling a lie—especially when the truth might serve his purpose better. "Doing like you. Following the bitch."

Interest popped into Skanland's eyes. "Is that so? You know the pretty lady?"

George nodded, thinking too much honesty might be hazardous to his health. "Sure do. Intimately."

"Intimately?" Carl's sour breath slid over George's shoulder. He swallowed the bad taste and hoped he wouldn't hurl.

"He means he's fucked her, asshole." Skanland chuckled and grabbed his crotch for emphasis. "And I bet she's hot in bed, huh?"

Happy that Skanland had bought his story, George winked, enjoying the opportunity to embellish his fib. "You don't know the half of it. She can suck the lid off a beer bottle. Of course, you gotta slap her around a little first. As an incentive, you know."

Skanland's interest jumped up ten degrees. "So she likes getting slapped around, huh?"

"Doesn't matter what she likes." George recognized a man who liked to beat up women. After all, it took one to know one.

The three men shared a laugh. Skanland abruptly stopped, scrutinized him, and waved his hand at Carl. "Let him go."

"Aw, do I have to? He's so...soft."

Huh?

Carl's fingers swept down George's arms to squeeze his elbows. With a grunt of displeasure, Carl reluctantly released him.

"Ugh." George stumbled forward a few inches before gaining his stability. Rolling his shoulders around and shaking his arms to loosen up the soreness, he glanced furtively around the enclosure for any possible escape route. "I told you my little secret." Fixing his gaze on Skanland, he added, "Now tell me yours."

But Skanland wasn't ready yet. He walked over to the side of the building and peered through a slot in the wall. "I bet you ain't too cozy with the female any longer." Turning back to him, he took out the toothpick and grinned. "Are you?"

Female? George swallowed the wad of spit he wanted to aim directly at the man's wide, flat forehead. Instead, he played along with the assumptions since they happened to be true. "Naw. The uh, female, has a little ego problem. She fired me and thinks she won't get punished for it. Nobody fires a man like me."

Skanland snorted. "Everybody fires a dick like you."

Rankled, George started to object, but Carl's wink caught him by surprise. *Did the big lug just flirt with me? Argh.*

"And what about her friend? She throw you over for him?" Skanland popped the toothpick back into his mouth.

George scowled, unhappy to be put in a position of ridicule. "The freak? He won't last long."

Skanland threw away the toothpick and stepped closer. The body odor from the man almost brought George to his knees. *Shit. Metrosexual he's not.*

"I think we have a mutual interest in those two. You want to pay her back? You lookin' to get rid of him? If so, I think we could do business. Whaddya say?"

Forgetting about the foul smell, George cocked his head. "I'd say…tell me what you've got in mind."

"We don't give a shit about your bitch. What we want is her boyfriend and his buddy. But I'm thinking once he's out of the way, you can move in on her."

"His buddy?" *Crap. Was there another one like Freak Man?* George darted his attention between the two men and knew they weren't lying.

"Yeah. The one in the parking lot."

George scowled at the squat man. "I don't know anything about a parking lot. So there's another one like the—like him?"

"And he's a big one, too."

George studied Carl and took a moment to let the news sink in. *Shit. If this big ape thinks the other one's big, then he must be really* big. Yet he knew an opportunity when he saw one. "Here's the deal. If you guys want to get both of the freaks, then listen up."

Skanland and Carl shut up, their interest leveled on him. Power unlike he'd ever experienced before rushed through him, and he smiled in delight. Neither one moved, waiting for him to lay out his plan.

George took a moment to bask in their attention, crossed his arms and adopted the stance Skanland had used earlier. "Okay, so here's what we're going to do."

☾

The hairs on the back of Tala's neck stood on end all the way home from the zoo. Glancing in her rearview mirror, she couldn't shake the uneasy sensation crawling through her. In fact, she'd had the same feeling all day long.

Is that car following me? As she'd done many times during the drive, she whipped her head around to stare at the headlights behind her. *I'm probably just being silly. After all, who'd want to come after me?* Her reasoning made sense, but

Devlin's warning still echoed in her mind. She shook her head and grumbled under her breath, "Great, Tala. Don't let Devlin make you paranoid."

When the car made a signal and exited onto a side street, she relaxed a little and blew out a puff of air. She wiped her palms on her jeans, consciously realizing for the first time how nervous she was. *Damn, I need to calm down.* "See? The car turned off. You're jumping to stupid conclusions, girl." She caught her worried expression and mirthlessly clucked at her mirror self. *Sheesh. Now you're talking to yourself full time. Not good, Tala. Not good.* But her feigned levity couldn't get rid of the uneasy feeling making her tense and edgy.

Tala drove on and tried to ignore the cars behind her. After what seemed like the longest drive home in history, she swerved into her apartment complex and pulled into her reserved spot. Gathering her purse, she checked the area around her, left the car quickly and jogged up the stairs to her apartment. Her breathing slowed only when she finally neared her front door. She fought the urge to call for Devlin, praying he hadn't gone anywhere.

Take it easy. If you don't, he'll think you're some kind of clingy girl. Or worse, a dick-whipped female. A tight high-pitched titter escaped her. Hurriedly, she pushed her key into the lock and twisted the doorknob.

Tala burst into the apartment. Stumbling over an empty pizza box, she fell forward and reached out for the nearby side table to keep from falling. "Shit!"

Devlin dropped his phone and sprang off the couch to catch her but rammed into her instead, sticking a slice of pepperoni pizza on the front of her shirt. Thick sauce smeared over her chest, and pepperoni dropped down the vee neck front, lodging between her heaving breasts.

"Oh, yuck." Tala peeled the pizza off her shirt and handed it to Devlin. She counted six pizza boxes scattered on top of the table, couch, and carpet, including the one that had tripped her. "I guess I don't have to ask what you've been doing all day."

The skin around Devlin's big velvet eyes crinkled with his smile. "What can I say? Except maybe 'Hi. My name's Devlin and I'm a pizza addict'."

She retrieved another chunk of pepperoni from inside her shirt and popped it into her mouth. "No shit. But couldn't you have put down the pizza long enough to say hello?" She giggled when he threw the other piece he was holding onto the floor and hauled her to him. "Devlin!"

His tongue licked across the swell of her breasts. Glancing up at her with sauce all over his mouth, he quipped, "Yum. You're the best piece in town." Another lick across her boobs had her squirming and giggling from the raspy texture of his tongue.

"Should I come back later after you've finished eating your female?"

Devlin and Tala jumped at the sound of the amused voice and together faced the speaker.

Devlin swung Tala to his right and away from Conrad. "What are you doing here?"

"I thought I'd better check in." Conrad waved a manila folder at Devlin. "I've got a couple of questions regarding the latest contract for the Chinese imports." His eyes glittered as he walked into the apartment, his gaze latching onto Tala's saucy breasts.

Devlin snatched the folder and flipped it open. Conrad had highlighted portions of the contract so it was easy to find the areas needing attention. "Tala, this is Conrad Vilmar."

Tala grabbed a dish towel from the kitchen counter to wipe off the sauce. "Oh, so you're Conrad."

"The one and only."

Devlin glanced up to see his lecherous friend stepping closer to his mate. "Thank God for that." He sent him a *back-off* look.

Conrad stopped and held out his palms. "Relax, dude. I know the score. But haven't we met before, babe?"

The smirk on his friend's face pushed at Devlin's last nerve. Obviously Conrad was talking about the time in the parking lot. But he'd yet to tell Tala that the wolf she'd seen was his best friend. Devlin tossed a questioning look at Tala, who blinked at him and switched on her frosty glare.

"No." Tala's expression left little doubt in Devlin's mind that she wasn't thrilled to meet Conrad. She fisted her hands on her hips and scowled. "And please don't call me babe."

Conrad arched his eyebrow at her. "Ah, feisty. I like that." He grinned at her, letting her in on his joke. "And don't call you babe. Got it." He walked around the room, picking up knickknacks and pictures to examine. At last he paused and gestured at the walls. "Love the wolf posters, by the way. At least that explains why you've hooked up with Dev here."

"I have an affection for wolves." She arched her eyebrow in an exact imitation of Conrad's gesture. "Or at least, most wolves."

So she's figured it out. Devlin laughed. *That's my girl.*

Fortunately Conrad could take as good as he gave. "Ooh, good one." He shot Devlin a questioning look, then tilted his head at her. "So you know?"

"Of course she knows. She knows about us and the rest of the pack." He decided to plunge ahead. "We're mated. I've already marked her twice."

Tala moved over to Devlin to snake her arms around his waist. "Yep. I'm Devlin's mate. And I'm guessing you owe me a repair job for my car. Those scratches are going to cost me a bundle to get fixed."

Conrad's surprise lasted briefly before he pointed at her and chuckled. "I definitely like her, dude. She's a good one."

"So? Whaddya say?" Tala broke free of Devlin's squeeze and stepped toward the big man. As she opened her arms for him, jealousy, pure and simple, crashed into Devlin's heart. "Want to give Devlin's mate a welcome-to-the-pack hug? And just maybe I'll forget about the repair bill."

Conrad grabbed Tala and hugged her. Resting his chin on her shoulder, he grinned at Devlin, daring him to break them apart. Devlin resisted the thought of wrestling his friend. That is, until Conrad's hand slid down and grabbed Tala's shapely tush. "Actually, we give a welcome-to-the-pack rump rub, instead."

Devlin lunged forward but wasn't as quick as Tala. Her hand whipped around to grasp Conrad's and bent it, wrenching his fingers backward toward the top of his hand. He hollered, pulling his hand away, and backpedaled away from her. Tisking at him, she slid into Devlin's arms.

"She's something, huh?" Devlin couldn't resist rubbing it in—a little.

"You got that right." Conrad massaged his sore fingers. "But does that mean the rump rubbing is off?"

Before Devlin could snarl his answer, the phone rang. He shook his head at Tala and beat her to the punch. "No, I'll get it. And if it's your work, I'll tell them you're busy meeting your new wolf pack."

"They'll never believe the crew I've gotten hooked up with. Oh, and tell them I'll give them a call back." Lifting her chin, she howled. "Wolf style."

Warmed by her quick acceptance of his friend, Devlin picked up the phone. "Wilde residence."

"Hey, Freak. Bitten anyone lately?"

Recognizing the voice, Devlin scowled and put his back to Tala. *The little man who beat the she-wolf. George.* "Fuck off." In one quick motion, he disconnected the call and took a deep breath. No need for Tala to know.

"Who was it?"

Crap, I should've known she'd ask. He let Tala's question wait a second before deciding to lie. "Wrong number."

"A little harsh weren't you? I mean, a wrong number is a simple mistake. There's really no need to curse at them."

"Meanwhile—" Conrad, as usual, wanted the center of attention on him, "—what d'ya say we sit—"

The jangle of the phone came again, interrupting his suggestion. "Damn." Devlin blocked Tala from getting the phone and scooped it up. Holding it close, he cupped his hand over the receiver and hoped his posture wouldn't relay his fury to Tala. "Talk."

"Don't hang up on me again, Freakazoid. I know all about you and your buddy. Just how many of you freaks are there?"

His hatred of George sent his blood boiling, but he managed to keep his tone level. "Don't call again." He started to hang up when he heard George shouting.

"You'll be sorry!"

"Is something wrong?" Tala frowned, concern mixed with curiosity on her face, and yanked on his arm.

"Naw. Probably just the pack wanting him to bring home some dog biscuits."

Yet Devlin could tell Conrad knew something was up. He concentrated on keeping the phone turned away from her and stuck to the conversation. "I don't think so." What he wouldn't give to be able to reach through the line and throttle the guy.

"Oh, but you're gonna want to hear what I have to say."

Tala inched nearer, forcing him to speak even softer. "Again. I don't think I do."

"Yeah, you do. Unless you want something to happen to pretty Tala. Something real bad."

Devlin squeezed the phone tighter, his knuckles turning white from the strength of his grip. Tala again moved closer, forcing him to put on an act. "Hey, buddy." Looking at Tala, he feigned a big smile, covered the phone and told yet another lie. "It's a friend of mine. And no to the dog biscuits. Although I am hungry."

Tala seemed unconvinced but took his not-so-subtle hint and headed for the kitchen. "You two have a weird way of relating to each other, whoever this guy is."

She trusts me and I'm lying to her. He thought about telling her and opted against the idea. *No, I have to keep Tala safe. Even if it means keeping secrets from her.*

Conrad, however, drew next to Devlin and narrowed his eyes to let him know he hadn't bought his lie. With his friend's sensitive hearing, Devlin didn't doubt he could hear everything.

He jerked his head at Tala in a silent don't-let-on message. Again turning his back to Tala, he spat out his whispered warning. "If you hurt Tala in any way, I promise you I'll snap your neck. After I tear the skin off your body in tiny strips. Then I'll let you die a slow agonizing death."

"And what? Eat me alive?"

This smile was genuine. "Yeah, but with lots of ketchup to take away the nasty taste."

The silence on the other side told him he'd hit home. Unfortunately, the silence didn't last long enough.

"Listen up, Wolf Man."

So he does know. George was brighter than he looked.

"If you want to keep Tala safe and sound, you'll meet me tomorrow at the downtown park around four o'clock. You and your freaky friend. And don't bring anyone else. Especially Tala."

"And why should we meet with you? You won't be able to get near her with us around."

Tala waved at him from the kitchen and held up a sandwich. Devlin smiled and nodded, silently thanking her.

"Don't bet on it, dog breath. You can't guard her twenty-four seven. I'll visit Tala when you're not around and she'll get a taste of my tender loving care. You know, like I showed the female wolf? Or maybe I'll give Tala a treat with a little booty action first. That's how you doggies like it, isn't it?"

Devlin tipped his chin at Conrad and waited for his agreement. The big man licked his lips and smiled, always ready for action. "Consider us there."

"Good doggy."

The resounding click echoed in Devlin's ear.

☾

"I don't get it. Why are you acting so mysterious?" Tala flopped on the bed to watch Devlin get dressed.

Just thinking about running her tongue over his toned abs, heading for the black hair below, made her mouth water. *I haven't had a dick sandwich in a long time.* She swallowed at the thought. *For at least four hours. Waay too long.* Her pulse quickened and the muscles between her legs tightened. *The man has a body other men would kill for and women would die for. And it's all mine.* She ran her tongue over her lips to draw his attention. *Come on, Dev, let me eat a hot dog.*

Devlin stopped buttoning his shirt. "Damn it, Tala. Don't tempt me." The low sound in his throat sent pleasurable chills through her. "I've got something I have to do."

I wish he'd growl for me. Growl while sucking on my tits. "With Conrad. Devlin, you're starting to really tick me off. This thing better be important."

"It is. I have to go. We stick together when threatened."

She quickly sat up. "Threatened?" *What the hell is he not telling me?*

He shot her a reassuring smile. "It's just an expression. I didn't mean it literally." But his comforting smile didn't last. Instead he acted nonchalantly—or tried to—and asked, "You're sticking around here, right? Until I get back?"

"Yeah, that's the plan." She studied him, searching for his hidden agenda. "So why the hurry? What's going on, Devlin? You're not telling me something. I know it." *What's he hiding from me now?*

He tucked his head, averting her scrutiny. "Don't worry. Nothing's going on. It's just business. I can't keep doing all my business by phone, you know."

Business my ass.

She slid her hands over her breasts and tweaked her hardened nipples to elicit another lustful look from him. Pouting, she put on her best sweet-and-innocent yet don't-you-think-I'm-sexy expression. "Wouldn't you rather do something fun with me?" She ran one hand over her breast and down her stomach. Pausing, she sent him a sultry look, then slid her fingers under her thong and played with the aching part of her body. "Come on, Dev. Get busy with me."

He let out an anguished sigh and turned away from her. "You, woman, are a devil in disguise. Get busy? So we've gone from making love to plain old getting busy?"

"Oh, Dev-lin." Her sing-song tone brought him around to face her again. Grinning, she whipped her teddy nightgown over her head and tossed the red silk at him.

He caught it and rubbed the lacy material between his fingers. *Oh, you so want me, my hunky wolfie. Give it up and take me.* Jiggling her breasts at him, she raised one breast upward and swiped her tongue over the brown tip.

Devlin's eyes gleamed with unmistakable lust. "You're killing me. You know that, right?" At her come-take-me look and wink, he moved closer.

Wanting to keep him moving toward her, she fell back on the bed, her arms flailing out to the side with a dramatic flair. She knew that her movement made her tits bounce appealingly. Skimming her hands along her body, she once more attempted to lure him onto the bed. She pushed her fingertips under her thong to play with herself again, this time spreading her legs for him to get a better view. "Come here, Devlin. I need you." She mewed, putting all her sexual frustration into the sound. "I can do this alone, but it's not half as fun."

If he hadn't taken her in his arms right then, she really

would have gotten worried. But his strong arms around her left her with no doubt. She ran her hands over his shoulders and rubbed her breasts against his chest. He took them in his hands, and helped her rub against him.

"You drive me crazy, Tala. You know I'd rather be with you." His eyes flicked to the bed. "In you."

"Then stay. Do work later." She tracked her tongue lightly under his chin. "You can do all the work you want after you work for me."

Taking her face in his hands, he pressed his mouth to hers, exhaling his warm breath into her. She drank up his taste, so sexy and familiar, and quivered. Parting her lips, she welcomed his tongue, dragging it inside, sucking it hard. His moan wafted into her, shooting down her throat to the rest of her sexually-tormented body.

Too soon, however, he broke their embrace. Yet before she could complain, he met her eyes, diving deep inside, searching for an answer.

"We're already mated, Tala. But maybe you'd like a traditional wedding anyway? With all your family and friends?"

How can one man be so sexy and so sweet at the same time? Tala, you are one lucky woman. "Devlin Cannon, are you officially asking me to marry you? Human to semi-human?" She wiggled her nose at him, hoping to prod him into challenging her jab.

"Real cute." He nodded. "And I am, Tala Wilde. So what do you say? Wanna marry the Wolf Man?"

"Will you follow me around for the rest of my life? Nipping at my heels?"

Devlin fondled her breasts, rubbing his thumbs over her taut nipples. "You betcha. I'll nip at your heels every day of the week and beg for a treat." He bent and bit her tit. "Unless you'd rather I nip at other things."

She pretended to play coy and consider his proposal. "Well, okay. I guess I'll have to say yes. Besides, you've already marked me and we're mated, so what else can I do?"

Devlin tugged her lower on the bed and she wrapped her legs around his waist. Rubbing the cleft between her legs against his jeans, she wiggled harder and was rewarded with his cock straining at the zipper. Soon she'd have his jeans off and his cock in her hand. Or mouth. Or pussy. She licked her lips, trying to decide which place to put it first.

Giddy with happiness, Tala kissed him long and hard. "My friends are not going to believe this."

"Will you tell them what I am? What you'll be? And, if you do, will they approve of me?"

She played with a strand of his silky hair, pretending that his caresses weren't heating her insides to the boiling point. "They'd better like you or I'll let you shift and scare the panties off them."

A wicked glint flashed in his eyes and the mischievous grin she'd come to love spread across his face. "Hmm. Scare the panties off the lady friends, huh? Sounds like a job I'd love to do."

She good-humoredly slapped him on the chest. "Watch it, Wolfie. You're all mine."

"And glad of it."

He kissed her again and she smiled into the kiss. *Now all I have to do is get his jeans off and—*

Without warning, he pulled away from her, jarring her out of her blissfulness. "Hey! Watch how you treat your future bride."

"Sorry." Unwrapping her arms and legs from him, he scooted off the bed and dug his phone out of his pocket. "Duty calls." He chastely pecked her on the cheek, fending off her attempt to bring him back onto the bed. "Gotta go."

Stunned, she lurched for his arm and held on. She knew something was up, knew she should keep him close, yet she didn't know how. "No. Come on, Devlin. Blow your friend off just this once."

"Blow my friend? Bleck, what a thought." He faked a shiver of disgust.

"Quit trying to change the subject. You know what I mean." Batting her eyelids at him, she tried one last proposition. "I promise I'll show you a good time." She tipped her head to look up at him seductively. "A really good time."

But his serious expression squelched her humor and he took her hands away. *He's way too serious. Something's definitely up.* A shot of dread coursed through her, reinforcing the urge to keep him by her side. "I know you're hiding something from me. Please tell me what it is." She fixed her eyes on him, not letting him move away.

Breaking free, he strode out of the room, calling to her as he darted through the apartment and out the door. "You've got it all wrong, Wilde. I'll get back as soon as I can and *then* we'll get busy."

Gaping, she stared at the emptiness surrounding her until she heard the door slam shut. *What the hell just happened? Since when does he ever turn down sex?*

The silence left behind after Devlin's departure pounded against Tala's nerves. She snatched up jeans and a T-shirt and tugged them on as she loped through the apartment. "No way, Devlin Cannon. I'm going to find out what you've got going on whether you like it or not."

She swung open the door and checked the stairs leading down to the ground floor. Grumbling under her breath, she grabbed her keys, shoved them in her jeans pocket and pulled the door shut behind her. Since Devlin wasn't driving—no way would he ever drive again if she could help it—she was determined to stay on his heels. At a discreet distance, of course.

Taking the stairs two at a time, she scanned the area around the apartment building. Off in the distance, she spied Devlin jogging down the sidewalk across the two-lane road running adjacent to the apartment complex. Pulling in a breath, she started after him.

Rough hands latched onto her, wrenching a shout from her throat. Two large men dragged her to the side of the building. Strong arms pinned hers behind her back while the other man hooked her legs under his arms.

Tala tried to cry out again, but the sound was suffocated against the cloth pressed over her mouth.

Chapter Eleven

The blackness slowly dissolved into a mist, changing from pitch black to gray then, at long last, to a dingy haze. Tala groaned, her head a heavy ball of stabbing pain balancing on top of her neck. "Aw, crap. I feel like shit."

"The effects of the drug will wear off soon enough."

Her attempt to move her arms sent painful pinpricks from her wrists to her shoulders. Coarse ropes bound her arms and legs to a chair with her hands bound behind her. She flexed her fingers, working to regain some sensation in them.

Widening her eyes hoping to clear her vision, Tala blinked at the squat man sitting across from her. Yet the clearer his image grew, the more she wished she couldn't see. The man was a poster child for Dirty People Against Baths, and his greasy strands of hair were a testament to his aversion to shampoo. His shirt, almost stiff with the grime clinging to the material, billowed over khaki slacks that hadn't seen the inside of a washing machine since they'd left the factory.

Tala glanced around the dimly lit room, furnished only with the chair she sat in and the cot he used. The overhead light hung from a wire in the ceiling while a black blind blanketed the one small window. An image of an old war movie flashed through her mind. "Where am I? Your interrogation room?" She shot him a piercing look and wished looks could kill. Or at least dismember. "I ain't tellin' you nothing, you Commie, you."

"Commie?" His broad forehead crinkled in a frown. "I'm no

Commie. Hell, I don't even vote."

"Figures." She rolled her eyes before glancing at the door. "And I don't suppose you're the sole survivor of some antisocial cult, huh?"

As if answering her question, a tall man with an I'm-so-stupid-I-don't-even-know-I'm-so-stupid expression barged into the room. "Skanland, the men want to know if they should—" He leered at Tala, running his gaze up and down her while his tongue snaked out to caress his upper lip. "Damn, she's hot."

Tala glared at him, letting him know he had as much chance with her as a slug would with a bunny. "Who are you jerks?" She sent a silent prayer of gratitude for the anger sweeping through her. Better anger than fear.

Skanland rose from the dirty cot in front of her, moving close enough for her to smell his foul odor. He pinched her chin and forced her to raise her head. She saw the hatred in his bloodshot tired eyes. "Such an ugly mouth on such a pretty lady. Or should I say, pretty bitch?"

"Yeah. Pretty bee-atch." The stupid man giggled.

Both Skanland and Tala shot Stupid irritated looks, but Skanland added a jab to the shoulder.

These guys are a joke. "You shouldn't say anything. Not until you've poured a gallon of mouthwash down your mouth. You reek, man."

"Shut the fuck up."

The sting of his hand across her cheek was unexpected. *He hit me?* Tala glowered at Skanland. "You do *not* want to do that again."

She prepared for the next slap, ducking her head right before contact. *Ha, ha! Missed me!*

"Ow! You hit me!" Stupid rubbed his arm, a hurt expression overtaking his blank one.

Skanland fumed, embarrassment evident in his scowl. "Then get out of the way, moron."

"I wasn't in the way."

Tala bit the inside of her lip to keep from laughing. "Are you two for real?" *Ladies and gentlemen, may I present for your amusement Squatty and Stupid.*

Stupid's tough expression dropped and he buckled under the other man's glower. "You shouldn't hit her again. We're supposed to swap her for the shifters. Besides, my momma taught me to never hit a woman." He shook his head vehemently. "Uh-uh. Momma always said, 'Carl, don't you go hitting women like your daddy did'."

Skanland gawked at him. His deep belly laugh vibrated against the walls of the room and he clutched his stomach before stumbling a few feet away. "A woman?" Pointing at Tala, he tried to catch his breath between guffaws. "She ain't no woman, you moron. She's a shifter."

Tala's mouth dropped open. *He thinks I'm a shifter?* Although first incredulous at his statement, she inwardly smiled as an idea dawned on her. Could they tell? Even though she hadn't actually shifted yet, could she be considered one? Devlin had told her hunters could smell a shifter even in human form, but not before the shifter had completely transformed at least once. So how could they tell? Either from her ancestral blood or from Devlin's marking her?

"She don't act like one." Carl bent closer to examine her. "Besides, hitting any female ain't nice. My momma said so."

Again Skanland scoffed at his big friend. "Crap, but you are such a girl. Did your momma truss you up in dresses when you were little?"

Carl's pink complexion told the story. "Well, we did used to have a good time trying on each other's clothes."

Tala met Skanland's eyes with a wicked grin. "Some bosom buddy you have there, Skanland. Emphasis on the bosom part."

"I told you to shut the fuck up." He raised his hand, getting ready to strike her. "Or do you need more convincing?"

Tala closed her mouth. *No need to antagonize the apes*

when I'm fresh out of bananas.

"But, Skanland, wouldn't she have shifted by now if she was one?"

Stupid does have a point. Dismay pushed away all the pride she'd felt a moment earlier.

"How's she gonna shift while she's knocked out? But it don't matter." Skanland's filthy hand pulled her shirt collar aside to expose the large mark of Devlin's bite. "One of them's marked her. She's his female and one of them now."

Carl grimaced at the mark on her shoulder. "Damn. Why would such a pretty woman want to do it with one of those things?"

Skanland let go of her shirt and shrugged. "Danged if I know. But once a woman lies down with dogs, she's no longer a woman. She's just another bitch in heat." He let his hand slide over her hair to finger the end of a strand. "'Course it doesn't mean we can't have a little fun before she starts shifting like the rest of the beasts."

Tala jerked as far away from him as her restraints would allow. "I wouldn't let you touch me with your skuzzy dick if you boiled your cock in hot water first." She grinned, issuing a challenge. Who knew, maybe he was just dumb enough to do it. "But you go ahead and try it, then I'll see."

Rage stiffened Skanland's body and again he raised his arm to hit her. She readied herself, prepared to dodge another blow, yet as he put his arm over his head, the door swung open and two more men shuffled into the room.

"Skanland, George called. They're at the park."

Fear pierced Tala's heart. "Who's at the park?"

Skanland cackled. "Your animal boyfriend and his pack buddy. They're getting the word about you right now. And soon they'll join us for a party."

All four men chuckled, hurling panicked signals through her. "What are you going to do to them?"

Skanland leaned over to rest his hands on the arms of her chair. "First, we're gonna trap 'em and give them a good neutering. Then, we're gonna skin 'em alive. I need a couple of new hides for my walls."

"Yeah, we're gonna have a shifter skinning party."

The joy on Carl's face sickened her and she tried to keep her terror from showing. However, judging by Skanland's expression, she failed. "But why? What do you have against them? What'd they ever do to you?"

Skanland's lips curled into a half-sneer, half-smile. "They're shifter scum. Freaks of nature that don't deserve to live." He rose and took a gun from one of the other men. Holding the rifle in front of him, he shook it at her. "And we're the ones who're going to wipe their kind—your kind—off the face of the planet."

What could she do? Nothing, no words, no action came to her. Would she be an unwilling witness to Devlin's death? Tears of helplessness welled up inside her. Yet one comforting thought still remained. *At least they'll kill me, too.*

"Okay, boys, let's go get ready for our guests."

☾

"Are you sure this is a smart idea?" Conrad loped alongside Devlin, jumping over the low barrier separating the park's perimeter from the sidewalk. "I mean, what're you hoping to gain by meeting with this guy?"

Devlin slowed to a jog and scanned the open grassy area for George. "Gain? Nothing except the joy of breaking his neck. Or, at least, scaring him so much he'll never threaten her again. I'll take either outcome."

"But he's got to have something else going on. After the encounter you told me about, he's not going to meet you in a park to talk. At least, not by himself. He's not that stupid, is he?"

"It's about time you two showed up."

Together they swiveled to find George leaning against a lamppost. Before he could say another word, Devlin's hands were around George's neck, his fingers pressing into his throat. With George's back against the pole, Devlin lifted him off his feet, propping him two feet off the ground.

"Look, you little asshole. I'm here. I did as you asked." Devlin let his fangs grow and the saliva flow into his mouth. He bared his teeth and pressed his nose against the squirming man's bulbous one. "But I'm warning you. If I ever so much as guess you've bothered Tala, spoken to her or come within twenty yards of her, I'll track you down and rip out your heart."

Conrad sidled up next to the two men and wiggled his fingers in greeting. "Hey, dude, how's it hanging?" He pointedly looked at the ground beneath him. "Or should I ask how're *you* hanging?"

George gurgled at him, an obvious plea for him to intercede. "Uh, Dev. He's turning blue. You may want to think about letting him live, especially since there're so many people watching right now."

Devlin, who'd forgotten the existence of anyone else, took a moment to check out the spectators. A group of people stood gawking at them.

Conrad leaned in to whisper. "Too many witnesses, dude. Come on, be a good wolfie and put the little man down."

Devlin growled, but relented. The guy's face was a mottled purple and blue. "Fine. For now."

George rubbed his neck, sucking in air with labored breaths. Once he'd coughed a couple of times, however, Devlin figured he was good to go. But the crowd lingered.

"Okay, folks. Show's over." Conrad flapped his hands, trying to shoo the people away. "Merely a little fuss between old drinking buddies. He's fine. No need to contact the authorities." Slapping George on the shoulder, he nodded and urged him to agree. "You're fine. Right, old buddy?"

Devlin slitted his eyes at George. "Sure, George. You're fine, right?"

George darted his gaze between them and the onlookers. Although his voice sounded strained, he managed to croak out the words. "Yeah. Right. Fine." He coughed again but plastered a halfhearted smile on his face.

Playing the game to the finish, Devlin slid his arm around George's shoulder and pulled him onto the path. "What's more fun than a little roughhousing between friends, huh?"

Conrad took up step on the other side of George, wedging his body between them. "Oh, for sure, dude. Good times for all."

As the three walked down the path together, the crowd they'd left behind began to disperse. Devlin took a deep breath and patted his captive on the cheek. "Keep walking and start talking. What's this all about?"

"Tala's waiting for you."

Devlin missed a step, but Conrad's hold on George kept them moving forward. "What're you talking about? She's at her apartment." A cold dread closed up his veins, hooked onto him, and he had to concentrate to keep his feet moving.

"Your friends from the other day are with her."

Devlin stopped, swinging the shrieking man in front of him. Yanking him closer, he snarled his words, his anger fighting a not-so-distant second to his fear. "Stop playing games with me, asshole, and tell me what's going on. Where's Tala?"

"Keep walking, Devlin. There's a cop not far behind us."

Conrad's warning catapulted him into motion again, taking George along with him. George, however, tried to drag his feet. Devlin let his eyes change color, hurrying the little man along.

"Keep your tone light and easy if you want to keep your tongue attached." He sniffed and picked up a familiar foul smell off George's body. Shivers sprinted down his spine. *Skanland. He's been around that damn hunter.* "Now talk."

George's words were weak but unmistakable, confirming Devlin's worst nightmare. "The hunters have Tala. They're keeping her in a house at the edge of town. If you—both of you—show up and turn yourselves over to them, they'll let her go."

☾

Tala strained against the ropes securing her to the chair, but the cords held tight. Afternoon light poked through the sides of the blind and caught dust particles floating in the air. She puffed and saw her breath in a swirl of dust.

Aw, hell. This is so not good. Fear threatened to overtake her, driving any spark of logic. *Hang on, Tala. Keep your wits about you. Look for anything that might help you escape.* But her quick perusal of her surroundings only confirmed what she already knew. *I am shit out of luck.*

Where is Devlin? Is he safe? Or has he already walked into the hunters' trap? Closing her eyes, she pictured him, lying in a pool of blood, killed while trying to rescue her. *I can't let that happen. No, I won't let that happen.*

Maybe she could signal to Devlin somehow? She had to tell him not to attempt a rescue. If she couldn't keep the hunters from skinning her hide—*oh, what a terrible thought!*—then she'd do her best to save Devlin's. Concentrating, she sent a mental message to him and prayed he'd receive her plea. *Devlin, hear me. It's a trap. Don't be a hero. Stay away. I can escape on my own.* She doubted he'd believe her lie, but she had to try.

Would he receive her warning? If Devlin heard her telepathic message, would he then heed her warning? Or would it only serve to enrage him and make him act recklessly? Her stomach tightened, making her nauseous.

She knew nothing could keep him away. In fact, he was probably already looking for her. Still she had to warn him. Again, she concentrated, putting all her energy behind the telepathic warning. *Devlin. Beware. Trap. Get help.*

Damn it all to hell and back. I sound like I'm telling Lassie to fetch Timmy's dad.

She worked her wrists back and forth, hoping to find her ropes loosening a bit. But with no luck. What if he didn't hear her warning? Could she get a message to Devlin some other way? Hadn't he said she'd called him to her? Remembering how he'd told her about hearing her call, she decided a howl was worth a try.

She took a few deep breaths so she could put as much force as she could behind her call. Just as she was about to take the final and biggest breath of all, a ludicrous thought struck her. *Who do I think I am? The big bad wolf in* "Little Red Riding Hood"*? Although, blowing down the house like the wolf in* "The Three Little Pigs" *would really help right now. Too bad this isn't a fairy tale.*

She shook her head and resolved to do her best. *You can do this. You have to.* She squirmed in her chair a minute, trying to get comfortable. Taking some more deep breaths and keeping her mind off the idea of huffing and puffing—*No. Don't think about the big bad wolf*—Tala sucked in a big intake of air, laid back her head and howled.

She pushed with all the strength she could gather, making her throat ache. One howl ended as she slid into another. And another. All while thinking, *Devlin, hear me. Be careful. They're waiting for you.*

Shit, but it's hard to howl with ropes across my chest.

The door banging open startled her, cutting off her last howl before she could finish.

"What the hell are you doing?" Carl scowled at her, confusion making his normal stupid expression seem imbecilic. "Are you howling?"

Tala put on her dumb blonde face. "Howling? Little old me?" *Such a big mouth you have, Grandma.*

When he didn't seem to buy her dumb routine quickly enough, she slid into Plan B, going into full flirtation mode. "Okay, you caught me." Batting her eyes at the idiot striding over to her, she adopted the sincerest yet sexiest expression she could and lovingly gazed into his malicious eyes. "I just wanted some attention. You can't blame a girl for wanting a little attention, can you?" She stuck out her lips, hoping for a sexy pout. "Especially from you."

Eck! Am I really flirting with this goon? Shit, how far will I go to save my butt? Not that far. But for Devlin? I'll go as far as it takes.

A glimmer of excitement sparked in Carl's eyes. Bending over, he licked his lips and got on his knees in front of her.

Oh, please, do not let this guy touch me. If he touches me, I'm going to puke. But at least she'd make sure she'd puke on him.

"From me?"

The creep nearly drooled on her. She swallowed the bile rising in her throat and fortified her game face. "Who else, handsome?"

He chuckled, a dirty chuckle filled with innuendo. "Yeah, I thought we had a vibe going on before. And I do like girls too."

She smiled a coy little smile. "Too? Me, too. Uh, men, I mean." Leave it to her to pick a bisexual bimbo. "I couldn't wait for the others to leave us alone. But then you left me and didn't return. So I had to do something to bring you back to me."

He skimmed his hand over her breasts and a wave of nausea hit her. *Keep yourself together, Tala. Don't lose it. For Devlin's sake.* Doing the exact opposite of what she'd like to do, she thrust out her chest and let him cop a feel. "You know, if you'd untie me—" she made sure he saw her glance at the cot, "—we could have some real fun."

His bushy eyebrows slid downward toward his nose. "Uh, I don't know. Skanland wouldn't want me messing with you."

She shot him a disappointed look and stabbed at his ego. "Are you telling me you're afraid of him? A big strong man like you afraid of such a little bitty man?" *God, please kill me now before my dignity sinks even lower.* Instead, she pouted as though he'd told her she couldn't have a pony for Christmas.

"'Course not. I'm not afraid of him. But Skanland runs things, you know."

"He wouldn't have to know. I promise I won't say a word. And afterward, you could tie me up again." When he started to protest, she continued, making one last ditch try. "I'd love to run my hands..." she licked her lips, "...and my tongue all over your body."

Score! Carl's jaw plunged to the floor and he couldn't get to the ropes fast enough.

"You promise you won't say nothing?"

"Oh, I promise, my big strong man." *Urgh! Bleck! Vomit!*

"Carl, you're dumber than I thought you were."

Tala's heart plummeted to her feet at the sound of Skanland's voice. *Damn him to hell and back.*

Carl snatched his hands away from the ropes like they were laced with acid, jumped to his feet and headed toward the door. "I wasn't doing nothing. I was just checking to make sure the ropes were real tight."

Skanland knocked Carl in the head and pushed him from the room. "You stay outta here." Turning to Tala, he jabbed his finger at her. "And you shut the hell up or I'll shut your fat trap for you."

Fat? She tipped her head to study her body. *Sure, I've shared a lot of pizza with Devlin lately, but I'm not fat. Am I?*

The door slammed closed behind Skanland, leaving Tala wondering what to do next. She shook her head and discarded the idea of howling again. Skanland might do something drastic like stuff a rag in her mouth if she made any more noise. Besides, if it had worked, Devlin would already be on his way.

So what do I do now? She slumped in the chair and let her mind wander. *If only Devlin was here. He could shift and take care of things.* The power he exuded when he shifted was twice a normal man's. If only she could shift, she might grow stronger, too.

Devlin had said she'd shift when the time was right. And Skanland had called her a shifter. Could the power be lying dormant inside her? Could she shift now if she tried? Deciding it was worth a go, even though she'd failed so many times before, Tala focused on one thought. *Shift.*

For several minutes, she chanted the word over and over in her mind. And waited. And waited some more. Tried again and waited. Yet after several attempts, nothing had happened.

Fighting the frustration boiling inside her, she stomped on the floor, tightening the ropes around her ankles in the effort. *Why can't I do this? Why don't shifters have a manual or a beginner's class?*

As her mind thought about devising a workshop—Shifting 101—she remembered another class she'd taken called Anything Is Possible with Visualization. According to the teacher, if she could visualize something happening—like getting a promotion or mastering a physical challenge—then she could make any dream, any ambition come true.

Shit, I can't do any worse than offering to sleep with Carl. Tala contemplated what she wanted to happen. She wanted to shift. To do so, according to the visualization class, she'd have to see herself as a werewolf.

Tala closed her eyes and imagined she was at home. Standing naked in her bathroom, she visualized her body in the bathroom mirror. *Whoa, maybe I am getting fat? No more pizza for me.* Shaking off the thought, she concentrated harder, forcing her mind to make the changes to her body in her vision. Sweat popped out along her brow, but she pushed harder, wanting the change more than anything else in the world.

Without warning, the form in her mind's vision altered. Her torso expanded, doubling the size of her ribcage. Her facial features morphed, elongating, stretching beyond human limits. Hair, golden and shiny, spread across her body and claws replaced her French-tipped nails. Glorious sharp fangs broke through her gums and she opened her mouth in a snarl.

Tala snapped her eyes open, eager to experience the real transformation. Grinning, she widened her mouth and yearned to feel the fangs she'd formed. Ready to see her claws, she glanced down.

"Skanland!"

Skanland appeared in the doorway behind Carl and both of her captors stared at her. Skanland cocked his head in wonder. "Holy crap. What happened to her?"

Chapter Twelve

"This is the address George gave us."

"Yeah, the rat gave us the path to the trap, dude."

Devlin surveyed the decrepit house. What little color was left on the exterior after years of neglect hung in strips of peeling paint. A broken-down picket fence sported the same dismal gray color as the house. The yard, overgrown with weeds, left images of vermin and bugs crawling through its jungle. A beaten-up mailbox was bent at an angle from the dried-hard ground and attached to a rotting piece of wood with yards of duct tape. "What a pit."

"Figures." Conrad spat on the sidewalk.

Devlin reached for the swinging gate hanging by one hinge. "It's not like we're moving in. Let's go and get Tala." But his friend's hand on his arm held him in check.

"Uh, Dev, we've got company."

Vicious growls caught Devlin's attention. Two large Dobermans stood a few feet away, their fangs dripping with saliva, ready to chomp on delicious flesh. Delicious wolf flesh, that is. "Aw, crap. Doggies."

"Big mean doggies, dude. The type who'd chew up a tasty wolfie like me in one gulp."

"And then eat me as their dessert." Devlin set his sights on the dog in front of him. "Good doggy. Nice doggy."

"Yeah, right. Can't you just feel the love, Dev?"

Devlin reached for one of the broken boards lying on the ground near them. Snarls erupted and the dogs lunged forward, stopping a few feet away from the fence.

"Hey, Dev, don't make any more sudden moves, okay?"

Devlin nodded, keeping his arms close to his body. "Agreed. But they're standing between us and Tala." He bent down, getting eye level with the dogs.

"Careful, dude. These aren't shifters you're about to introduce yourself to."

"I'm getting to know the leader." Devlin sought out the eyes of the bigger Doberman, searching for the mind behind the angry dark eyes. Yet when fear ripped through his chest, halting his breath, Devlin wasn't surprised. Fear often hid behind anger.

He searched the other dog's mind and came to a similar conclusion. "Someone's hurt both of them."

A snarl came from Conrad, echoing the sentiments squeezing his chest. "Three guesses who."

He shook his head, dismayed at the pain he'd picked up from the dogs. "The hunters have them locked up most of the time with very little food or water. Keeps them mean." He exchanged a glance with his friend. "Even if we didn't have to get past them to save Tala, I'd have to help them."

"I'm with you on that." Conrad squatted beside him. "Just as long as I don't lose an arm in the process."

"Okay, maybe just a foot instead."

"Not funny, dude. Not funny at all."

Devlin renewed his focus on the dog. "Okay, boy. Let's get to know each other." Going to his knees, Devlin poured his thoughts into the Doberman.

The dog cocked his head to the side, listening. After a few minutes of the exchange, the dog whimpered, lay down and rested his head on his paws. The other dog, having moved to one side of the leader, squatted down and placed her head on her paws, too.

Devlin smiled and reached through the fence to pet the bigger dog's head. "Thanks. I'll return the favor." Standing up, he opened the gate and stepped inside the yard. "Coming?"

"After you, dude."

Devlin chuckled at the uncertain expression on his friend's face and took the lead, stalking toward the house. The dogs rose, following on their heels.

"You know they're probably watching, right?"

Devlin nodded without glancing around. "No doubt about it."

Conrad pushed ahead of him to stomp up the broken steps to the front door. "Then let's quit playing games and get this party going."

Leave it to C-man to take the most direct approach. Although this time, Devlin couldn't argue with his friend's logic. Together, they stripped off their clothes, piling them in a spot by the door. "Hurry up. I have a feeling some old lady's spying on us from across the street."

"Then it's her lucky day, huh, dude?"

Conrad banged on the door for several minutes.

Finally, the door flung open with two hunters standing in the frame, their guns poised and ready. They glanced down at the men's private parts, then turned to check each other's reaction.

Devlin grinned. "Hi ya, boys. I hope we're not overdressed for the party."

☾

"What?" Tala scowled at Carl and Skanland. "What're you rejects staring at?" Did they have to gawk at her like she was a three-headed frog?

"Damn." Carl stammered another couple of expletives

before repeating Skanland's earlier question. "What happened to her?"

The other hunters joined them, skidding to a stop when they saw her. Skanland reluctantly inched forward, acting as though he expected her to be contagious. "I think she's starting to change."

"You mean, like she's a little bit werewolf?"

"No, you moron. Being a little bit werewolf is like being a little bit stupid. Not possible. Either you're stupid or you're not." He rolled his eyes at his cohort. "And in case you aren't sure, you are."

Who are these guys? Tweedledee and Tweedledum? Tala squirmed under Skanland's persistent scrutiny. Other hunters joined them at the door. "How about you goons telling me what you find so fascinating?"

He squinted at her and leaned closer. Reaching out with his index finger, he slid his finger along her jaw. "Weird. Really weird."

Tala whipped her head to the side and snapped at his finger, missing his digit by centimeters. "Don't touch me, you pervert."

"Oh, sure. I'm the preevert."

His short bark afterwards made her wince in disgust. "The word's *pervert*, not *pree-vert*, you pervert."

He fumbled in the pocket of his pants and brought out a cosmetic compact. "I ain't the *per*-vert here. You're some kind of mutation." He opened the compact and held it in front of her.

What is this guy up to? Her stomach flopped, unsure if she wanted to look into the small mirror. *But knowing is better than not knowing, right?* Skanland snickered and she made her decision.

With all the dread of a mother checking out her truant child's report card, Tala dipped her head and stared into the mirror. Shock rocked her body. Slowly, she turned her head to better examine the sight reflected in the glass.

Soft golden fur covered the left side of her face, running from the curve of her jaw down to the middle of her chin. Fascinated, she moved her head from side to side, comparing the two parts of her face. While the right side was clean and hairless as usual, the left side sported a virtual rug of animal hair. "Oh, my God."

"God has nothing to do with monsters like you." Skanland thrust the mirror closer to the end of her nose. "Take a gander at yourself. You tried going wolf, didn't you?"

A spark of excitement sent her heart soaring. But why hadn't she shifted all the way?

Skanland saw her smile and whipped the compact back into his pocket. "Just so you know. You go all the way, you die." He straightened up and headed for the door.

She coughed a sarcastic laugh. "Hey, Skanland."

He turned. "What?"

"Just in case you aren't sure...going all the way with you isn't happening." His lurch in her direction only deepened her resolve to piss him off. "Oh, Skanland?"

"Now what?"

She feigned an expression of interest before asking the question she knew he couldn't and wouldn't want to answer. "Why do you carry a ladies' cosmetic mirror?"

An immediate stream of red burst up Skanland's neck and rushed into his face. "Shut up, bitch!"

Carl was the only hunter bright enough—*now there's a frightening thought*—not to snicker at her question. Instead, he covered his laughter by clamping a huge hand over his mouth. But the other two yokels laughed like they'd never heard anything so funny in their whole lives. Then they couldn't keep their mouths zipped, adding insult to injury.

"Yeah, Skanland. What's with the makeup mirror? My momma used to carry one like that."

"Gotta put on some lipstick? You gotta hot date tonight? Is

he gonna get lucky?

The chunkier hunter nudged his friend in the arm. "'Course not, Rims. Skanland won't even kiss goodnight. He wouldn't want to mess up his makeup."

"But, Skanland, sweetie, you can always bend over and take it in the a—"

Skanland's hands wrapped around the man's neck, cutting off his last word. "Shut the fuck up or I'm going to mess up your face. Do you hear me? Shut the fucking shit up!"

Carl gripped Skanland's shoulders and pulled him off the choking hunter. "They're just teasin', man. They don't mean nothin' by it."

Skanland, whose complexion was slowly returning to normal, broke free of Carl's hold. "I carry that thing because..." He paused, unable to finish his sentence.

The men were as entranced as Tala by his possible reason. In fact, they were so anxious to hear what he had to say that none of them said a single word.

Skanland glanced around at their rapt attention and stumbled for an explanation. "I, uh, I have it because..." He squirmed a minute longer before tensing up and glaring at them. "It's none of your damn business. Get back to your posts. Those mutants could arrive any minute now."

A loud knock reverberated through the small house, shaking the walls around them. The men stared at each other a few moments, then they raced from the room, leaving Tala alone.

"Devlin?" Tala strained against her ropes and tried to see into the hallway. Howls changed to growls, snarls, and barks. Shouts from human men mixed with the sounds of fighting and loud bangs, crashes and gunshots came from another part of the house. "Hey, I'm in here!"

The Doberman who skidded to a stop at the door was not the rescuer she'd hoped for. *Uh-oh. Right species. Wrong breed.*

Long white teeth flashed at her and she held her breath, praying he'd go away. But the dog stood his ground, snarling and dripping saliva.

"Oh shit." Tala spoke as softly as she could, not wanting to excite the dog any more than he already was. "Good doggy. You're a nice doggy, right?" When he didn't leap and tear her face off, she took a shallow breath and dared to hope she could escape certain death. "Go find your master and leave the nice lady alone, okay?"

"Okay. But there's no way in hell I'm calling Devlin my master."

Daring to take her eyes off the dog, Tala looked up to see a nude Conrad standing a few feet behind the brute. *Keep your eyes on his face.*

Conrad grinned at her. "In fact, Dev's always been more like a pest. Tagging along on my dates, looking to me for help, having a lap dance with the hooker I just paid for. You know what I mean." He shrugged. "But I guess someone has to take care of the dude."

"Whew, I am so glad to see you!" Next to Devlin, Conrad came in a close second.

He dropped his gaze down to his penis, then back up to her. "Of course you are. I'm every woman's dream."

She laughed, more out of relief than at his joke. "Can you get rid of him? Then get me outta here?"

He tilted his head in question and pointed at the dog. "Get rid of him? What for?"

Was he serious? "So he won't chew me up and eat me alive."

Conrad chuckled, flinched when a terrible crash came from the other room, and snapped his fingers. "Go along, Brutus. I think Devlin could use your help."

Brutus snarled in answer, took one last hungry look at Tala, then padded down the hallway toward the noise.

Tala's heart skipped a beat. "Devlin's here? Well, don't just stand there. Untie me. Let's go help him."

Conrad walked over to work on her bindings. "If you say so. But he seemed to be enjoying his time alone with the boys."

Tala pulled the rest of the ropes off her arms, not expecting what happened next. Conrad clasped her chin and examined the fur alongside her jaw. "Hmm. Looks like someone's tried going wolf. And didn't quite make it past the cub stage." Bending forward, he sniffed her, paused, and swiped his coarse tongue over her fur.

Tala lurched away from him. "Yuck. What the hell do you think you're doing?"

"Just welcoming you to the pack, babe."

"I thought I already got the rump rub welcome." She frowned at his smirk. "And don't call me babe."

A loud boom echoed from the fight in the other room. Tala jerked, startled by the intensity of the sound, and ran toward the noises of battle with Conrad on her heels.

She tore into a larger room containing living room furniture and skidded to a stop. Or, at least, the room *had* contained living room furniture a few minutes ago. Now the debris of a sofa, chairs, end tables and a television littered the room. Guns, bent and broken, were strewn across the floor and bullet holes decorated the walls. Devlin, in full wolf splendor, stood in the middle of the fray striking out at the three men attacking him. The dog stood next to him, an unflinching comrade in arms.

Damn. Talk about magnificent. She stared at Devlin, mesmerized as he slashed one hunter while bending the arm of another. She heard the snap of the man's arm breaking but kept her concentration on his face. Devlin raised his head and saw her. A howl, ferocious yet joyful, erupted from his lips.

A growl wafted over her from behind and she turned to find Conrad morphing into his wolf form. He flew by her and slammed into a hunter poised to shoot Devlin. The gun went off, hitting Conrad in the leg. With a ferocious roar, he chomped down on the gun, yanked it out of the hunter's hands and bent the barrel in half. The hunter, too stunned to move, slobbered in fear. With a ferocious roar, Conrad picked him up and hurled him across the room.

"Conrad, you're hurt!" Tala stepped over an unconscious hunter but came to an abrupt stop when Conrad shook his head.

He winked at her, then snapped his jaws down on another hunter's crotch. The man's scream sent a shudder down Tala's spine. *Oh, that's gotta hurt.*

Taking Conrad at his word—er, wink—she searched for the hunters' leader. *Where the hell did Skanland go?* A yelp from the other room sent her spinning to the right.

She raced into the kitchen, stopping when she saw a horrific sight. *No!* Skanland stood over another, slightly smaller Doberman, a butcher knife white-knuckled in his hand. Blood dripped down his wrist. The dog, whimpering and wild-eyed, locked eyes with her.

Help me.

Did I just hear that dog talk? Tala's mouth dropped open. The Doberman hadn't barked, but she'd heard her cry for help, nonetheless. *Wow. Devlin didn't tell me about that.*

A ferocious anger grabbed her, making her too furious to think. But no thought was necessary. Instead, she let the power within her build, surging through her veins at an incredible speed. Her breath shortened and fangs grew in her mouth. Claws shot out, replacing nails.

Tala glimpsed her reflection in the mirrored door of the microwave and widened her mouth to expose long, sharp fangs.

I'm shifting. And it's about time. Glorious elation filled her and she lifted her head and howled.

Startled, Skanland brandished the knife at her. "Damn bitch is trying to shift again."

What's he mean, trying *to shift?* Tala caught her image in the glass of a large picture hanging on the wall. Fur grew in tuffs all over her human-shaped face, but didn't cover the entire area. Her mouth, however, was contorted enough to make room for the fangs protruding over her lips. Still, not much else had changed. *Oh, come on, already. What's a girl gotta do to get a little hair on her chest?*

She studied the claws bursting from the ends of her fingers, but the rest of her body remained human and unchanged. *Why can't I get the hang of this?*

"I should have killed you when I had the chance."

Torn from her disappointment, Tala looked up in time to deflect Skanland's thrust as he tried to stab her in the chest. She roared, both from fear and anger, and instinctively struck out. Skanland flew across the room, banging against the wall with enough force to rattle the pictures. He scrambled to his feet with the butcher knife still clutched in his hand.

At least I'm getting stronger. Tala leapt over the injured dog and grabbed Skanland's wrist, driving his knife-wielding arm over his head. His putrid breath hit her face, making her stomach revolt, but she held on and squeezed.

His eyes widened at her strength and a small cry escaped him. Although he tried to throttle her with his other hand, she thwarted the move, bending his arm behind his back. She howled, delighting in her power.

"Talk about Call of the Wilde. Want some help?"

Tala glanced over her shoulder at Devlin, Conrad and Brutus standing in the doorway. Her gaze fell on Conrad's leg. "Are you okay?"

"What? Have you thrown me over for the big lug? Don't care to see if I'm okay?"

"You look like you're okay." She almost laughed at Devlin's jealous tone. "Didn't you notice his gunshot wound? Conrad got shot."

"Aw, it's just a flesh wound." Conrad passed his tongue over the area and wiped away the blood. "See? It's almost healed."

Devlin nodded toward Skanland. "Good enough. But now that we're sure Conrad's going to live, do you want a hand with him or not?"

She hurled Skanland's body at them. "Yeah. You can take care of him." The hunter flailed, trying to regain equilibrium yet failing. His body landed against the two waiting wolves.

Devlin caught one arm while Conrad twisted his other. "You want to do the honors?"

Conrad's eyes glittered with delight. "Thanks, Dev. Don't mind if I do." Snarling, he dragged the struggling man into the other room. "Come on, asshole. Let's give the lovers a little privacy."

Tala turned to the dog lying on the floor. She hurried to her side and knelt down to examine her wounds. "Damn, this looks bad."

A touch of fur skimmed the side of her arm as Brutus lay down next to his mate. His pitiful whimpers cut a slice through her heart. "Don't worry, boy. We'll do everything we can for her."

Devlin fell to the floor beside her and returned to human form—very *naked* human form. Very naked, sexually erect human form. The familiar lurch in her abdomen brought an image of Devlin pumping his long hard cock into her, her legs wrapped over his shoulders. She licked her lips and turned toward him before reality finally stopped her. "Devlin, this isn't the time or the place." *Oh, you are such a hypocrite.*

He saw where she was looking and cupped his hands over as much of his shaft as he could. Jutting his chin toward the female, he broke the hold his manhood had on her rapt attention. "Will she live?" Yet before she could answer, he pulled her closer. "Are you all right? Really all right? Damn, I'm glad to see you."

The concern, the worry she heard in his voice made her search his face. His arm around her sent warm tingles racing down her spine while an overwhelming impression of reassurance filled her soul. She had to admit the sensation was as wonderful as having sex—maybe even better. *He loves me.*

"Uh, I know. I can tell you're glad to see me." She giggled, the light titter of a girl in love.

Snuggling against her, he whispered in her ear. "Kind of hard to hide my happiness in my present condition."

Adrenalin of a hormonal kind flowed through her, racing her heart. Visions of Devlin sucking her tits, stroking her, pulling her on top of him made her ache with need. Yet it was the next images of Devlin holding her close, cuddling against her through the night, that made her head reel and her soul soar. *Oh what you do to me.*

Another stronger whimper came from Brutus, coaxing her to return to her patient. Smiling, she pulled away from Devlin to examine the female's injuries.

Keep your mind on the dog, Tala. This is no time to think about jumping Devlin's bones. But later...

Her tongue touched the tip of a fang, reminding her that she was still in wolf form. Or, at least, partial wolf form.

"Is she a friend of yours?" If she'd asked this question about a dog before meeting Devlin, she'd have thought it a joke. But not now.

"Yeah, you could say so." Devlin reached out to put his hand on the dog's head. "She's hurting a lot."

"I know. I can sense it." She placed her hand on his arm. "We need to get her medical attention right away or she won't survive. Go find something to wrap around these wounds to stop the bleeding."

Devlin nodded and moved away. She knew he wouldn't fail her or the dog. Murmuring soft words of comfort, she held her palms over the worst wounds and waited for his return. Fortunately, she didn't have to wait long.

"Here." Devlin dumped a few rolls of bandages and tape on the floor beside her. "The hunters had a first aid case in the bathroom. Seems only right we're using it on the dog and not wasting it on them." He started tearing off a strip for her.

"Besides, I don't think there's enough bandages in the world to put them back together."

She gritted her teeth at the sudden fury inside her, nodded at the dog, and started bandaging the most severe wound. "As if I'd want to."

"How're you two doing?" Conrad stood over them in clothed human form, worry etched on his face as he studied the injured dog. He dropped a wet cloth and a pile of clothes onto Devlin's lap. "I thought you might need these."

Devlin rose, wiped the bloody signs of the fight off his body and started pulling on his jeans. "Good thing we stripped before we came to the rescue."

Tala couldn't stop a groan. "Hey, don't cover up on my account." *Behave, girl. For now.*

Devlin flashed his any-time-any-place grin and finished getting dressed. Growing somber, he glanced from Tala to his friend. "Did you take care of the hunters?"

"Yeah. They won't bother anyone ever again."

"What does that mean?" Tala checked each of the men. Their expressions sent cold chills down her spine.

"It's not a pretty sight. Are you sure you want to know?"

The sadness in his eyes gave her the answer. "Not yet. I think I've seen enough for today." Swallowing hard, she shook the gruesome feeling away and focused on the dog. She wrapped the last of the bandages around the dog and wiped her bloodied hands on a cloth. "Let's get this poor girl some medical attention. In fact, let's take her to my office at the zoo. It's closer than my clinic."

Moving with the utmost tenderness, Devlin slipped his arms under the wounded dog. As he lifted her, his eyes found Tala's and shot her a pointed look. "You might want to go to full human form before we get to the zoo. I'm not sure how you'd explain those teeth and your patches of hair to your coworkers."

"Yeah, you look like you mated with a poodle."

Conrad's booming laughter heightened her frustration level. Why was this so funny? She snarled at him and followed Devlin from the room. "Tell me why, Devlin." But he didn't answer, instead nodding at his friend to lead the way.

Conrad ran ahead of them, opening the front door, then the gate with a set of keys. "I bet one of these goes to the hunters' car." He tossed them at her and she caught them with one hand. "I think you'd better drive, don't you?"

Cradling the dog, Devlin slid into the back seat with his fellow shifter piling in after him. Tala jumped into the front and looked into the rearview mirror in time to see her fangs recede into her mouth. Her hands, human hands, gripped the steering wheel.

Devlin cradled the dog in his lap. Brutus, standing alone in the yard, raised his head and yelped a few short sad barks. "We need to come back for him as soon as we can."

"How about I call a friend of mine who's great with animals? I'll have him come and pick Brutus up."

"Sounds good."

Their gazes met in the rearview mirror and a silent message zipped between them. *Why can't I change all the way?*

The look in his eyes softened, changing from a hot desire to comforting warmth. "Don't worry. You will. But for right now, concentrate on getting all the hair off your face."

Chapter Thirteen

Tala and Devlin slid into the front of the car.

"So? What'd your coworkers say, Tala?" Conrad leaned forward in the rear seat.

"I didn't give them time to ask. Besides, Devlin's presence intimidated them so much they couldn't get a word out, what with their chins sitting on their chests. But they'll take good care of our friend."

"Yeah, I thought old Jim was about to keel over from a heart attack when I snarled at him. The lightweight."

Tala slapped him on the arm. "You didn't have to be so mean, you know."

Devlin laughed and buckled his seatbelt. "Maybe not, but I couldn't resist."

"Yeah, right." She hid her grin—why encourage him?—and pulled the car onto the road. "Boys, we've got some unfinished business to deal with."

"Like taking care of a certain disgruntled ex-employee?" Devlin followed his words with a low rumble in his throat.

"Exactly. Now if only I knew where to find him. I can't remember George mentioning any friends." She paused, then snapped her fingers. "Wait a sec. I remember the guys at the zoo joking around about George's fascination with strip joints. And one strip joint in particular called *The Lucky Lady*."

"I know the place. It's a hole-in-the-wall joint downtown."

Tala's bemused glance caught Conrad's innocent one in the mirror. "Are you a regular there?"

"Hey, a dude's gotta do what a dude's gotta do. I sometimes troll for willing females, uh, women there."

"Willing females?"

Tala started to ask more, but Devlin held up his hand, stalling her. "Don't. You do not want to go there." She caught his meaning and dropped her questions. "Well, I'd say the strip joint's as good a place as any to hunt down old George. He's probably already there celebrating getting us skinned alive."

"Then let's get our own party going." Tala laughed. "Except he'll be the one getting skinned alive."

"That's my girl." Devlin high-fived her.

Tala steered the car toward downtown, following directions from Conrad. Before long, they'd managed to park and make their way inside the hovel of a bar.

Tala swallowed, hoping to siphon a little air in through the gunk circulating around her. A dense layer of smoke, stale air and cheap perfume threatened to enclose her in a shell of bad smells. She wrinkled her nose and peered through the blanket of smog at the dimly lit stage where one stripper worked the pole and another gyrated at the end of the platform. Neon signs promoting various alcoholic drinks hung on walls of an indeterminate mud color while topless waitresses cruised around the room with trays expertly balanced on one hand. A long bar, filled with male customers, ran the length of the wall on the opposite side of the room.

"Wow." Devlin crooked his head to the side, following the stripper's act as she held her body upside down on the pole, then spiraled clockwise. "How does she do that?"

An uneasiness clenched Tala's stomach. Recognition of the sensation dawned on her, stunning her in its passion. She was jealous. Plain and simple. Green-eyed, hot-tempered, stay-away-from-my-man jealous. "Uh, yeah. She's limber and strong. I think we've established as much."

"Limber and lusty. Just the way I like 'em." Conrad scooped a drink off the tray of a passing topless waitress. When she started to protest, he flipped a twenty-dollar bill at her and her glower morphed into a practiced smile.

He and Devlin stood side by side, transfixed by the two women on the stage. Neither one's attention left the dancers, except when a third stripper swayed out from behind the stage curtain.

"Okay, boys. Let's keep our eyes on the prize." Tala had to tug on Devlin's sleeve twice before he noticed her. "Our ball's in play." She winced at his chuckle. "You know what I mean."

"Um, sure. Whatever you say. I only have eyes for you anyway."

A derisive snort from the other shifter didn't help her deteriorating disposition. "Don't forget, guys. We're here on a mission, remember?"

"Right you are." Conrad coughed and pointed toward the bar. "Check him out at two o'clock. If I'm not mistaken, that's our little squealer making a meathead sandwich between two big blobs of silicone."

Tala scanned the bar, but with the crowd as thick as it was, she couldn't find George. "You mean next to the blonde waitress?"

"Blonde?" Conrad narrowed his eyes as though seeing the woman for the first time. "Oh, hey, yeah. I guess she is blonde."

Of course, all he'd noticed were her gigantic breasts. "Urgh. Men are such animals."

Devlin slid his arm around her shoulders and gave her a reassuring squeeze. "Some more than others. But in a good way, huh?"

Both Conrad and Tala rolled their eyes and spoke at the same time. "Oh, pulease."

Grinning, Devlin shook his head. "You guys are getting too chummy for my comfort."

She and his friend exchanged a telling look and all three of them, in sync, turned toward George. He raised his head from between the woman's breasts and took a swig from his drink. Tipping the glass, he poured a few drops of the clear liquid onto the blonde's large boobs, grabbed the breasts and plunged his head back between them. Men on either side of him cheered and slapped him on the shoulder, urging him on.

Tala shuddered, a wave of nausea shooting up from her stomach and into her mouth. *And to think I used to think he was an okay guy.*

"Tala? You okay?"

Devlin's velvet tones broke through the bad thoughts and she waved away his concern. "Yeah, I'm okay. Just thankful I don't have to deal with that asshole any longer. At least, not after tonight."

"Well, okay then. Let's get the creep before he hires the bitch for a backroom session."

"A backroom session?" Tala cringed, already guessing what it meant.

"You don't want to know." Devlin started toward George with Conrad and Tala following on his heels.

The wall-mounted television flickered, replacing the scene of a football game with one of Tala's public service messages. Her face, smiling at her from the set, unnerved her even before George added his two cents.

Pointing at the screen, he shouted in a loud and drunken voice. "Hey, there she is. The Bitch of the Beasts."

A few men guffawed and the blonde waitress took the roll of bills George clutched in his hands. She peeled off half of the roll, stuffed the rest into his shirt pocket and waved for the bartender to refill his glass.

"I'm telling you guys, stay away from her. She may look hot, but she's as cold as ice inside. Even if she is great in bed. The broad can suck the skin right off your dick and you'll love every minute of it. But then when she talks, nothing but shit comes out."

Tala stopped, frozen with shock. *Damn him to hell and back! He's telling lies about me. And worse, lies about me having sex with him.* Numb, she stared at him, unable to think beyond hearing his words repeated in her head.

His audience responded with titters and jeers. "And to top it off, she loves animals. Especially the big wolves. In fact, it wouldn't surprise me if she got some doggy action once in a while. If you know what I mean."

He gyrated, pretending to hump an invisible Tala, and a roar of laughter exploded around him. Grinning, he downed the rest of his drink and called for another.

"Too bad she'll never get the chance. 'Cause right about now she's giving it up for some friends of mine. And it's going be the last time she ever spreads her legs. For anyone."

A fat, balding man next to George scanned Tala from top to bottom. Soon, a slow leer slid across his blubberous features. Nudging George, he stuck a chubby finger toward her and asked in a voice loud enough to be heard above the raunchy music. "Think again, man. Looks like the animal lover's tracked you down."

George moved in slow motion, his bleary eyes socking into Tala. "Tala? How the hell did you get away—"

Devlin's fist connected with his mouth, dissolving his next words into howls of pain.

☾

George's head jerked back and forth like a jack-in-the-box. Blood ran out of his nose, staining the front of his paisley shirt. "Argh!"

Devlin, Conrad and Tala formed a semicircle around him, trapping him against the bar. The men and women around George scattered, unwilling to get involved in the dispute.

George snatched several napkins from the counter,

clutched them to his nose and held up his other hand, begging them to stop. His eyes bugged wide and he stammered, trying to get keep Devlin from attacking again. "Wait! Hold on."

Devlin snarled and drew back his arm for another blow. Tala, however, hooked him by the arm, keeping him near her. "No, Devlin, you can't beat him up."

The wild force emanating from Devlin struck her, hyping the power growing within her. She saw no visible signs of him shifting. At least, not yet.

George called to the people surrounding them. "Someone call the police. Get help. This guy's going to kill me." When no one budged to come to his aid, he whimpered and called to the bartender. "You! They're going to wreck the place if you don't get some cops in here right now."

But the bartender shook his head, picked up a baseball bat lying on the counter behind him, and rapped it against his palm. Frowning, he moved around the bar to stand with his back to Tala and her men. "Everyone keep away. I wouldn't want my customers or my girls to get hurt." He skimmed his eyes over George before adding, "But I'll make an exception with you."

"Looks like you're on your own, George. Defenseless. With no one to help and no one to do your dirty work." Devlin rubbed his hands together. "And you're all mine." In a low whisper, he asked Tala, "Tell me why I can't beat him up."

Tala caught the look Devlin and the bartender exchanged. *Does he know this guy? Or is it just a guy thing?*

George's bloodied mouth curved into a pitiful half-smile and he reached out a hand to her. "You won't let him, will you, babe? Don't let him hurt me."

Tala arched a brow and slapped his hand away. "Why do men want to call me that? Do. Not. Call. Me. Babe." She delighted in his wince. "Dev, I didn't mean you couldn't beat him up. I just meant you shouldn't do it right here. You know. In front of witnesses."

"Oh, right. Gotcha."

The bartender snorted. "Don't worry none about witnesses, sweetheart. These folks know better than to talk about anything that happens at Max's. Isn't that right, folks?" He nudged her again and winked. "I'm Max, by the way."

A low murmur from the crowd confirmed his claim and Tala, once more, thought she noticed a bond, a kinship pass between Devlin and the man. "Do you two know each other?"

Conrad, however, obviously wasn't in the mood to exchange pleasantries. "George, you're going to do exactly what I say."

Tala sensed the change in the two shifters. Raw power undulated in the stale air around them as each of them allowed a partial shift to happen. Two sets of fangs, each as dangerous as the other's, replaced teeth, and full lips curled back into similar snarls. Two sets of deep brown eyes morphed, replacing the cool darkness with brilliant furious amber.

Concerned about the crowd seeing them, Tala checked Max's reaction and was shocked to find him smiling at the shifters. With a wink at her, he pushed the people farther away from their group.

"You're not good enough to lick my friend's boots." Conrad's already stretched lips widened into an evil smirk. "But do it anyway."

Surprised at the command, Tala watched in awe as the terrified George fell to his knees. Crawling over to Devlin, he bent over and swiped his tongue over the toe of one boot. Between licks, he sobbed, tears dropping to the dusty floor.

The crowd behind them, including George's former supporters, burst into jeers to taunt the groveling man. Laughter joined the jeers, making George cry even harder.

"I don't believe what I'm seeing." George continued to lap up the grime off Devlin's boots. The sight should have thrilled her. Yet, she couldn't help the uneasiness clenching at her stomach. The order burst from her lips before she'd even thought the word. "Stop."

George halted, but didn't get up. His body shook with unbridled fear and he waited for the next command.

Tala placed her hand on her chest, knowing she couldn't allow this to continue. Grasping Devlin's arm, she hoped he'd understand. "I don't want him tormented. I don't want you sinking to his level. He's the real animal. Not you." She looked down at the pitiful man at their feet.

The amber fury in Devlin's eyes faded and soon she gazed into the soft brown eyes she loved. "Let him go. He won't bother us any more."

"Now hold up. Don't I have a say in this?" Conrad growled at George, sending him into another volley of shakes. "How about we have a little more fun first?"

Devlin pulled her to him. Warm comfort, mixed with the ever-present attraction, flowed through her, followed by an intense rush of uncontrollable lust. She inhaled his masculine, dangerous aroma, drinking in everything he was, everything he had to offer. "Let him go. We can go home and make up for lost time in bed." Rising on the tips of her toes, she slipped her tongue inside his mouth, promising him more.

He groaned a half-human, half-animal sound and kept her against him. "Whatever you want." Bending over, he yanked George to his feet. "If you ever come within a hundred yards of Tala, I promise you I'll pluck out your eyes and have them for appetizers."

"Bleck, dude. Talk about nasty food." Conrad scrunched up his face and swiveled away to ogle one of the strippers. "I can think of a dozen other things better to eat."

Devlin shook George again, eliciting a series of yelps from the terrified man. "You're getting off easy this time, asshole. Now get lost." He flung the trembling man away from him, leaving George to stumble toward the back of the club.

Devlin good-naturedly jostled Conrad, recalling the day's events. "You and me, C-man. We take care of our own."

"And what about this guy?" He hooked Max in a headlock, playing with the brawny bartender. "I knew he was one of our kind the minute I caught his scent."

The bartender broke free, sauntered over to pour three drinks and set them on the counter. "Here's to the pack. Whoever's pack it is." Raising one of the drinks in a salute, he waited for them to join him. All three downed the booze in simultaneous gulps. "I haven't had this much fun since I went hunter-hunting."

Devlin offered his hand in greeting. "Devlin Cannon of the Cannon Pack. And this ugly mutt is my best friend, Conrad Vilmar."

Max accepted the handshakes. "Max Branson. Swift Pack. Glad to be of service." He quickly poured another round. "Should I pour one for the lady? Providing she wants one when she returns."

"Sure." Devlin turned to check for Tala. "But where'd she go?"

"She headed off toward the ladies' room a minute ago." Max jerked his head toward the neon sign over the adjacent hallway. "Is she a new convert?" He poured them all another drink. "I can smell shifter in her, but she hasn't completed a total transformation yet, has she?"

Devlin scanned the hall for Tala. *Guess she needed some time to herself. After all, like the man said, she's new.* "Not all the way, but the full transformation won't be much longer." *I wish she hadn't gone in the same direction George had.*

The three let a comfortable silence envelop them. Each of the shifters lifted a glass, nodded at the other, and gulped down their drinks. Max left the bottle on the bar and moved off to serve another customer.

Devlin poured another shot, swallowed it and cleared his throat, hoping to dislodge the growing knot of unease. "Thanks for standing by me, Conrad."

"Yeah, sure. I'm always saving your sorry ass." Conrad

punched Devlin's shoulder. "Now that includes your mate's."

My mate. A nervous tingle ran down Devlin's spine. He leveled his focus on the hallway again. "I don't like this. Tala's taking way too long in the restroom."

"Shit, Dev, you know females. They can spend hours primping." Conrad shrugged and downed another drink. "But if you're so worried, why don't you—"

Before Conrad could finish his sentence, Devlin strode over to the hallway and headed down the long dark hall. A flickering neon sign boasting the word *Bitches* hung lopsided over the ladies' restroom door. Devlin tapped the shoulder of a young woman leaning on the wall next to the door. "Do me a favor, will you? Go inside and check on my girlfriend."

"In there?" The passion-pink-haired woman blinked at Devlin before shooting him a take-me-home-and-fuck-me smile.

Just how dumb is this female? Hiding the annoyance churning inside him, he returned her smile and kept his tone light. "Uh, yeah. In there. She went inside awhile ago and I'm worried about her. Maybe she fell in the toilet?" He chuckled through gritted teeth. *Come on. Gather what few brains cells you have and think.*

As he'd half expected, his joke went straight over her head. "Really? You know what? My roommate, Missy, fell in the sink once." Her smile grew in megawatts. "Hi, I'm Stacy."

Attention, World. Dumb and Dumber are roomies.

"How does a person fall into a sink?" Conrad sidled up next to him and slapped him on the back. "Get sidelined, dude?"

The girl flipped her hair over her shoulder and reached out to skim her fingers over his chest. "Missy and me went out partying and got like really drunk. So by the time we made it home, we had to like pee like really, really bad. And since I got dibs on the potty first, she decided to use the kitchen sink."

"Look, we don't have time—"

"Hush, Dev. The lady's telling a story."

Stacy flashed Conrad a flirtatious smile. "Anyway, she got up on this like really, really tall stool and turned around. But when she tried to squat over the sink—you know, how girls squat over potties?—she lost her balance and fell in." She ran both hands over Conrad's shirt. "She bruised her butt up and made it like really, really purple."

Their joint laughter raked over Devlin's last nerve. "Great story. Now can you check on my girlfriend?"

"Oh, yeah. A woman was in there, but she left. With a man." She batted her long fake eyelashes first at him, then back to Conrad. "I'll take her place, if you want. With both of you."

He took her by the arms, none too gently. "Where'd she go?"

"Shit! I don't know. You're hurting me!" She yelped, squirmed out of his hold and hurried down the hallway.

A man? Had George taken Tala? Panic leapt through Devlin and he shoved through the door and into the dirty bathroom. Open doors showed three empty stalls.

Checking under the other two closed doors, Devlin's nerves prickled along the top of his skin. He rotated, checking to see if he'd missed anything in the tiny restroom. He clenched and unclenched his hands, matching the chant throbbing through his head. *Tala's in trouble. Tala's in trouble.*

"Dude, take a look."

Devlin followed his friend's gaze to an open window large enough for a person to crawl—or be dragged—through. He stared at the window, caught the scent of something sickeningly familiar and moved to the window sill to get a better view. Steeling himself, he ran his finger along a thin line of red on the bottom of the frame.

Shit. No. Prepared for the worst, he sniffed the all too-familiar aroma. *Damn.*

Conrad came up behind him. "Is it...?"

"Yeah. It's Tala's blood."

Chapter Fourteen

Tala's world flipped upside down. Her head banged against the window frame of the bathroom. "Shit!" She shut her eyes against the pain stabbing from her head into her neck. A hand clamped around her throat, strangling the air from her and she froze, trying to regain her feet.

"You're gonna pay, you bitch."

George! Thank God he's choking me so I don't have to smell him. Snarling, she clasped her hands together and brought them up between his arms, breaking his hold on her. Surprise ripped the sneer from his face.

Tala touched her head where blood had oozed from a gash across her already-healing forehead. "George, you should've gotten away while you had the chance."

Suddenly, a tremendous power rushed through her, allowing the animal lying dormant within her to awaken. Her wolf bristled, sharpening its claws to break free.

George's wide eyes told her the change she felt coursing through her body was a total transformation. *Finally.*

The wolf roared alive in her, but this time she was ready. Instinctively, she directed the power, letting it ebb and flow through her veins. Forcing herself not to think, only to react, she waited for what would come.

Bones grew, crunched, and bent as her body altered with the conversion. Pain burst throughout her body, but somehow she knew the change was worth it. Hair sprouted, not in small tufts, but all over her. With a small cry, George whirled and scrambled for the restroom door.

A tingling sensation on her forehead made her reach for the wound again yet she no longer felt the gash. Instead, her fingers—*claws!*—skimmed over ridges forming her new brow, her alternate face. Fangs, glorious, long, razor-sharp fangs jutted out from her elongated jaw and she stretched a different grin, a wolfish grin. Her hair shortened, leaving fur in its place. She growled, enjoying the vibration the sound made in her throat.

George yanked on the doorknob, but couldn't get it open. His eyes, wide and round, shone with a wild madness borne of terror. "No! Stay away from me!"

Heat inside her, glorious and untamed, burst into a full flame. With a snarl, she leapt for him, snagging his ankle and yanking him to her. She pounced on top of him. His scream sent chills over her, not from the horror of the sound but from the delight she experienced in hearing his cry.

Out of the corner of her eye, she glimpsed her image in the full-length mirror at the end of the room. Cocking her head, she stared at the sight.

Wow. That's me. Cool. Very cool. The golden wolf in the mirror lifted the corners of its mouth in a welcoming smile. She'd definitely shifted. And definitely all the way.

Damn, if only Devlin were here to see this. To see me. She preened, proud of what she saw. *Because I look good. Damn good.* She winced at the state of her clothes. *I shredded my clothes but it was worth it.*

With difficulty, she broke away from her reflection and dropped her head close to his cheek. A snarl, surprisingly vicious, snaked out of her and she blew her hot breath against his neck. She bit him, barely piercing his skin with the tips of her fangs, but it was enough to keep him yelling. Ecstasy raced through her at his scream. Until, that is, a warm wetness soaked her leg.

"Oh, damn it all to hell and back, George," she sneered and hopped off him. "Get yourself some Depends." She didn't know if he understood her mangled words, but it didn't matter.

A terrified George tried to scramble away, but she ignored his struggles. She hooked one long claw under his belt and lifted him, puckering her canine lips. "So? Whaddya think, George? I make one gorgeous wolfie, don't I?"

When he didn't answer—unless the incoherent babble was an answer—she shook him a little. "As much as I'd love to stay like this..." Standing and taking him along with her, she glanced longingly at her new body, then shifted to human form in one quick continuous move. *Wow, I'm catching on fast!* "To think I actually felt sorry for you earlier." She gave him another quick shake, just for good measure. "Come on."

Flinging the door open, she stalked out, almost knocking a pink-haired woman down in her haste. Ignoring the expletives the girl hurled at her, Tala dragged George toward the rear of the building. In quick order, she found the strippers' changing room and pushed George inside.

Several pairs of bored eyes fell on them. Although she held George two inches off the floor, no one questioned her. "I guess nothing much surprises you ladies any longer, huh?"

A heavily rouged, bleached blonde rose from her stool in front of the large vanity mirror to stride over to them. Dark, seen-it-all eyes scanned them and she hoisted a tight-fitting bustier over ample breasts. "You got that right. I'm Maggie." Maggie slipped her rhinestoned fingers under one of the slits in Tala's shirt. "Interesting outfit you got there."

"Uh, it's the new shredded look." George squirmed in Tala's hand, but couldn't form words that made any sense. "I was wondering if you'd like to try out a new act tonight." She tilted her head at him and added, "A comedy act."

A penciled-in eyebrow arched in response. "You talking about him?"

"Hey, I know this guy." A chubby brunette, who looked like

she'd be more at home in a high school pep squad than in a strip joint, pointed at George. "He's a real creep. Always treats us like dirt and doesn't tip."

Tala clucked her tongue in sympathy. "Figures." Would the young stripper help her? "Do you think you might have some clothes that would fit him?" The other strippers gathered around them.

"You mean like stage clothes?"

"Exactly. Like maybe a hot pink thong or something? Granted, he'll stretch them out, but I'll buy you new clothes. I promise. You see, George here wants to go on stage." Shaking him elicited a small squeak. "Don't you, George?"

The ladies checked each other's reactions before turning to dig into their personal stashes of costumes. Within minutes, Maggie handed Tala a large brassiere and thong panties. Another girl's pink robe and feather boa completed the ensemble.

Holding them up against George's skin, Tala and nodded her approval. "Oh, my. Pink is your color, Georgie."

Tossing her captive to the floor, she turned away from the strippers, allowed her fangs to peek through her stretched lips and snarled her command. "Put them on. Now. You've got a show to do."

Although George was shaking badly, he managed to choke out a defiant response. "A-and if I d-don't?"

"Hey, he can talk, after all." Maggie chuckled, egging the other women to throw barbs at George. "We're waiting, Georgie."

Tala widened her lips more, adding a low growl for emphasis. George, horror paling his complexion, unbuttoned his shirt, then swapped it out for the big bra.

"Keep going, George." Tala crooked her finger at his slacks.

"Yeah. Get the panties on. I paid good money for the lacy thong, but it'll be worth it to see you in them." The little brunette wiggled her rump, demonstrating how to shimmy into the thong.

George, seeing Tala's warning look, dropped his pants in a hurry, stripping his jockey shorts along with them. But Tala stopped him before he could take off his socks.

"No. Leave those on. And I think we'll add a pair of high heels, too."

A pair of four-inch silver heels appeared on cue, tossed at George's feet.

Once dressed, the chubby man shivered before them. The strippers jeered and clapped their approval. The tight bra pinched into his man-breasts while the thong showed what little package he had to offer.

"Hmm. He sure doesn't fill out my thong much. Maybe we should pad his crotch."

Tala helped him slip on the silky robe and wrap the feathery boa around his neck. "Maybe some makeup would do the trick?"

Three girls hurried to get their cosmetics. While one added rouge to his cheeks, another added eye shadow, and the third applied an apple-red lipstick to his lips.

After letting the women have their way, Tala crossed her arms and admired their work. "Okay, Georgie. It's show time."

Tala pushed George out of the dressing room, leading the giggling group of women down a dimly lit hall and onto the stage area behind the red velvet curtains.

The loud raunchy music ended. A stripper broke through the curtains and stared at the man standing before her. "What the shit?"

"Don't ask, Barbie. Just go out there and announce a very special act." Maggie studied George for a moment before adding, "This is Gorgeous Georgina, the Gal Pal of the West."

Barbie paused for a moment, then flinging the curtains aside, swayed onto the stage.

"Please, Tala. Don't make me do this." Surprisingly, George once again gathered his courage to oppose her. "I won't do this."

"Lookie, lookie. He speaks again."

Tala ignored the ladies' taunting remarks. "Do this or I'll finish what I started in the restroom."

Maggie's mouth fell open. "You two? In the bathroom?" Her surprise morphed to dismay. "Oh, honey, you can do so much better."

Yuck! Does she think…? Oh, hell no. Tala shook her head, vehemently denying the woman's assumption. "No way. It's not what you're thinking. Trust me."

Barbie's voice rang out, drawing the attention of the audience. "Gentlemen! Listen up!"

George turned white and struggled against Tala's hold. "No, please!"

"We have a very special treat for you tonight. Straight—or maybe not so straight—from his life in the closet, *The Lucky Lady* proudly presents for your amusement Gorgeous Georgina, the Gal Pal of the West."

A generous applause filled the air and Maggie drew the curtains out of the way. Stepping behind George, Tala placed her hands on his shoulders and pushed him on stage.

Pandemonium broke out with catcalls, insults and boos erupting from the male audience. The disc jockey, catching on to the joke, broke off the fast-beat music he was playing, substituting it with the stereotypical bump-and-grind stripper music.

Tala peeked through the split in the curtain and hissed at George. "You better start dancing or they're liable to get really mad. Not to mention how mad I'll get."

A forlorn George glanced at Tala, then scanned over the audience. Slowly, in gawky, awkward movements, he moved his hips to the rhythm of the song. Soon the men surrounding the stage got involved in the joke and took up a chant.

"Take it off. Take it off."

George baby-stepped to the middle of the runway, stopped

and clutched the boa close to his chest. Yet, although he cowered in front of the boisterous crowd, his hips continued to bump to the left and right, keeping with the beat of the music.

The strippers gathered around Tala to sneak glimpses of the show. Soon George loosened up, growing bolder with each second. Tossing the feather scarf in a flamboyant gesture, he twirled around, executing a perfect pirouette.

The move surprised Tala, but his expression surprised her the most. "Oh, my God. I think he's actually enjoying this."

"Looks like Georgina may have started a whole new career tonight." Maggie guffawed and slapped Tala on the arm.

☾

He needed to learn to drive. Before he did anything else, he'd learn how. Jogging down the streets, even in wolf form, was slower than traveling in a car. But at least as a wolf, he could cut through yards. The full moon above beckoned him, calling him to hunt, but he couldn't let anything keep him from finding Tala.

Devlin had searched the club, but couldn't find her, getting no help from the closed-mouthed strippers. Hell, he hadn't even been able to catch her scent because of all the smoke and grime in the place. Then a fruitless search outside the strip club had led to no leads. No smells. No tracks. Nothing. It wasn't until he discovered the car was gone that he decided to pray she'd gotten away and gone back to her apartment.

He left Conrad at the club to keep looking and headed home. With luck, she'd either get in touch with him or return safely. If she didn't, then he'd find one ex-zoo employee and tear him apart, inch by agonizing inch.

Her scent hit him and the relief coursing through him invigorated him. *She's alive.* Rounding the corner, he glanced at the one lamppost shedding a hazy yellow glow over the area behind her apartment. Another light shone from the second story window of her apartment, highlighting a shapely shadow on the blinds. He inhaled, caught the spicy, tantalizing fragrance of her, and smiled.

Her form played across the blinds, gliding back and forth, arms outstretched as if in flight. The enticing shape, alluring in silhouette, dipped and weaved, dancing in time with the familiar, sensual music. Her movements entreated him, flaring the desire within his soul to a fever pitch. Grinning, he flew up the stairs and burst inside.

The music, seductive and sultry, played over him and his mouth fell open at the sight of her naked body dancing around the room. She slid her hands along her body, skimming over her firm, round breasts, and his shaft responded. She flicked her tongue over her top lip and moved her hands up and through her hair.

She was more beautiful than ever. His shaft throbbed for her, but it was his heart that swelled with love.

Spinning again, she performed a perfect twirl and landed with her arms outstretched, welcoming him home. "What took you so long?"

His hand slid over her breast, tweaking her nipple. Tala laughed, locking her hand behind his neck. "I missed you."

"Yeah?" He cupped both breasts in his hands. "I'm not the one who disappeared. You scared the hell outta me."

"I knew you'd figure out where I went." Gyrating her hips, she swayed with the music, rubbing against the rough denim material of his jeans. "And I didn't disappear. I was just busy having some fun with the ladies."

His gaze jerked up from devouring her body, eyebrows dipping in confusion. "You mean the strippers? What the hell were you doing with them?"

"Oh, nothing much." She pushed her tits against his palms. "Just helping someone start a new career." When he looked at her quizzically, she quipped, "I guess you were busy looking for me and missed the special show. But don't worry. I'll tell you about it later. After all, don't we have better things to do right now than talk?"

He favored her with one of his lazy smiles. "When you're right, you're right."

"Good. Then let's get busy." She stretched to her tiptoes and brushed her tongue lightly across his lips. He groaned and slipped his hands to her waist, possessing her body as he'd possessed her soul.

His nostrils flared, a sure sign that he was turned on and ready to play. She loved how well she knew him now. How the glint of amber in his eyes told her his animal was near the surface. And all she had to do was let him out.

"Do you want to move to the bedroom?" His tone was husky, filled with desire.

"No." Tugging him down, she knelt. Knee to knee, she ran her hands up to his neck, taking a firm hold on him. "I want you to take me where you first saw me."

He buried his face in her neck and his words warmed her skin as they warmed her heart. "I loved you from the first second I saw you."

She sighed and kissed him. Not only with lust, but with every ounce of love she had for him. He met her tongue as it skimmed over her lips and they played together, teasingly, lovingly, savoring each other's taste. Closing her eyes, she concentrated on the texture of his mouth, the curve of his lips, the nip of his teeth. Although familiar, his flavors were intoxicatingly new.

At last, he pressed his mouth to hers, dragging her tongue into his mouth. He gripped her hips and his fingers traveled toward the middle of her ass to meet at the valley. Downward he continued until he could take both her cheeks in his hands. He spread her, cupping her forcefully, sucking on her tongue. She pressed against him, flattening her breasts against his rock-like chest. Rubbing against him, she arched, wanting him impossibly closer.

Devlin moved his fingers deeper, moving them into her, exciting her, making her tighten around him. He broke the kiss to lick his way down her neck, along the scar left from his mark to nibble at the roundness of her shoulder. He was all to her, everything she'd ever yearned for.

Needing to catch her breath, she pulled away. Amber eyes met hers and she thrilled at the power lying within them. "Devlin."

He answered exactly the way she'd wanted him to. Tenderly, he lowered her to the carpet and slid beside her. His gaze ran the length of her, taking in every inch. She rejoiced, happy that she had put that look of heat in his eyes.

"I have to have you, but I want to take this slowly." His tongue sneaked out to tickle her tit. "But I'm not sure how long I can last."

"Take me any way you want." She took his face in her hands, needing him to see the sincerity on her face. "I'm yours and you're mine."

He growled deep in his throat and buried his face in her hair. He smelled her, drawing in her scent. Slowly, he trekked his fingers over her breast, making an easy circle around her areola. She arched, urging him to take her nipple, but he was true to his word and took his time, making her happy and irritated all at the same time.

He traced his fingers around her tit several more times, moving his fingers closer and closer in smaller circles, nuzzling her neck and murmuring soft words of endearment. Finally, his fingers tripped over her nipple and the muscles between her legs tightened. "Devlin, you're torturing me."

He chuckled wickedly. "You ain't seen nothing yet...babe."

"Babe?" Yet before she could admonish him, he took her tit in his mouth and rubbed the other between his finger and thumb. She inhaled, forgot what she'd wanted to say, and stared down at him. The wicked gleam was still in his eyes, sending a turmoil of unreleased desire swirling in her abdomen.

Pushing her breasts together, he suckled on both tits at once. She bit her lower lip and reached out to run her hands over his broad shoulders. Muscles rippled and she couldn't decide which sight she liked better: the sight of him pulling on her taut buds or the expanse of his shoulders above her.

"Devlin, I'm not sure I can last very long either."

He let her nipples pop out of his mouth and studied her. "You can if I can. And you will."

Suddenly, he reared up, pulling his body upward until his cock hung over her face. She grinned and reached up for him, but he jerked his body away from her. "Uh-uh. This is my time to play. Besides, if you blow me, I'm a goner."

She started to argue. He was probably right, but that didn't mean she liked it—especially when the large mushroom cap was so temptingly close that she could reach out and flick it with her tongue.

She'd decided to do just that when he moved away, dragging his cock over her chin to bounce on her chest. He swayed his hips, swiping his shaft under her chin, skimming it into the hollow at her throat. She groaned and he chuckled at her. "Feeling a bit frustrated?" She narrowed her eyes and reached up to take him in her hand, but he was too quick for her. "Uh-uh-uh. No touchie for you. Not yet anyway."

Brushing her hands away, he continued to draw his shaft over her, in between her breasts, down the cleft between her ribcage and over the quivering muscles of her stomach. She watched him and decided turnabout was fair play. Gripping her breasts, she brought them to her mouth and slid her tongue over the tops of them. Then she pushed them together and sucked her tits into her mouth. She jiggled them, keeping her tongue playing over the tender nubs.

He paused, his eyes growing glassy, and ran his tongue over his lips. But her payback didn't work as planned. The lustful glint in his eyes was soon replaced with a gleeful glint.

"Good try, Tala. But since I've already tasted your tits, I can handle the teasing."

She hid her surprised reaction and made a soft yearning sound deep in her throat. Her reward, the rush of desire, spread across his face. He gritted his teeth and scowled. "Damn, but you sound sexy. Okay, you got me. Let's quit tempting each other."

When he slipped a little lower, running the tip of his engorged cock over her curly mound, she nodded once and wrapped her legs around his waist. He bent to kiss her ribcage and tracked his lips along the curve of her side. But still he didn't enter her.

"Devlin, please." She couldn't help the whine in her voice and didn't care. All she wanted was him inside her. "I thought we were getting serious now."

He looked up at her and the heat in his eyes nearly scorched her with its intensity. Together, they paused, each waiting for that moment when they would join.

"Mates forever."

She nodded. "Forever."

Keeping his gaze on hers, he slid into her and, although she was oh-so-ready for him, she gasped, her body instantly electrified with the feel of him. He rocked against her, into her, at first slow and easy. But then she could see him losing his control, his features taking on a strained expression, his jaw moving and he began to move faster, deeper, shoving into her. She clung to his arms, locking her feet behind him, and held on.

She tried to keep pace, thrusting her hips against him, but he moved too quickly for her to keep up. At best she could only match one buck for every two of his, their stomachs meeting in sweaty slaps. Fucking Devlin was like riding a bronco. The best she could do was to hang on and enjoy the ride.

When he left her, taking his cock abruptly from her, she cried out, then tried to arch higher as though she could force him back inside. Instead, he took her legs, making her unlock her feet, then pushed her knees toward her chest. With a flick of his tongue, he dove lower and sank his head between her legs. She held her breath and waited, anticipating the feel of his kiss against her pulsating clit. Still, she was unprepared for the shock.

"Oh, shit!"

She could swear she could feel him smile against her.

"Devlin, please, oh, please, oh—"

He lashed at her, pressing the fullness of his tongue against her and dragging it over the top of her mound, down over her clit, along the slit and then up again. She grabbed her knees, holding her legs for him, and closed her eyes. *Oh, please, oh, please, oh, please.* What she was begging for was unclear since he was doing everything she wanted and more.

Soul-shaking shudder after shudder ripped through her. She thrashed her head back and forth while her body trembled from her release. She cried out, this time not in frustration, but in joy.

The darkness behind her eyelids swirled, lights flickering with each stroke of his tongue. She tried to follow his movements—suck, flick, bite—but soon became lost in the sheer ecstasy of his attack. He groaned, the hot air striking her clit and sending shivers of another orgasm from her pussy to spread across her abdomen. Her muscles clenched as though trying to catch his tongue. The sounds he made lapping up her wetness nearly drove her insane.

When his fingers slid into her, she knew she'd never think clearly again. He moved his fingers, stroking, pushing into her, while his tongue continued to lash at her clit. She shrieked, shaking under his hold.

"Damn it, Devlin. Are you trying to kill me?"

He stopped—*don't stop!*—to answer. "If I am, then what better way to die?" He lowered his head, propping his chin on her patch of curly hair. "Tell me what you want, Tala. I want to please you."

She glanced down at him, waiting a moment to let her lust-fogged eyes focus and grinned at him. "Anything?"

He raised his eyebrows in wonder. "Yeah, anything."

"I want you to dance with me." She giggled at his surprised expression.

"Are you kidding me?" He flicked his gaze downward, then back to hers. "You want me to stop doing what I'm doing—to dance?"

With her breathing almost back to normal, she let her legs fall to his sides. "Yeah, I want to dance. I want us to dance while you make love to me."

He took a second to think about what she'd said. Then in one easy movement, he rose, taking her with him. Yet before she was barely on her feet again, he reached behind to grasp her buttocks and yanked her upward. She laughed, draped her legs around him and twined her hands behind his neck.

He smiled at her, lowered his head to nuzzle her neck and began to sway with the music. His cock tickled the inside of her legs, reminding her of how he'd felt inside her, and she leaned back, thrusting her lower half against him. He growled with a rumble against her neck and sank into her.

Rocking with the music, he held onto her as she rode him, bending her body to better move along his shaft. He lifted her higher, shoving his cock deeper into her until she was sure he'd push all the way to her throat. Together they danced.

She tightened her muscles around him, imagining holding his cock inside her forever. When he pulled out, the deliriously hot friction drove her own hunger higher until she was certain she'd pass out.

"Oh, damn, Devlin. Fuck me. Ooh. Please, please, please—" She sucked in a breath and held it as yet another orgasm tore her apart. She clung to him, her arms shaking along with the rest of her.

Soon, however, Devlin picked up speed, moving at twice the

tempo of the music. "I don't think you're dancing to the music any more."

"What music?" he murmured against her skin.

She smiled and closed her eyes, wanting all her other senses to tell her about him.

He feathered kisses and nipped along her shoulder. She pressed against him, melding their bodies together. She copied his actions, nipping when he did, licking when he did, and enjoying the flavor the mix of his sweat and musky odor gave her. She tracked her fingers through the hair at the nape of his neck and rubbed her tits against him. Knowing he would hold her, she trailed her hand down his back, reveling in the sensation of rippling muscles under her fingers.

This is the man I've always dreamed of. My wild man. My mate.

When his breathing grew more labored, she knew his release was near and she wanted every drop of him inside her. Tightening her hold on him in every way, she drew him to the brink and pushed him over the edge. He tensed, squeezed her tighter and groaned, thrusting into her harder than he ever had before. Bellowing, he released and burst his seed into her.

When his shudders finally stopped, she took his face in her hands and met his eyes. "Now, Devlin. Do it again. Make me yours again."

He leaned away to look into her eyes. She saw the brown give way to the amber and a joy of realization whipped through her. When he opened his mouth wide, she welcomed the fangs she saw and tilted her head. With a roar, he sank his teeth into the curve between her shoulder and neck, marking her again.

Instead of crying out, she sighed, delighting in the feel of his fangs breaking through her flesh. Warm stickiness flowed over her shoulder down to the hollow between her breasts. She let loose, letting her wolf take over, and opened her mouth for her fangs to grow. With a small yelp, she released, her final climax shuddering into her and echoing the pain in her neck.

As one, they slowly slipped to the floor.

She rested on top of him, eyes shut, letting her breathing even out. Her hair, sweat-dampened, lay spread across his chest and she listened to him, riding the rise and fall of his chest. His arms circled her, making her feel safe. She sighed in contentment and flattened her hands underneath his back.

I want to stay like this always.

"Tala?"

"Hmm?"

"Will you come with me?"

I'll go anywhere with you. Yet instead of voicing the words, she lifted her head to question him. "Where?"

"To the mountains. To the pack."

His dark brown eyes were still flecked with gold, letting her know the animal within him was still stirring. She knew he was asking for more than a mere vacation to the woods. She'd known he would ask her, but had put off thinking about her answer. Could she leave her family? Her work?

Yet, when she looked into his eyes again, she knew her decision had been made from the first moment she'd met him.

"When do we leave?"

He studied her, relief flooding his face. When he saw that she'd seen how relieved he was, he busied himself, playing with an already taut bud. "Is next week good for you?"

She nibbled at his ear, wanting to hear him groan in pleasure. "I'll live wherever makes you happy, but continuing my work is important, too." She paused and held her breath.

"I know and I'd never take that away from you."

She arched an eyebrow and shot him a pointed look. "As if you ever could."

He chuckled and she relished the sensation the sound made in his chest. "Yeah. As if." He pushed a stray strand of her hair out of her face. "We can live in both places. Think of the first-hand experience and knowledge about wolves that you'll gain when you stay with the pack."

"Deal." She rubbed her breasts against his skin, enjoying the way her nipples felt against his hard chest. "I shifted, you know. All the way."

Devlin fondled her breasts and she wiggled her bottom over his crotch. No harm in teasing him a little more. He half-heartedly growled in warning. "Hey, being a shifter gives me extra strength, but even I don't recover that quickly. You're going to kill me, woman."

"Well, to quote someone near and dear to me, 'then what a way to die, huh?'" She poked him playfully in the chest. "Seriously, though. You should have seen me in wolf form. I was amazing. And one hot bitch, if I do say so myself."

"*My* bitch." He stroked her hair, making her wish he'd stroke somewhere lower. "You're always amazing. And beautiful."

"But as a werewolf? Who knew?"

"I knew." His hands clamped onto her rump, making her gasp. He pulled her mouth to his and scorched his tongue into her mouth. Warm sweet juices slid between them, swirling around.

Breaking free of his kiss, she placed her hands on his chest and leaned back, tossing her hair over her shoulders.

He rained light kisses over her neck. "You know, we'll have to get up at some point."

"Are you sure?"

Devlin chuckled and kissed the palm of her hand. "Pretty sure. I like making love on the carpet, too. But rug burns are the shits."

She giggled, turned his hand around to blaze kisses along the long lifeline of his palm. "Devlin, will you do something for me?"

"Anything."

"Good answer." Yanking him up, she snatched her robe

lying on the chair nearby and tossed him a towel from the laundry basket. Once he'd wrapped it around him, she took his hand. "Come with me, Devlin Cannon." Pushing open the sliding glass doors, she went to the railing of her balcony.

His arms slid around her waist, while the towel covering his body tickled her calves. Nuzzling her neck, he skimmed his tongue along her shoulder blade to her already-healing wound, sending a happy shiver down her spine.

"The scar will be bigger this time." He continued to lick her, holding her next to him.

"Do it with me, Devlin."

"Uh, I think I already did. Didn't you notice?"

She turned and playfully nipped him on his chin. "No, you boob. I want to howl." She angled her body, smiled at him and lifted her eyebrows in question. When his quiet response came, she altered her gaze, raising her eyes to the creamy moon above them.

Together, they lifted their heads and howled at the moon.

About the Author

Beverly Rae's witty, sexy, action-packed romances leave readers experiencing a wide range of emotions. As a multi-published author, Beverly is always working on her next book, taking the "usual" and twisting it into the unusual.

To learn more about Beverly, please visit www.beverlyrae.com. Send her an email at mailto:info@beverlyrae.com or join her Yahoo! Group to join in the fun with other readers as well as Beverly: http://groups.yahoo.com/group/Beverly_Rae_Fantasies.

Romeo and Juliet never had to worry about being skinned alive.

Howling for My Baby
© 2009 Beverly Rae
A Cannon Pack Romance, Book 1

Sydney Skeller's father is spitting bullets over her reluctance to join the family business as a shifter hunter. The last thing Daddy needs to know is why—she yearns for a lover who's man enough for a relationship but animal enough to give her the wild ride of her dreams. After a treadmill mishap lands her in a tangled heap with Jason Cannon, she wonders if she's finally found her beast, er, man. One session in bed and one bite later, she's sure. Now if only she can keep her father from mounting Jason's head on a wall…

Jason is all man on the surface, but wolf shifter down to the bone. He's more than ready to stop "playing the pack" and find his one true mate, and Sydney of the luscious curves is the woman of his dreams. Finding out that she comes from a family sworn to eradicate his kind isn't a deal-breaker. But her outrageous plan for him to masquerade as the wolf in hunter's clothing, right under her father's very nose, could be asking more than he ever expected to give.

Warning: Readers, be aware of stranger side effects. These side effects may include but aren't limited to biting strangers, asking furry strangers to bite you, purposely falling off treadmills to collide with handsome strangers, enjoying hot sex with wild strangers, and baying at the moon to meet other moon-influenced strangers. If you notice any of these side effects, contact the author immediately. You may be in her next book!

Available now in ebook and print from Samhain Publishing.

Nitro? Meet glycerin…

Biting Nixie
© 2009 Mary Hughes
A Biting Love Story

Punk musician Nixie Schmeling is a hundred pounds of Attitude who spells authority a-n-c-h-o-r and thinks buying insurance is just one more step toward death. So she really feels played when she's "volunteered" to run the town's first annual fundraising festival. Especially when she finds out it's to pay for a heavy-hitting, suit-wearing lawyer—who's six-feet-plus of black-haired, blue-eyed sex on a stick.

Attorney Julian Emerson learned centuries ago that the only way to contain his dangerous nature is to stay buttoned up. He's come from Boston to defend the town from a shady group of suits…and an even shadier gang of vampires. But his biggest problem is Nixie, who shreds his self-control.

Nixie doesn't get why the faphead shyster doesn't understand her. Julian wishes Nixie would speak a known language…like Sanskrit. Even if they manage to foil the bloodthirsty gang, what future is there for a tiny punk rocker and a blue-blooded skyscraper?

And that's before Nixie finds out Julian's a vampire…

Warning: Contains more eye-popping sex, ear-popping language and gut-popping laughs than can possibly be good for you. And vampires. Not sippy-neck wimps, but burning beacons of raw sexuality—this means passionate blood-heating, violent bloodletting, and fangy bloodsucking. Oh, and cheese balls. Those things are just scary.

Available now in ebook and print from Samhain Publishing.

The ultimate battle is waged with one's heart.

Going the Distance
© *2009 Mandy M. Roth*
Paranormal Deathmatch, Book 1

Extreme fighting champion Quinn Padgett once had it all. Fame, fortune, freedom. One fateful night it was all stripped away, and for two years the alpha male has endured a torturous life, doing the bidding of a madman in a different kind of ring. The Deathmatch, where the only rule is kill or be killed.

It's as primal as it gets, and Quinn must draw on all his werewolf instincts to survive. Especially with Carri. Her very presence brings him to his knees, demanding he do all to protect her.

Carri had no idea how close danger lurked until she witnessed her boyfriend's sick idea of "entertainment". Now all she wants is to get away from the bastards who are hell-bent on ridding the world of that which they do not understand. But her boyfriend's reach is long—and brutal. Quinn is her only hope. And the only man who awakens a fire within her, body and soul.

As Quinn and Carri go on the run in a fight for their lives, they find themselves engaged in an even deeper and more dangerous battle—a battle of the heart.

Warning: This book contains a kick-ass alpha male, a crazed madman, towel-dropping sexual tension, smokin' hot sex, a woman who is more than capable of taming the beast, and the normal "Mandy" death, destruction and mayhem.

Available now in ebook from Samhain Publishing.

GREAT CHEAP FUN

Discover eBooks!
THE FASTEST WAY TO GET THE HOTTEST NAMES

Get your favorite authors on your favorite reader, long before they're out in print! Ebooks from Samhain go wherever you go, and work with whatever you carry—Palm, PDF, Mobi, and more.

WWW.SAMHAINPUBLISHING.COM

CPSIA information can be obtained at www.ICGtesting.com
Printed in the USA
LVOW092139060612

285027LV00001B/63/P